Antiques dealers might sometimes be cutthroats, but they were courteous cutthroats and would seldom risk embarrassing another dealer—unless, of course, they could make a profit by it. The etiquette went with the role and the territory.

Maggie sat on the folding chair in her booth and exchanged muddy sneakers for dressy sandals, thinking about what she had seen at Show Management. Susan Findley and Vince Thompson. Odd. She pulled out her sales book and the mahogany stationery box she'd inherited from her grandmother and now used as a cash box for good luck.

This show was going to be very, very interesting.

Even without last week's murder.

SHADOWS AT THE FAIR

"Fans of John Dunning's mysteries [will] enjoy this solid start to a new series."

—*Library Journal*

"Wait seamlessly weaves information about antique fairs [and] prints into the narrative. . . . [T]he premise is intriguing and the mystery credible."

—*Booklist*

"Homicide and antiques combine smoothly in this well-crafted mystery. . . . Full of fascinating information. . . . This solid debut will appeal to cozy fans who appreciate a realistic background."

—*Publishers Weekly*

"This new series hits the spot. . . . You'll learn a bundle about antique prints and 'the business'. . . . Highly recommended. More please!"

—*Mystery Loves Company*

AN ANTIQUE PRINT MYSTERY

SHADOWS at the FAIR

LEA WAIT

POCKET BOOKS

New York   London   Toronto   Sydney   Singapore

This book is a work of fiction. Names, characters, places and incidents are products of the author's imagination or are used fictitiously. Any resemblance to actual events or locales or persons, living or dead, is entirely coincidental.

POCKET BOOKS, a division of Simon & Schuster, Inc.
1230 Avenue of the Americas, New York, NY 10020

ISBN: 0-7434-5620-3

First Pocket Books printing July 2003

10 9 8 7 6 5 4 3 2 1

POCKET and colophon are registered trademarks of
Simon & Schuster, Inc.

For information regarding special discounts for bulk purchases,
please contact Simon & Schuster Special Sales at
1-800-456-6798 or business@simonandschuster.com

Front cover illustration by Joyce Patti

Printed in the U.S.A.

For Elizabeth Park, who introduced me to mysteries; for Sally Wait, who introduced me to antique prints; and with thanks to Louis Luciani, retired Irvington, New Jersey, police detective, for his attempts to enlighten me regarding police procedures.

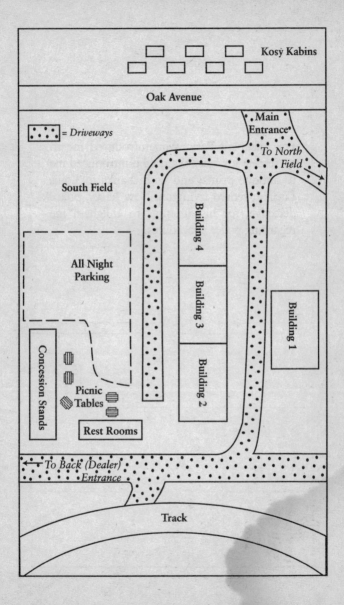

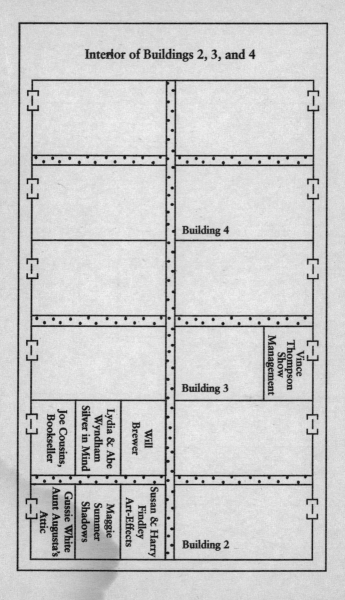

Interior of Buildings 2, 3, and 4

Building 4

Building 3

Vince Thompson Show Management

Joe Cousins, Bookseller

Lydia & Abe Wyndham Silver in Mind

Will Brewer

Gussie White Aunt Augusta's Attic

Maggie Summer Shadows

Susan & Harry Findley Art-Effects

Building 2

March 18 . . . Don Worthington, local antiques dealer and Kiwanis member, died last night in a one-car accident on Brookside Boulevard. Worthington, who appeared to have fallen asleep at the wheel, was returning home from an antiques exposition in Columbus. (Ohio Evening Star)

April 14 . . . Fire took the lives of two Scranton men late last night. Thom Reardon and Paul Moskowitz died in the apartment over their antiques shop before they could be reached by members of the Scranton Fire Department, said a spokesperson this morning. The men had apparently been sleeping when the fire broke out. They are presumed to have died of smoke inhalation. (Daily Times, *Scranton, Pennsylvania*)

May 3 . . . Yesterday, auction attendees in Sharon, Connecticut, were shocked by the discovery of the body of James Singleton, a Massachusetts antiques dealer, in his truck outside the auction house. Police reported Singleton appeared to have ingested a toxic substance. The medical examiner's investigation is pending. (Hartford Star, *Connecticut*)

May 22 . . . Well-known local antiques dealer John Smithson, a resident of Croton-on-Hudson, collapsed in his booth during the Westchester Antiques Show today. Smithson was declared dead at the scene by local paramedics. (Westchester Tonight, *Channel 6*)

Chapter 1

—✦—

Snap-the-Whip, *wood engraving by noted American artist Winslow Homer (1836–1910). The most famous of Homer's wood engravings, published by* Harper's Weekly, *September 20, 1873. Double page. Country boys playing a game outside their schoolhouse, with mountains beyond. Notable because it was the basis for two later Homer oil paintings also called* Snap-the-Whip, *often pointed to as most representative of Homer's accurate depiction of nineteenth-century American life. Price: $1,700.*

"Booth number and admittance card?"

The man looking through Maggie's van window was a far cry from the student in faded jeans and Grateful Dead T-shirt whom Vince usually hired to check in vans at the dealer entrance to the Rensselaer County Spring Antiques Fair. This man was a cop.

"Booth two twenty-three."

He looked down at his clipboard. "Name?"

"Maggie Summer. Security seems a bit heavy this

year." A brass nameplate was pinned on his chest. The chest's name was Taggart.

"Yes, ma'am. After that incident at the antiques show in Westchester last week, we wanted to make sure there were no problems here. Admittance card?"

Maggie reached into her worn red Metropolitan Museum canvas bag and pulled out a gray card tucked among rolls of masking tape, business cards, two small hammers, a portable telephone, and the latest Toni Morrison book. "What incident?"

"Dealer murdered. Poisoned. It was in all the local papers."

"I'm from New Jersey. I hadn't heard." Maggie swallowed hard. Was it someone she knew? A poisoning at an antiques show? Bizarre. "Has anyone been arrested?"

"Not that I know of. Westchester police are investigating."

"Why the concern here?"

"Just insurance. A lot of the same dealers who were in Westchester last week are here today. Don't want the public to be worried." He looked at her. "Or the dealers. Nothing for you to be nervous about. We've doubled security. Only authorized people are allowed in." He looked down at the paper she'd handed him. "Maggie Summer . . . Shadows Antiques. Do you have a picture ID?"

"They don't require photo licenses in New Jersey."

He waited.

"If I'd been heading for an airport, I'd have brought my passport. What about an employer ID with a picture?" She searched through her bag again. The ID was at the bottom. As she pulled it out, coins, tissues, and pencils fell onto the floor. A truck behind her beeped. "Just a minute!"

He looked at the photo, then at her, and grinned. "You've colored your hair. Looks good."

She smiled and reached for the card. Maggie's long, dark brown hair was her one vanity. She tucked back a strand that had escaped her braid.

"Decided to go back to school when your kids left home, Ms. Summer?"

"No kids. I teach at Somerset County College."

"That must be why it says 'faculty' on the card."

A droll fellow, Officer Taggart. The truck in back of her was beeping steadily now.

"Here's your entrance permit." He taped a green label printed SPRING SHOW—DEALER just above the inspection sticker on the inside of her windshield. "Park over in the south field. As soon as you've finished unpacking, move your van to the back of the lot so other dealers can unload. You staying on the grounds tonight?"

"No. Living it up at Kosy Kabins." They weren't so cozy and they weren't exactly cabins, but the motel was just across the street and had indoor plumbing.

"Okay, then. Your vehicle must be off-premises by ten tonight, after the preview, and you may not reenter the fairgrounds until eight A.M."

Maggie nodded. Same routine as always. With one difference this spring—a dealer had been murdered at a show ninety miles down the road in Westchester last week. She put her faded blue van in gear and felt a surge of anticipation as she passed the brilliant pink and red azaleas separating the driveway from the exhibit buildings on her left and the fairground track on her right. It was spring, she loved this show, she was about to see some of her favorite people, and she might even make some money. Many people who lived in New York City, two and a half hours south, had second homes in this area or made it their weekend getaway spot. Their purchases alone made the show worthwhile.

She'd done it for eleven years; so far the worst thing that had happened had been putting the wrong price tag on a wood engraving of Winslow Homer's *Snap-the-Whip*, the most famous of his wood engravings, and having to sell it for $170 instead of $1,700. She still winced at the memory. It was good to be back. And if strengthening security meant more Officer Taggarts, then she had no complaints. This was her time for some spring sunshine and fun. She didn't intend to worry about anything.

Not even murder.

Chapter 2

——∽——

Wall Street & Broadway: Ways of Getting and
Spending Money, *wood engraving published by
Harper's Weekly, September 2, 1865. Elegant
Wall Street men and their families . . . balanced
by a tough bar, on Broadway. Surrounded by
vignettes showing various means (elegant and
rough) of "robbery," "burglary," "murder," and
"flight." Price: $60.*

Maggie passed several dozen vans in the fairgrounds
parking areas, recognizing some. There was the red
and white PASTIMES license plate advertising its owners'
shop name. The truck cutely bearing OLDTHGS plates.
And the station wagon labeled ANTQLADY.

Every year there were a few new dealers, but most
people who were offered a contract came back to a
prestigious and profitable show like this one. An
available booth usually meant someone had gone out
of business or died. Antiques dealers had no mandatory retirement age.

There was no sign of her friend Gussie's van—a
tan model with Massachusetts wheelchair plates. Not

here yet. But there was Abe and Lydia Wyndhams' motor home. Strange couple. She pulled into a space a little farther along the line. The Wyndhams lived in their van, traveling up and down the country with their silver and jewelry. At their ages—at least in their midsixties—most people would want to settle somewhere.

Maggie hoped she wouldn't be living on the circuit in twenty-five or thirty years. It was a rough life. But maybe the Wyndhams were staying in the motel this year. Usually they camped on the fairgrounds. Many dealers roughed it occasionally to save money on show expenses, but the Wyndhams did it all the time.

Susan Findley was unloading near the same entrance. Maggie climbed down and waved at Susan. Four hours of driving wasn't too bad, but her back was stiffer than it would have been ten years ago, when she was in her twenties.

Susan and her husband, Harry, about Maggie's age, or maybe a little younger, were enthusiastic and perpetually negotiating their next big deal. Susan looked good, as always, her hair in the latest shade and style. Today she was a blonde, with a touch of silver in the front. She also looked as though she'd lost more weight. Maggie waved again.

She'd have plenty of time to catch up with them—the Findleys had the booth on one side of hers, and her friend Gussie had the booth on the other side. Susan was a big talker. She loved to gossip between customers. Nobody kept a secret from Susan. And her energy level was incredible; maybe a result of the vitamins, herbal teas, honey, and fruits and vegetables she always carried in a small cooler and constantly consumed. Maggie had never quite decided whether Susan really knew more than anybody or if she was a hypochondriac.

Susan waved back as she balanced an Art Deco pedestal and a pile of Chinese embroidered hangings on a small dolly. Susan and Harry seemed the perfect couple. Even in their better days Maggie and Michael had never been as close as Susan and Harry. Sometimes during the past winter Maggie had thought of them. Energetic, attractive, interested in the same things, they lived and worked together in a loft in New York City and, according to Susan, had active social lives. Some people shared their children; Susan and Harry shared their business.

Maggie and Michael had shared neither children nor business. They had been too busy living their individual lives to focus on having children, and it had just never happened. Too bad. Maggie had always wanted to be a mother. Just not quite yet. In the meantime she had her teaching, and her antique-print business, and Michael's job selling insurance had kept him on the road most of the time. Too often she'd been at the college, or out of town herself, buying or selling prints. Maybe they could have made the marriage work. Maybe neither of them had tried hard enough.

Just five months ago—three days after Christmas—those possibilities had ended. It was Christmas break and the sky had threatened snow. Maggie had been curled up in her big red chair near the fireplace rereading an Agatha Christie when the phone rang. It was the emergency room, reporting an accident.

"Your husband is here. He's all right, but we'd like to keep him a few days for observation."

Everything would be fine, she had told herself as she pulled out the overnight case Michael kept packed for quick business trips. It held the things he would need in the hospital. She decided to add an extra pair of pajamas.

The Tiffany's receipt was under his navy-and-white-striped pajamas. Tiffany's receipts are pale blue. This one was for a diamond and sapphire bracelet. There had been no diamond and sapphire bracelet under Maggie's Christmas tree. Michael had given her new software for her computer and an espresso machine.

She hated espresso.

Maggie had read the receipt, folded it neatly, put it back in the drawer, and continued packing Michael's small leather suitcase. By the time she got to the hospital there was more information.

"Your husband seems to have had a minor stroke. He lost control of the car, but he was lucky. He didn't hurt anyone else, and only his leg was broken."

Only his leg. That was good.

"He's in some pain; we're going to keep him here and run some tests."

Of course. Tests. The next call came at four-thirty in the morning. Apologies. It had all happened too suddenly. It had been massive this time. There wouldn't be any more tests. It was over.

At the age of forty, Michael was dead.

At thirty-eight, Maggie was a widow.

She had found the receipt for the bracelet at two-thirty in the afternoon, and he had died at four-thirty the next morning. After fourteen years he had left her twice in fourteen hours. No time to question; no time to argue; no time for explanations or apologies. Only time to grieve, and then to rage.

Her marriage was gone, but Susan and Harry still had each other. They were lucky. Maggie told herself not to be jealous.

It was time to get on with her life.

Chapter 3

———❦———

Woman in a Feathered Hat, *Harrison Fisher*
(1875–1934), famous American illustrator
whose pastel portraits of beautiful women
appeared on the covers of many magazines,
including Puck *and* Cosmopolitan. *From*
American Beauties, *1909. Price: $90.*

Abe and Lydia Wyndham had just finished draping
their tables in black and were beginning to hang a
few prints for decoration. Maggie decided to check
those out later. Usually the Wyndhams just hung
some *Godey's* fashion prints or gold-framed mirrors
to fill up space, as many dealers did: nothing that
would be competition for a print dealer. But you
never knew what they might have come up with this
year.

Susan had vanished after placing the pedestal
under a spotlight in her booth, leaving the Chinese
embroideries to be arranged or hung. The Findleys
must have been here at dawn: their Art-Effects booth
looked almost finished, and Harry was now helping
Joe Cousins, the nerdish antiquarian-book dealer

whose booth was next to the Wyndhams', unpack some cartons of first editions and private printings. Harry and Joe looked like mismatched bookends. Harry was tall and slender, with neatly sculptured dark blond hair and designer jeans. Joe was short, a few pounds overweight, with slightly scruffy brown hair, wire-rimmed glasses, and, today, a brown cardigan buttoned unevenly, creased slacks, and baggy white socks.

Harry and Joe waved, and Maggie waved back. "Hello! Good to see you both!" She took a quick look at her space to make sure the four eight-foot tables she had ordered were in place. She hadn't known that Harry Findley and Joe Cousins were friends.

Dealers often hired porters to help bring inventory in from trucks or vans, or they brought friends or relatives to help. They almost never helped each other. No time or energy was left after setting up your own space.

But first she had to check in. Vince Thompson's Show Management booth was at the far end of building four. He looked up from piles of dealer envelopes, admittance cards, advertising posters, future show contracts, and promotional notices for the buyers' trips he organized each year to London, Paris, and the Far East.

"Maggie!" He stepped around the table and gave her a hug that was, as usual, a little tighter than necessary. "I was so sorry to hear about your husband— but you're back! And you look terrific! You've lost some weight, haven't you?" His cologne smelled expensive, and slightly exotic. Maggie grinned, moving back from his hug, shaking her head and accepting the compliment. Vince was a charmer. His wavy black hair and mustache were elegantly touched with a little gray this year, but Vince was holding his own. Today he looked tired, though. He had probably been up most of the night supervising booth construction. Or involved in other activities. Vince's other activities had always kept him far too busy to be married or have a family.

So where was the young, attractive assistant of the season who was usually there to share his motel room, serve coffee, and admire Vince should anyone else fail to do so? Either no one was playing that role this year, or she was off doing errands. Knowing Vince's record, probably the second.

"Yes, I've lost a few pounds. I've taken up long walks," Maggie said. Quiet time; thinking time. "It was a rough winter, Vince, but it's over. Thanks for saving my booth when I couldn't make the January show." Vince expected his dealers to do all four shows he promoted each year; Maggie had canceled out of his January show knowing that might take her off his dealer list. Illness or death was no excuse: she knew one dealer who'd done the show with two broken arms and a bandaged head because Vince said he'd have to be there or lose the space. Booths at a Vince Thompson show were coveted.

"Always for you, my dear. My favorite print dealer? Always a place for you."

Vince must not have found another print dealer to replace her.

He began sorting through his paperwork again. A handsome bronze Chinese lion, a carved ebony letter box, a scrimshaw-cased Japanese sword, and a pair of jade bookends were almost lost among the clutter on his tables.

"Going into the trade?" Maggie asked. "These are all lovely." Vince was also wearing an unusual jade and gold tiepin that looked as though he'd picked it up in Asia: one of the side benefits of being in antiques.

Maggie glanced down at the three marcasite *M* pins on her red Somerset County College sweatshirt. She and Vince were dressed to play different roles, but they were both obviously in the same business.

"That stuff isn't mine; it's on loan. I'm just an entrepreneur. And a voyeur." He leered comically at the Asian antiques. The look would have had more impact if it hadn't been so close to his normal expression.

Maggie ignored his mime.

"I really like the lion; it is a 'temple lion,' isn't it?" She reached over and touched the ornate animal. Its body was embellished with scroll-like curls, and two small horns were on its head.

"Some people would call it that. Or a 'temple dog.' But it's really a smaller version of the immense bronze lions that guard the sacred way, or Shen-tao, on the way to the tombs of emperors of the Southern Dynasties. They're called chimeras."

"I didn't realize you knew Chinese art."

He shrugged. "I've led enough antiques-dealer tours to Hong Kong and Singapore to know some of the basics. I'm no expert." He looked down at his balance sheet. "That's a balance of eight hundred and seventy-five dollars before setup."

She reached inside her tote bag for her business checkbook.

"What's the story about a murder at the Westchester Show? I hadn't heard."

"Awful situation. John Smithson."

"John Smithson!" He'd always had a booth down the aisle from Maggie's. Architectural details and turn-of-the-century wrought-iron furniture. A friendly, rather pale young man. They'd shared the coffee and soda run at last fall's show.

"He was doing the Westchester Show last Saturday and just keeled over. No one could do anything. Right in the middle of the customers and everything. Really upsetting. Some customers asked to have their admission fees refunded."

"Why did the officer at the gate say it was murder?"

"Seems John had been taking medication, and some of his capsules had been tampered with." Vince hesitated. "It probably had nothing to do with the antiques show, but it got a lot of publicity around here, so I wanted to make sure we didn't lose any customers because of it. The local police agreed I could have extra security. I was lucky to fill John's booth space at such short notice. A fellow named Will Brewer, from near Buffalo, called and said he was in the area and could fill a last-minute cancellation. So it worked out."

For everyone except John Smithson.

"Actually we have several new dealers here this spring as a result of deaths."

Maggie shivered. "Who else died?"

"Jim Singleton, Don Worthington, and Thom Reardon. Must have been a rough winter."

For sure. She hadn't known any of those dealers—

at a 250-dealer show you only got to know the people whose booths were near yours. "There are a few deaths every year; that's what happens in a business where lots of people go into the trade when they've retired from other jobs."

"You're right. It's not unusual. Although, come to think of it, all of those fellows were young. One car accident; one fire. I don't know about the other one. Sad."

Vince took another sip from his coffee cup. TAKE THE MONEY! was imprinted on its side in green.

"Have you seen your neighbors yet—Susan or Harry Findley, or Joe Cousins?"

"All of them—they were unloading and setting up when I walked by."

"Have you been in touch with anyone? I mean, since last fall's show?"

Maggie handed Vince the check for the balance of her booth rent. "No. Not really. I've talked with Gussie White and exchanged Christmas cards with other people, but that's about it. You know what it's like—being off the circuit and all."

Vince looked amused. "Well, you'll have a lot to get caught up with then. Glad you're back."

"Been looking forward to it. Refreshments for the dealers this year?"

"All the coffee and tea you can drink until the show opens. Just around the corner, outside, under the overhang."

Maggie shook her head. "No coffee or tea for me; what I really need is a diet cola."

"You're on your own for that. There's a machine near the rest rooms."

"No problem. My major priority is unloading my van. I want to get my prints inside the building before it rains."

Maggie stuck her envelope of show papers in her now overflowing canvas bag.

"I'm on my way."

"Good show!" Vince said.

Yes, thought Maggie. Let it be a very good show.

Chapter 4

———✍———

Raiden *(Japanese god of thunder)*, *1902 print from portfolio* Mythological Japan, *published in New York. Raiden has a fierce expression, two goatlike horns, and is surrounded by eight drums. He is endowed with the power to produce thunder by striking the drums with more or less vigor. Price: $40.*

The soda tasted cold and metallic and delicious. Some days Maggie felt diet soda was the one constant in her life.

She took another deep drink from the icy can, then walked to her van and started unloading table covers, piling them on a small dolly, along with all the tools of a print dealer doing an antiques show: drill, hammer, nails, wire, wire cutters, string, and large clips to hang pictures; pegs and clamps for the Peg-Boards she'd attach to the back of her tables; masking tape to secure table covers and for any last-minute repairs to mats or backboards; scissors and razor-blade knives; tape measures; levels; and a large box of adhesive bandages for occasions when her aim wasn't perfect.

At every show the equipment bag seemed heavier. Next show, for sure, she'd splurge and hire a porter.

Inside, between sips of soda, she covered her tables with navy material and tacked her SHADOWS—PINE CREST, NEW JERSEY sign on the back wall of the booth.

She'd named the business Shadows because that's what old prints were—outlines of worlds to which the doors have closed; shadows of pasts that have vanished except for memories and remembrances. She often borrowed prints from her business to illustrate lectures on American civilization or women's studies at the college.

Lydia and Abe Wyndham were arranging cases full of nineteenth-century cameos, garnet bracelets, and silver flatware on their tables across the aisle. Vintage jewelry was always popular at antique shows. The kind Grandma *should* have left you.

"Glad you're back," Lydia called out. "We missed you in January."

"Glad to be back." Maggie tried to look busy. Once Lydia started talking you could forget about working. The older woman crossed the aisle, her omnipresent cup of herbal tea in hand. "Sorry to hear about your husband, dear. All things come to an end, and we can't second-guess the Lord, you know. When he closes a door, he opens a window, I always say."

Yes, she did.

"And isn't it just awful about that nice young John Smithson?" She took a step closer. "They say he was poisoned."

"It is awful. But awful things do happen—I guess the antiques business isn't exempt."

"Vince has certainly increased security around

here. I'm glad. I've always been nervous about leaving all of our jewelry and silver here overnight with just a watchman for protection. Vince says he's going to make sure there are police here all the time. And he's even sleeping in his van this year as an extra precaution."

"He is?" Maybe Vince was anticipating a decrease in the number of customers at the show, and therefore a direct decrease in revenue to Vince. It wasn't like Vince to deprive himself of a comfortable hotel room with an attractive assistant. Maybe the situation was more serious than Maggie had assumed.

Lydia was still chattering. "The man they gave your booth to, in January? Not at all pleasant. Just not our type of person at all." She looked around and lowered her voice, although her husband, Abe, was the only one nearby. "He had lots of those art nouveau statues—you know the kind? I told Abe, 'Don't be throwing any stones, now,' but Abe almost decided we wouldn't do this show again. I had to talk him into it." She gave a quick nod toward Abe, who was arranging jewelry cases on their back tables. "Sometimes he can be stubborn, you know."

Maggie didn't know. "I guess we're all stubborn sometimes." Abe didn't look as though he had the energy to object to anything. Even his mustache seemed to be hanging at a dejected angle this year. "But I'm glad you're here. It's like coming home, to see everyone." Art nouveau statues? Maggie guessed some of them were not clothed quite properly. Lydia and Abe wouldn't have approved.

"Maggie, I'm really hoping you can help me. Have you got any of those prints from nineteenth-century herbals? The kind that show the plant and lists its uses? I'd love to give my niece back in Iowa prints of coffee and tea plants as a wedding gift. She's getting married in August, and she drinks coffee, and her intended is a tea drinker."

"I think I have some that might do." Maggie remembered sticking coffee and tea prints into her portfolio of miscellaneous trees and bushes that are used medicinally.

Lydia put her hand on Maggie's arm. "Don't bother about looking through everything today. We'll both be here all weekend. Just sometime before the show closes. I know we're all busy as bees with setting up today."

Maggie nodded. "No problem." She had hardly started to set up. The opening tonight, and then two long days, would leave plenty of time to look through portfolios. She'd just have to make sure she didn't forget or sell those prints to anyone else.

Harry Findley was arranging early children's books on one of Joe Cousins's back tables. "I notice Harry's helping Joe set up his booth."

Abe Wyndham suddenly appeared next to his wife, at least a foot taller than she was, and half as wide. "I don't think we need to talk about that in public, do we?" He put his arm around his wife's shoulders and steered her back to their booth. "Dear, where did you pack the silver-plate miniatures? I was sure they were in the same carton as the dressing-table bottles, but I can't seem to find them."

"They're right where we always put them, in the green carton." Lydia looked at Maggie and shrugged as she moved back into her booth, pointing.

"Maggie!"

She covered the distance between her booth and the outside door in a moment. "Gussie!" Maggie bent down and gave her a big hug. "Now the show can begin! You look great—new hairdo!"

"I was forty-seven last month. I decided to celebrate." Gussie reached up and touched her hair, cut in a sophisticated ear-length wave. "Like it?"

"Love it! I've been thinking of trading in my mop, and you are an inspiration!" Gussie did look great, but Maggie had no intention of cutting her own hair. She'd worn it long since her student days, and it was a part of her that she didn't plan to change. "New wheels?"

Gussie spun her electric scooter around. "Cool, right? The doctor says I'm supposed to stop stressing my muscles, so I gave in and she wrote a prescription for this beauty. Cost a few pennies even so, but when I go, I go in style. Want to drag?"

"No way, lady. You'd beat me; no contest. Have you checked in with Vince yet?"

"My assistant is taking my check over as we speak. Told you I was getting lazy!"

"Assistant? Who?" Gussie had always insisted on total independence. She hadn't mentioned an assistant in any of their telephone calls during the winter. Maybe that new man in her life had come along. What was his name? Jim? Yes, almost certainly Jim.

"Do you remember my sister's son, Ben?"

Maggie nodded; she had first met Gussie's nephew when she'd visited the Cape eight years before. He had been twelve at the time and had just received a community service award from the mayor for having found a toddler who had wandered away from his mother on the beach. The award had received a lot of media attention in the area because Ben had Down's syndrome.

"Well, I needed a little brawn, and Ben needed to get away from home and be a little more independent, so we've decided to be partners when I do shows. He helps me out at the shop when we're at home. It's company. Ben loves meeting people and traveling, and I love not having to look for porters, and not worrying about someone dumping cartons into my van without caring which one holds the iron banks and which the German bisque dolls." Gussie grinned. "We're giving it a season's trial. So far it's working even better than I thought it would."

"And who's watching your shop while you're out gallivanting?"

"Aunt Augusta's Attic is in good hands. My sister is keeping an eye on it. I can't afford to close down for a couple of days when I do shows. You're lucky to have a full-time job with a steady income!"

"And you're lucky not to have to commute to a full-time job every day!"

They both smiled. It was an often revisited exchange.

"Having Ben help out is a terrific solution. But I thought maybe you'd brought Jim along so I could meet him!"

"Not this time. Rensselaer County is too far from his law practice for a long weekend this time of year. Too many real estate issues with the summer people. You'll meet him when you do the Provincetown Show in July. You are coming up this year?"

The Provincetown Show was a good one; it was a

lively community to visit, and usually a profitable show. And Cape Cod certainly beat the New Jersey suburbs as a great place to be in July. "Wouldn't miss it. I sent in my contract six months ago. And then I'm heading Down East to do a couple of shows in Maine."

"Well, Jim will be on the Cape this summer, I promise."

Ben appeared at her shoulder.

"Ben, you remember Dr. Summer? She has the booth next to ours."

"Glad to meet you again, Dr. Summer." Ben grinned and pumped her hand.

"I'm Maggie, please, Ben. Welcome to the antiques business."

"Did you have any trouble getting us registered?" Gussie asked.

"No problem, Aunt Gussie. Here's the envelope the pretty lady asked me to give you." Ben handed her a white envelope like the one Maggie had picked up earlier.

"Pretty lady, huh? Watch it, young man." Gussie shook her head, turning to Maggie. "I guess Vince has another one this year."

"I haven't had the pleasure. When I checked in, Vince was by himself. Obviously a temporary situation."

The sky darkened and they heard thunder in the distance.

"See you when we get this stuff unloaded," Gussie said as she and Ben turned back toward their van while Maggie hurried toward hers. She lifted a large blue plastic carton from the van onto her dolly. Next year definitely a porter.

Maggie had decided to feature Currier & Ives prints on the side panels of her booth, and Winslow Homer wood engravings on the back wall. The rest of the prints were arranged in categories (botanicals, fruit, anatomy, ships, shells, butterflies, children, maps, sporting) along the tables, and on two easels near the aisles. It took a lot of climbing up and down to hang the framed prints evenly, to ensure that customers could easily read the sign and price on each print, and to arrange the matted prints so customers could browse through them easily. Maggie was up on her ladder for the fifteenth time when she heard Gussie's voice from the next booth.

"Ben? I have plenty of coffee. You don't have to get any more." Maggie saw Ben heading back toward the Show Management area.

"Maggie, I think Ben is enamored. That's three cups of coffee in the past hour."

"Youth!" Maggie shook her head.

She rearranged the anatomy prints so that the skeletons were in front of the more clinical cutaways of eyes and ears and decided to separate the prints of dogs from those of other animals. People would patiently sort through a stack of dog prints trying to find one that "looks just like our Ebony."

She put the Nast and McLaughlin Santas in back of a large collection of prints for children. Santas were popular all year among dealers and collectors, but May was not the time to feature them for general-interest customers. In the spring people were more interested in selecting botanical or fruit prints for recently redecorated kitchens or dining rooms.

She stood back and looked at the booth. Not bad. And definitely time for a break. Preferably a liquid one. And preferably not cola. She checked her watch. Almost four-thirty. An hour and a half to go before the show opened.

Susan and Harry Findley were still not in their booth. Maggie peeked in. Susan and Harry had diversified this year. In addition to the Art Deco glass and furnishings they usually featured, the Findleys had added some late-nineteenth-century American furniture, and some Japanese and Chinese carvings and prints of the same period. They also had a Chinese temple lion—chimera, she corrected herself— that looked very much like the one she'd seen on Vince's desk earlier. The booth fit together nicely: late-nineteenth-century Americans had been fascinated with Asia after Commodore Perry's trips to Japan and his negotiation of the first American-Japanese treaty in 1854. The art brought back from Asia during that period had a heavy influence on early-twentieth-century furnishings.

Across from the Findleys' booth the new dealer from Buffalo was unpacking dollies loaded with Colonial kitchen and fireplace equipment. All six feet of him, including his full beard, was dripping.

It must still be raining.

"Got lost. Just arrived." He waved as he noticed Maggie looking his way and raced back toward his van. There was always at least one dealer tucking a final carton under the table covers two minutes before the show opened. This year it looked as though that dealer would be Will Brewer.

The Wyndhams had put sheets over their cases and a BOOTH CLOSED sign on the chair blocking the entrance. With two of them to set up, they had probably already finished and gone to clean up. Maggie, too, had a change of clothing in her van for tonight. Travel and setups for a show this large took most of the day; there was seldom time to go to a motel and change.

"Hey, Gussie," she called. Ben had returned with coffee at least one more time, she was sure. Peeking around the wall, she realized that, despite frequent trips for coffee, two people worked faster than one. Aunt Augusta's Attic was totally set up. Hand-carved wooden and black-haired china and Door of Hope Mission dolls stood and sat in cases on the back wall out of reach of eager hands, miniatures were in a case to the left, and all manner of tin and iron cars, trucks, banks, and games were on the right table. Gussie had a couple of prints, she noted, and checked them out. Good—only some Kate Greenaways. Nothing that competed with her booth: she had those prints (at lower prices, because they weren't framed) and more.

Gussie and Ben had obviously taken off. Maggie decided to get a drink of water and change, then have a real drink. They say you shouldn't drink alone, so she'd give it another thirty minutes before she broke the rule.

The fairgrounds rest rooms were large and relatively clean, but far from new. They were in a separate building, on the east side of the parking lot, close to the four exhibit halls. During the show they'd be full of customers. Today the ladies' room was quiet. Maggie exchanged pleasantries with a dealer she'd never met before (Connecticut—art and Depression glass) who was also changing from jeans into a long skirt.

The antiques dealers' uniform, Maggie thought, as she folded her jeans and sweatshirt and straightened the panty hose she'd put on under them in the morning. Like gym class—all the girls getting freshened up after working out. But no showers here.

She put on a blue square-necked blouse to match her long dark-red-and-blue-patterned India cotton skirt and added some brass Victorian earrings. No necklace; she'd have to wear her dealer's identification badge anyway. But she pinned one brass *M* to her waistband for luck. Probably once part of a turn-of-the-century sign, it went with the earrings and was different. You never knew what a customer might want to talk about.

A little lipstick and blush, and Maggie unbraided her hair, which fell in full waves almost to her waist. I'll never cut it, she vowed. She shook her head and checked the way the earrings hung. Just right. She curtsied to the cracked mirror, threw her jeans and shirt into the garment bag she'd brought, and headed for the door.

She ran directly into Gussie. "Maggie—you look terrific, by the way; I love the pin—you won't believe what I just saw. Stroll—slowly, don't make a big deal about it—down the aisle near Vince's desk. And don't stop to flirt with any admirers along the way."

Maggie laughed. "Small chance! Do I look that great?"

"Just go! I'll meet you back at the booths. Ritual sherry in ten minutes, okay?"

"You got it. My turn to tote. I've got the bottle and glasses in my van." Maggie again started for the door. "And I'll check out Vince's area on the way."

What could Vince be up to?

Chapter 5

—⟋—

Tenth Commandment, *wood engraving by noted American artist Winslow Homer (1836–1910). Published by* Harper's Weekly, March 12, 1870. *Single page. Woman kneeling in church pew while peeking at elegant gentleman, who is looking back at her. Price: $250.*

Maggie hoisted her red canvas garment bag over her shoulder and headed toward the Show Management desk. What could Vince be doing? She'd seen Vince and his women before. She'd seen the coffee turn to something a little stronger about this time of day—or earlier. She'd seen Vince throw dealers out whose merchandise didn't pass his vetting as genuine antiques, and she'd seen dealers begging for a day's leeway on paying booth rent because times were rough. How much more exciting could Show Management get?

Gussie said to be subtle, so Maggie walked through the adjoining aisle first, checking out the competition. Dealers this year were displaying more oak and pine furniture; one dealer she didn't remember from previous years featured early posters. She wondered if he was replacing one of the dealers who had died and shivered as she passed the booth.

She paused in front of an exhibit of country pine furniture. That pumpkin pine mirror over the dry sink would look just right in her front hall above the small bureau she used for the gloves and hats and miscellaneous whatevers that were always filling the drawers. Maggie pulled a tape measure out of her skirt pocket. Thirteen inches by eighteen. Perfect.

They were asking $350, which was a little high for pine, but it was late-eighteenth-century pumpkin pine, that rare and slightly orange shade of pine that increased a piece of furniture's "country feeling," and its price. A dealer's discount would bring it down a bit.

No one was around. Maggie noted the name and location of the dealer. Booth 3-04. I don't believe they really call their business Pine Away, she thought. She grimaced as she left a note that Maggie Summer in booth 2–23 was interested in the mirror—would they quote a dealer's price?

She started toward her booth, focusing on the mirror, and then remembered—"Check out Show Management"—and turned around. I must be losing my memory!

She heard voices from Show Management before she could see the booth.

"Susan, we've been over this a thousand times, and this is not the moment."

"I don't know why! Vince, I'm tired of playing all these games. I'm tired, period. I set up my own booth, and then play gofer for you all day, and suddenly you're too tired to do anything for me. You promised I could have it back for the show. I've got a customer coming in to see it!"

"The reception is going to start in an hour. You need to get cleaned up, and so do I. We can talk after the reception. Right now I have to go shave and begin acting like a host, and you have to act more like the lady you're obviously not."

Maggie turned the corner just in time to see Susan Findley land a well-aimed palm on Vince Thompson's cheek. Maggie ducked back into the adjoining aisle before either of them could spot her.

Well! Gussie was right. That certainly was an interesting spectacle. Where was Harry? It was definitely time for sherry.

She walked quickly toward her van, holding her long skirt up and picking her way carefully between the puddles and mud in the field. At least the rain had stopped. She passed Susan's van and Joe's (a recent, navy blue model with J. COUSINS, BOOKSELLER in gold on the side, much more elegant than Joe himself) and the Wyndhams'. They had moved to the "park all night" area, a different part of the field from where people like her were parked, who'd be leaving for the night after the show closed. She hung her garment bag just inside the van's side door and pulled out a well-worn cooler containing glasses, a bottle of good Portuguese sherry, and a packet of cocktail napkins. Ben was over by Gussie's van, not far away. "Hey, Ben! Sherry for you?"

"No thanks, Dr. Summer—I mean, Maggie. I'm not twenty-one yet. Besides, I'm in training."

"Training for what?"

"I run races. I'm on a team. I'm going to practice on the track back there, behind the bathroom buildings, while you and Aunt Gussie are at the reception." Ben bent to tie his running shoes.

"Good idea, Ben. Much more interesting than standing around with us oldies."

"Yes." He nodded, still concentrating on his running shoes.

"Have fun." He was such a polite, kind young man. Gussie was lucky. Maggie headed back to her booth, cooler in hand. Alcohol wasn't encouraged for dealers at shows, but at most shows no one came right out and banned it. On a reception evening it was almost required. Abe Wyndham sometimes glared, but even Lydia was known to borrow a silver thermos from someone else's booth and add something to her herbal tea. Years ago Maggie and Gussie had decided that antiques shows were not the places to be hefting cans of beer, and that they weren't the type to add bourbon to their cans of diet ginger ale. They had settled on their own quiet bit of elegance.

Sherry was reserved for shows, and especially, for just before show openings.

She and Gussie would make an optimistic toast to the spirits of customers to come, and Maggie made a silent plea that this show be an especially good one. Once the show started, antiques-dealer etiquette required everybody to respond only "good show" or "not bad" if anyone other than their closest friend asked how they were doing. Too many shows were not good for too many people.

Antiques dealers might sometimes be cutthroats, but they were courteous cutthroats and would seldom risk embarrassing another dealer—unless, of course, they could make a profit by it. The etiquette went with the role and the territory. Dealers would rarely admit that they hadn't even made booth rent or, just as rarely, brag that they had sold enough for a buying trip to Great Britain and a vacation in Tahiti. Profits, or the lack of them, were private.

Maggie sat on the folding chair in her booth and exchanged muddy sneakers for dressy sandals, thinking about what she had seen at Show Management. Susan Findley and Vince Thompson. Odd. She tucked her sneakers under the table covers with her now empty cartons and portfolios and pulled out her sales book and the mahogany stationery box she'd inherited from her grandmother and now used as a cash box for good luck.

This show was going to be very, very interesting.

Even without last week's murder.

Chapter 6

—⁂—

Spectacled Owl, Siberian Owl, and Butcher Bird, *hand-colored steel engraving by the Comte de Buffon (1707–88), French naturalist who devoted his life to his forty-four-volume* Histoire Naturelle *(1749–94), the first study of natural history that attempted to classify animals and plants. This engraving, 1792. Price: $75.*

Maggie had just finished pouring about three inches of sherry into each of two slender but not irreplaceable wineglasses when Gussie motored up, dressed in black silk pants and a Chinese silk jacket embroidered with red and gold lotus blossoms.

"*Très* chic!" Maggie nodded approvingly. "Your sherry awaits you!"

Gussie raised her glass and together they chimed, "May they!" For some reason that neither of them now remembered, they began each show they did together with the same toast, short for "May they buy!" Any resemblance to the phrase *Mayday*, signaling a disaster, was purely intentional.

"So," said Gussie, putting down her glass on the

table edge nearest to her booth, "did you see them?"

"I sure did. But I don't think they saw me. Susan and Vince were having an argument about something. She even slapped him!"

"Well, when I was there, they sure weren't arguing. They were, shall we say, mingling closely. A good thing I was driving at a leisurely pace; if I'd been going faster than a crawl, I would have crashed right into them."

"Would they have noticed?"

Maggie and Gussie grinned like two teenagers who've caught the head cheerleader with the math teacher.

"But where is Harry while all whatever-this-is is happening?" Maggie realized that she hadn't even spoken with Harry today; just waved in his direction as she set up.

Gussie shook her head. "I don't know. I saw him earlier—you did, too—helping Joe. I haven't seen either Harry or Susan near their booth all afternoon."

"You're right. When I first got here, Susan was bringing in that pedestal she's put in the middle of her booth. She must have hung those embroideries on the quilt frame while I was registering, because I didn't see anyone near the booth after that. I did take a look before I went to change, though. Did you notice how they've diversified their stock this year? I really like one of their Japanese prints."

"Harry and Susan seem so perfect together." Gussie sipped the sherry. "I've always been a bit envious. Before last winter, I was even a bit jealous of you and Michael. I've been divorced too long, Maggie."

Maggie smiled ironically. "What we saw at Show Management didn't exactly illustrate that 'perfect couple' scenario for Harry and Susan. And, of course, you know what happened with Michael and me."

"You're right. Mouth opened before brain was in gear. I know how rough a winter it's been. I'm sorry we don't live closer, so I could have been some sort of a help to you."

"You're a good and kind friend, Gussie. But I felt the same way about the Findleys. They seemed to have the perfect setup." Maggie took another sip of her sherry. "And, no matter what the situation with Harry, Susan is making music with Vince, but it sure wasn't harmonious when I was there!"

"It was pretty tuneful when I saw them. If Vince ever put his hands on me, the way he was . . . well, he isn't my type. But it just doesn't make sense. Could Susan really be—seeing—Vince?"

They were silent for a moment. "Seeing Vince" involved a lot more than a visual experience, and with Vince, "seeing" was always a temporary situation. Vince kept moving, in every sense of the word. Between his shows and his antiques tours he was rarely home. And he was rarely alone, home or away. But Susan certainly was a great flirt. Always had been.

"If Susan was going to have an affair, why Vince?" Maggie shook her head. "She always seemed smarter than that. A little spacey. But not dumb."

"And to jeopardize her marriage to someone as terrific as Harry. And do it right under his nose!"

"If we saw them, then so did half the dealers here."

"Well, she does look terrific, as always. Although I think this time she's lost a little too much weight."

Maggie nodded. Susan was usually on some new health kick. Last year it had been radishes. She'd eaten at least a bowl or two during each day of the show, swearing they would guarantee smoother skin and more energy in one easy, nutritious package. Between customers she was always popping some sort of pill guaranteed to keep her young and beautiful forever.

"Well, whatever she's doing this year, she looked tired to me."

"Maybe she ran out of radishes."

"Or maybe this year it's kumquats!"

"The only thing sure about Susan is that every year it's something different."

"Maggie. I just thought. Susan was at Vince's Show Management area. She's probably the 'pretty lady' Ben spent half the afternoon checking out!"

"Well, she's a little old for him, but only by ten or twelve years, I'd guess."

Gussie shook her head. "I still can't put the whole picture together. There must be an explanation."

Maggie reached down below the table covering for the bottle to refill their glasses.

"What is it that you ladies need explained?"

"Susan!"

Susan, appearing from the direction of her booth, looked more like a guest at a cocktail party than an antiques dealer waiting for customers. The green brocade dress she was wearing featured a low neckline that framed a large carved-jade pendant.

She gave Maggie and Gussie each a fast hug and a big smile. Whatever the problem had been with Vince, it didn't appear to be bothering her now.

"It's me—in person! Sorry I didn't have a chance to chat with you guys earlier; I was helping Vince. But it's almost magic time, so here I am!"

Maggie reached out and clasped Susan's hand for a moment and took a good look at her. Susan had always been tiny and slim. But today her cheekbones were almost protruding, and the low neckline on her dress just accentuated her collarbone. Maybe it was true you couldn't be too rich, but Susan was a walking illustration that you could be too thin. Her hair, even blonder and frizzier than usual, was loosely curled and accentuated by the silver streak in the front.

Maggie tried not to stare at her. "Susan, what a beautiful dress. And that incredible necklace makes your eyes look so green!"

"Thank you. Actually, the green contacts help, too. I just needed to try something new, you know, so this year it's my eyes. Terrific?" Her eyes were definitely the color of strawberry leaves.

"It is certainly a new look! Gussie and I were just saying we hadn't seen you in hours." At least not in your booth, Maggie thought. "But I did admire your inventory!"

"Thanks! I've gone international this year! Found all kinds of wild stuff on Vince's buyers' trip to Hong Kong and Singapore in early April. I've got tons to tell you. What a year! Not to be believed." Susan paused and looked serious for a moment. "Maggie, I heard about Michael. I'm sorry."

"I appreciate that, Susan. It was a hard winter. But life goes on. And where's Harry? I haven't spoken with him today, either."

"'Where is Harry?' The question of the year! Harry's

gone." Susan gestured dramatically in the general direction of the ceiling.

Maggie and Gussie looked at each other while Susan recovered from her histrionics.

"Well, no, I don't mean he's disappeared or anything. But he's gone from my life. Or at least my legal life."

"Harry's here at the show, isn't he? I saw him earlier, helping Joe set up."

"Exactly. That's it."

Gussie shook her head. "Susan, you've lost me."

"I thought everyone would know by now, actually. It's been the talk of the circuit."

"What, Susan? I've been off the circuit—and Gussie lives in Massachusetts. We hadn't heard anything."

"Harry. He and I are still the best of friends—the best! In fact, he's buying out my share of Art-Effects, and we've almost got the paperwork done. It's complicated by the divorce and all, but since we're all in agreement, it's pretty clear."

Maggie raised her hands, then let them fall. "Susan, I'm sorry, but this has caught me way off base. You and Harry are divorced?"

"Will be next week. Harry has been in analysis for a long time and finally decided that he needed to be his own person."

"Well, that's fine," Gussie said. "But why can't he be his own person and be married to you?"

"Because Harry's own person is not married. In fact, Harry's own person is not even heterosexual. In fact, Harry's own person is in love with Joe. Which is why you saw them together earlier."

"Susan, how awful for you." Maggie reached out

and touched Susan's arm. Many dealers were gay, of course, but to have your own husband decide that he preferred men to women . . . what an awful blow to your ego!

"No, actually, it's wonderful! I'm playing the field; I'm having fun! And Harry and I are still friends, so I really haven't lost anything. I mean, he and I were always close, and all, but, you understand, sex was never a big thing with us, and now—life is a party! It's like being a teenager all over again, with lots of people to choose from, only now I'm old enough to know how to play the games!"

"Susan, I hope you do. Those games have lots of rules. And lots of liabilities." Gussie looked worried. "Do be careful, dear."

"I am, I am. I'm a big girl, Gussie. I can take care of myself. And I don't have anything to worry about. You see, everything is just wonderful! Everyone's got what he wants. Harry and Joe have each other, I'll have the money for my half of the business, and the world is full of possibilities! The old married-lady bit just wasn't my scene. I mean, Harry and I did pretty well for the last eleven years, but I've been too fettered. Now I can be me! When Harry and I met, we were just kids, out to set New York on its heels. We had lots of friends, went to lots of parties, and made some money. But over the years Harry has gotten too serious. First he wanted us to open a shop and stop just selling at shows and out of our loft. And now this thing with Joe; wanting to settle down with one person, when we could have had each other and the world, too! Well, that's not for me. I'm not ready to settle in and make chocolate chip cookies, you know?"

No; Susan didn't look like someone who owned an apron, much less a cookie sheet. Unless she used one to reheat vegetarian pizza.

Vince's voice on the public address system startled all of them. "Dealers, please return to your booths. The six o'clock reception is about to begin."

"Oh, you've got to let me go and get organized. I have to make sure my cash box and sales books are in order, just in case a customer comes near." Susan laughed. "We'll have lots of time to talk later!"

She turned and danced the few steps to her booth and disappeared behind the wall separating her space from Maggie's.

"Do you believe?" Gussie arched her eyebrows and looked after Susan.

The sound of a carton being opened in the booth across from Gussie's distracted them in the preshow quiet.

Joe Cousins was unpacking one last carton of leather-bound "decorator books" and arranging them on the shelves beneath his J. COUSINS, BOOK-SELLER sign. As they looked, Joe stood up, and Harry reached over to straighten his tie.

Lydia Wyndham was arranging some pink azaleas in a silver vase on one of her tables, while, standing at the other side of the Silver in Mind booth, Abe smiled and raised his can of soda toward them.

"Good show, ladies."

Maggie and Gussie raised their glasses back toward him. "May they!"

Chapter 7

———

Godey's Fashions for April 1867, *hand-colored
steel engraving, double foldout page from*
Godey's Ladies Book, *the first successful
American ladies' magazine; each issue featured
several colored plates of the latest fashions.*
Godey's *was a decisive voice in determining
Americans' morals and taste. Engraving of
five ladies in elaborate outside attire, including
one in mourning riding habit, with horse.
Also, child in red dress feeding swan.
Price: $60.*

The opening reception was civilized and predictable.
Well-dressed and well-coiffed couples strolled the
aisles, sipped chardonnay or martinis, and made the
usual comments as they walked by.

"Dear, how cute! What do you think it is?" (An eigh-
teenth-century wire flyswatter.)

"You know, my grandmother had one just like
that. We threw it out with all her junk when we
moved her into assisted living, you know." (A mid-
nineteenth-century flow-blue china platter.)

"Very nice . . . but the color wouldn't fit in our living room." (An Audubon egret print.)

"You know, I should tell my decorator about these things." (Victorian silver and crystal cosmetic bottles and jars.)

"I always did like mahogany." (A cherry sideboard.)

Dealers smiled patiently at prospective customers, sipped cups of whatever, and wished for a customer who was serious enough to appreciate the beauty and the value of merchandise they had spent months gathering and hours displaying, and maybe, if they were really optimistic, for a customer who'd buy something.

One redheaded woman in a chartreuse suit spent twenty minutes going through a portfolio of Maggie's hand-colored steel engravings of garden plants from William Curtis's *Botanical Magazine,* an annual published by the Royal Horticultural Society in London from 1887 until World War I. Maggie was lucky to have about seventy in stock. The best botanical artists worked for "The Magazine" or "Curtis," as it was called. Printings were limited, and highly thought of. That translated to "hard to find" and "valuable."

The woman examined the prints carefully, sorting them for color and symmetry. Finally, after she'd chosen six flowers that she liked in various shades of blue and burgundy, her husband joined her.

"What do you think, dear?" she asked. "Wouldn't they look stunning on the side wall in the dining room? We could mat them in dusty rose to match our drapes, and frame them in gold."

Her husband took about two seconds to wave them aside. "Boring. Why don't you just get one decent bright painting instead of bothering with all those dull flowers?"

The carefully chosen set of six prints went back into the Curtis portfolio, and Maggie wrote off her hopes of a good sale. Small Curtis prints were now going for over $100 each, and even with a discount for buying six, a $600 sale would definitely have made the evening worthwhile.

Lydia Wyndham, who had been watching the whole incident, came over and whispered, "Just like they say: one in the hand is worth two in the bush. I'd rather a single customer anytime than a married one with the husband or wife at the show. Eighty percent of the time they won't agree, and that means the end of the sale. Never knew it to fail. Would you like a cup of lemon verbena tea? I have a thermos of hot water in my booth."

"No, thanks, Lydia; I have something to drink." Maggie indicated the sherry next to her cash box. "But thanks for asking!" Maggie never drank tea, but she believed in keeping her options open. "Between you and Susan, I never lack possibilities for tea during this show."

"It's fun; we usually bring a few new favorites to share. Last year Susan was really into hibiscus. That's a little sweet for my taste. But if you want to try anything, and like it sweeter, I always keep a little raspberry honey set aside, just in case."

Maggie nodded. She couldn't tell raspberry honey from maple syrup.

Her next customer was a young man who picked

out two late-nineteenth-century male fashion prints. Engravings of men in elegant black suits and dapper mustaches were much rarer than women's fashion prints.

"What credit cards do you take?"

"Sorry; just checks and cash." Maggie sighed as he put the prints back. Some dealers took credit cards, but she had never bothered to go through the necessary paperwork. She only did a dozen shows a year, and most customers were comfortable giving checks if they didn't have enough cash with them. Occasionally a check bounced, but that was just one of the risks of doing business. Most antiques show customers, like most people in general, were honest. But she had lost several good sales in the past year. . . . Maybe it was time to check into whatever would be required to join the plastic world.

Michael could have helped me with that, she thought automatically. The numbness she had lived with for months was now gone, and so was the raw pain, but the deep, everyday pain remained. The really awful part, Maggie thought, was that I don't miss Michael as a person as much as I miss the life I had always assumed would be there for us, together. All the things we had planned to do "someday." Have children. Spend more time together. Cruise down the Rhine.

Late at night, hugging her pillow and allowing the tears to come, she still missed their dreams, and their tomorrows, and tried not to think about the mystery woman who had received a Tiffany bracelet for Christmas, or to wonder whether she was mourning, too.

On this opening night of the spring fair, Maggie

felt a new edge as she sat and greeted customers. Michael's insurance hadn't equaled his income. Community college teaching was a solid profession, but was not particularly well paid. She might have an empty bed. But she didn't intend to have an empty bank account as well.

"That's a very special Winslow Homer wood engraving," she said, smiling at the woman in a black suit and red blouse who was peering at one of the walls in her booth. "One of his Gloucester series, his most popular. It was published in *Harper's Weekly* in 1873."

"But it's black and white!" The woman, who managed to look Maggie's age only with substantial cosmetic help, was doubtful.

"Winslow Homer was one of America's greatest nineteenth-century painters. At the beginning of his career he worked for *Harper's Weekly,* a nationally known American newspaper. In the nineteenth century newspapers weren't in color. Homer would sketch on location, and an engraver would take his sketches and make the actual wood engraving used by the newspaper to print the sketches. Remember, this was before photography was common, and people's only view of places they had never seen was through engravings." Maggie paused. "Homer's wood engravings have been featured in recent exhibitions at the National Gallery in Washington, and at the Metropolitan and Brooklyn Museums."

"Nice. But I'm really looking for something red, to match my sofa."

The woman walked away. Making a living selling prints was not easy.

Between smiling at customers and sipping sherry (she was on her second refill) Maggie couldn't help watching Susan, who was standing outside her booth, laughing and talking animatedly with everyone who came by. She had also spent quite a bit of time talking with Will Brewer, the new fellow with the Colonial kitchen wares, who had somehow gotten his booth together in time for the opening.

And there were customers. Maggie sold one nine-by-twelve-inch 1890s *Hickory Dickory Dock* chromolithograph. "It will just be perfect in my new grand-baby's room," cooed a large, graying woman in a pink-flowered dress who twice dropped her check-book in her efforts to pull out baby pictures. "Isn't Nathaniel the cutest thing ever? Aren't his eyes just like mine?"

Maggie would happily have praised any baby photo as she wrote up the sale.

"I'm going to put that picture in a really cute blue frame and send it right down to my daughter in Atlanta. I'm making up a package of very special things for Nathaniel. He's my very first grandbaby, did I tell you?"

Abe, across the aisle, was still reading his worn copy of *The Bible in a Year*, while Lydia had made at least one sale: a Victorian silver christening mug, to the same grandmother who had just bought a print from Maggie. Perhaps the woman had also stopped at Gussie's booth. The toys from Aunt Augusta's Attic would be ideal for a new grandma.

Gussie stuck her head around the end of her booth. "Refill, please?"

Maggie reached for the bottle she'd tucked behind

the table draping. "We'd better save some room for dinner. Do you and Ben have any major plans?"

"He's still working out, as far as I know. He's to meet me at the motel after the show closes. I'm really exhausted. Not sure I feel up to going out. But there's a Pleasin' Pizza down the street that delivers."

"Sounds gourmet enough for me. Mind if I join you? I do like anchovies, but between my aching muscles, this sherry, and hearing about Susan and Harry's problems, a plain cheese pizza is about all I can handle tonight."

"You've got a deal if we can add mushrooms."

"Sealed. How're sales?"

"One good one: a miniature Victorian china tea set. That's it so far."

"Well, if you can say 'good sale,' you're ahead of me."

"Saturday's when the buyers come; you know that, Maggie. Tonight's museum night. Most people are just here to admire."

"And be admired. I know. But I always hope. And how's the view from your booth?" Maggie nodded toward Joe and Harry, across the aisle from Gussie. Their booth had several browsers or first-edition seekers.

"They've made a few good sales, from what I've seen."

"I didn't mean sales . . . isn't this whole situation strange?"

"Maybe for you and me, but they all seem to be acting very civilized. Joe and Harry are just Joe and Harry. Harry doesn't know much about books, but I've already heard him talk three customers into buying first editions. Joe's smiled a lot, like always, and said very little. Harry's hustling should help his sales. I can't believe Susan isn't upset, though. If Michael had even looked at another woman, wouldn't you have wanted to shoot him?"

Maggie blanched.

"Oops . . . sorry! But . . . another man! I don't think I could have dealt with that at all."

"Me, neither." Maggie was glad to change the subject. "Actually, I dated someone once, several centuries ago, pre-AIDS and all, who was bisexual. Hal was handsome, charming, appeared devoted—and every time he smiled at a waiter in a restaurant, I got nervous."

"Maggie, you're incredible. I couldn't have coped at all."

She shrugged. "He read *The New York Times* and *Maine Antique Digest;* he liked art exhibits and the theater; he didn't constantly keep comparing me to his previous girlfriends. None of that was too hard to take."

"Well, maybe you should have cloned him!"

"Not a perfect situation, though. It turned out that I wasn't paranoid for suspecting the waiters. He left me for Jason, who worked the dinner shift at the Wild Mushroom."

They grinned at each other, and Gussie shook her head.

"I love it! Well, they say you're only paranoid when no one is following you."

Maggie nodded. "Only thing was—it wasn't me they were following!"

She turned to respond to a portly gentleman with

a white beard who was admiring a print on the back wall.

"I remember a picture just like that hanging in my grandmother's house on Block Island while I was growing up. That was the early fifties. Could it be the same? She said it was from a calendar she got from her insurance company."

"No, that's an original Currier and Ives. Starting in 1936 the Travelers Insurance Company did reproduce Currier and Ives prints on calendars they sent their customers, so your grandmother might have had one of those, but this isn't a reproduction."

"How can you tell? It looks just like the one my grandmother had. It was right above the shelf with her cookie jar, so I remember it well. As soon as I walked into your booth, I smelled gingersnaps."

"What a great reason to like a print! But this is an original *American Homestead—Spring*." Maggie reached over to take the print down. "It was published in 1869 and is one of the most popular Currier and Ives scenes. In fact, it's in the New Best Fifty. That's a list dealers use to identify the most popular Curriers. It was reproduced often, but you can tell this is an original in three ways. First, it's exactly 7.15 inches high by 12.8 inches wide." Maggie pulled out her tape measure to demonstrate. "Second, it's printed on medium-weight rag paper. Did you know rag paper was really made by tearing up cotton rags and then adding a bonding agent? All Currier and Ives prints up to 1870 were printed on rag paper; then they started to use rag paper with some wood pulp added. Most reproductions are printed on paper made entirely from wood pulp."

The man listened intently. "And what's the third way to tell it's not a reproduction?"

Maggie reached over in back of her cash box and picked up a large square magnifying glass. She flicked on a light in the handle and gestured for him to look at a corner of the print. "See? The lines in the picture are made up of tiny nonsymmetrical dots. But the color is solid."

He focused on the trees next to the farmhouse and nodded.

"In a reproduction you'd find very tiny connecting lines between the dots . . . and the color would look like tiny dots, too. That's because, in an original, the color was added by hand. It's watercolor. You can see three original Currier and Ives prints of the same subject and the colors won't be identical. They were colored in an assembly line; each person in the line added one color."

"Well, I have to have it. If it isn't exactly like the one I remember from my grandmother's kitchen, that's all right. I think she would have liked this one even better." He pulled out his wallet.

If it reminded him of his grandmother, that was fine. So fine, in fact, that she could take it to the bank. A darn nice sale. She had gotten a good buy when she'd bid on this particular print at an auction in Maine, and the profit she had just made would pay most of her booth rent. In fact, maybe she could afford to both pay booth rent and buy that pumpkin pine mirror.

While she had been talking with the *Hickory Dickory Dock* customer, the Pine Away dealer had passed her a note quoting a dealers' price of $250 on the mirror.

The crowd was dwindling. Maggie looked at her watch; it was eight forty-five, and the show closed at nine. Almost over.

"Gussie, I'm going to stop at a booth over in building three before I leave tonight. They quoted me a price on a mirror I covet, and I feel affluent. I'm going to let them know they've sold it."

"Fine. I'll meet you back at the motel. I'll be in the cabin with the ramp and two rooms."

"I'll find you. Go ahead and order the pizza. In fact, it's on me."

"That must have been some sale! You don't know the bill you're in for. Ben is twenty, and still growing!"

"I'll cope. Tomorrow I'll eat tuna salad and watch the parade go by. Tonight, let's celebrate being alive."

Chapter 8

—❦—

Anatomy—Osteology: Cranium, *wood engraving, 1808, from a medical textbook. Six human skulls, seen from the left side, to illustrate anthropological differences in human anatomy. (Skulls are Georgian, Turk, Negro, Calmuck, and [2] Caribs.) Price: $75.*

"Any food tastes better with good company." Gussie moved her laptop computer to the back of the bureau to make space for the pizza box. "And I ordered some diet sodas. Sherry doesn't really go with pizza."

"Fine. I have no desire to face opening day with a headache if I can help it," agreed Maggie, settling herself in a large chair near the table and reaching for one of the soda cans.

"Ben should be here any minute. He left a note on the van seat saying he was going to walk a few more laps to cool down. I'm glad he's using up energy and doing something for himself while I'm busy. This is kind of a holiday for him, being away from home. And he has his exhibitor's badge, so he can get on and off the fairgrounds without me."

"He certainly does have energy." Maggie took a slice and added some red pepper and garlic salt from packets that Pleasin' Pizza had included. "My idea of a holiday wouldn't be slogging around on a muddy track."

"You're not a twenty-year-old boy. Ben has been working out for years now. It started with physical therapy when he was younger, because of the muscle weakness that comes with Down's syndrome. He really enjoyed it, and now he competes regularly. Competitions give him a chance to do a little traveling, and he loves meeting people and seeing new places."

"I think it's great for both of you. And, speaking of you, tell me more about this new love of yours before Ben comes back and we have to make sure our conversation is 'G-rated.'"

"Maggie, Ben is twenty! And he has quite an eye for the girls. Witness his interest in Susan. I suspect he wouldn't have been running around the track all this time if he'd realized she had a booth so close to ours!"

"So—tell me about Jim."

"Very nice, very professional, and very well-meaning."

"You make him sound like Mr. Rogers, not like a romantic hero."

"Well, not quite Mr. Rogers. But Jim is predictable. And a little too serious."

"Gussie White. With half the women in this country looking for a nice, intelligent, caring man who isn't afraid of commitment, are you saying you've found one?"

"Maybe it's me: maybe I'm not ready for a serious relationship. Or maybe just not quite yet. Sometimes late at night I have visions of myself crippled and dependent, and I just can't understand why Jim would choose me instead of a woman who can walk more than a few steps, and who isn't exhausted from taking a shower in the morning."

"Spoken by someone who runs her own business, owns and keeps up her own home, and has always had a fairly full and—from what I've heard—a fairly spicy social life? You're talking as though you're a decrepit old woman!"

"I am forty-seven. And when I was younger I could do so much more! Oh, Maggie, I keep seeing myself as the skinny kid with heavy braces and crutches who sat on the sidelines and took attendance in gym class. After I had polio it took four years of therapy just so I could walk by myself. And that was walking with braces and crutches. Those years were hell. The pain. The humiliation. Not being like the other kids." Gussie shook her head. "But even that was nothing compared to attending school for the first time after getting out of the rehab hospital. I was seven. My mother had brushed my hair and braided it and bought me a new dress. It was red, my favorite color, with short, puffed sleeves and smocking on the top, and long enough to cover most of my braces. I was so excited about meeting other children who didn't have to think about how to walk."

Maggie put her slice of pizza down.

"I remember standing at the door of the classroom and the teacher asking if I'd need a special desk. The other children were staring at me. Sarah May, who had long red pigtails and freckles, giggled. Some of the other kids pointed at my legs. At lunchtime I sat by myself with my favorite sandwich, cream cheese and jelly. My mother had made it so I wouldn't have to balance a tray in the cafeteria line. I heard the other kids talking and saw them looking at me." Gussie looked straight at Maggie, and there were tears in her eyes. "Maggie, I went to that school for three years. And for three years they called me 'the polio girl.' No one knew who Augusta White was. But everyone knew who the polio girl was. That's why I worked so hard to be like other people. And I was. I never had as much strength as other people, but I did my physical therapy exercises, and I swam, and by the time I was in junior high, I could walk without braces. My parents even paid for me to go to private school, where no one knew what I'd been like when I'd had the braces and crutches. But you never really overcome polio. When I first met you, Maggie—that was about ten years ago, right?"

Maggie nodded.

"Remember I walked with braces and crutches then? Well, I had just put them back on. I'd had twenty-five years of freedom before my muscles started giving up. Now doctors know that forcing muscles weakened by polio won't work for a lifetime. Children who have polio now are told they have to wear braces for life. If they don't, they'll end up like me, in a wheelchair in their forties. Now my superterrific motorized scooter is the only thing that keeps me going." Gussie took a sip of soda.

Maggie hesitated. "Gussie, I'm sorry. I never knew

what to say. You never talked about your disability, and you never asked for help. You never seemed to need any!"

"You're right. But now I'm looking fifty in the face, and I'm in this scooter all the time, except for the couple of steps I can take with my crutches to get to it. Thank goodness I can still do that! Thank goodness my arms are strong." Gussie flexed one in triumph and looked at it. "In thee do I trust! But I can't set up my booth alone anymore. Ben's help is keeping me on the circuit a little longer, but I'm already planning for the day when buying trips will be the only times I leave my shop for business. I've modified my house so I can be on the first floor most of the time, and I have a chairlift to the second, where I leave my old wheelchair. From a practical standpoint, I'm making the accommodations neces-sary. But, emotionally, when I think about having a serious long-term relationship with someone . . . I just want to be sure Jim understands what my limits are." Gussie grimaced. "You see, Maggie, I'm really just beginning to understand them myself."

"But Jim's watched you making changes to your life, so he knows what it's going to take."

"You're right. Of course Jim knows. And the facts don't seem to have turned him off. He's still around! And our . . . physical relationship . . . is pretty darn good. I guess I'd just like some chimes to ring. Some-thing to let me know I'm making the right decision."

"Listen, lady, it all sounds pretty darn good to a widder woman like myself."

"Did you and Michael hear bells?"

"That's a personal question!" Maggie was silent a

moment. "A few, I guess; maybe some cowbells, at least at the beginning. Come to think of it, a few jingle bells at this point in life would be nice."

"I have some great sleigh bells hanging in my shop. I could cut you a deal!"

They were both laughing and reaching for a second slice of pizza when the door opened.

"Aunt Gussie—"

"Ben! Great. You're back, and we haven't eaten all the pizza yet. Go and get washed up. We'll save you at least four slices."

"No—thanks—I mean—Aunt Gussie—I need help. I didn't know what to say, so I didn't tell the policeman, and I just came here, and I don't know what to do." Ben stood just inside the door, dripping with sweat and mud. He looked more like a seven-year-old than a twenty-year-old. A seven-year-old who had just seen a ghost. "Please, Aunt Gussie. It's bad. There's blood. I think I just killed someone."

Chapter 9

❧

Wild Fowl Shooting, *hand-colored steel engraving by Henry Alken (1765–1851), major English artist/engraver who, after a first career as a horse trainer, specialized in sporting prints; 1820. Two men with guns and dogs hiding on hillside and watching wild geese landing on a lake. Period frame.*
Price: $185.

"Ben, sit down, and calm yourself."

Ben sat on the edge of the nearest chair, but he didn't look calm. He looked panicked.

"Ben, what happened?" Maggie went over and put her hand on his shoulder. "One step at a time."

"I was walking around the track. People were leaving the buildings where the booths are and going to their vans. The people staying all night park near the bathrooms, you know? That's near the track. I could see the lights and hear the people. I just kept going, because I was beginning to get tired, but I wanted to go around the track a couple more times. Like I told you. I have a big meet in Hartford next week. And then I saw that lady—the pretty lady from Show Management. She was talking to a man."

Maggie and Gussie exchanged glances. "How could you see them if you were on the track?"

"I was coming around near the entrance. I'd almost finished my workout. I was walking slow, you know, to cool down. They were over by the driveway, where all the flowers are."

"The azaleas?"

"Right. All those red and pink flowers. They didn't see me at first; I don't think they thought anyone was out there."

That area near the back entrance to the fairgrounds was behind the rest room buildings and the concession stands. It wasn't far from the south field, where people were settling into their vans for the night, but there was no logical reason for anyone to be there unless, like Ben, they were interested in the track. Or interested in not being seen. The back entrance was open during setup, but was always locked before the show opened and would stay locked until it was time to pack out on Sunday night. Anyone leaving the show area tonight, customer or dealer, would have to use the front entrance. Security was tighter that way.

"So, you saw a woman and a man talking. That doesn't sound so awful."

"But it was! She was yelling at him, and he was yelling at her, and . . . it was bad." Ben's eyes filled, as though he were about to cry. "They were saying bad words. I don't say words like that, Aunt Gussie. I never say words like that."

"I know you don't, Ben. You're a good boy."

Maggie looked at him steadily. "What did you do?"

"I didn't know what to do. I wanted to stop them. And then the man pulled something out of his jacket. He was going to hit her. I know he was. And she started saying, 'No, no, you can't,' and I yelled at the man to stop and ran up to them, and then I pushed him, and she ran away and he fell down, and then everything was quiet. He was just lying there, near the flowers. I reached down to help him up, but he didn't move, and there was blood."

Ben raised his right hand and showed them a narrow streak of blood on his palm.

"I ran after the lady, but I couldn't find her. There were lots of people over by the vans, and I almost ran into some of them. I didn't know where she'd gone, and I was scared. So I came here." Ben took a deep breath. "And I guess you're going to call the police to put me in jail, right?"

Maggie looked at Ben. "How hard did you hit him?"

"I ran toward him and then I pushed him. Not really hitting. But he fell down. I don't remember. But he didn't get up."

"Did you recognize him?"

Ben shook his head. "No."

"Well, whoever he is, we need to find out how he is."

"Are you going to call the police?"

"We may have to. But not yet. Let's go and take a look at the situation first." Maggie had already picked up her canvas bag and moved toward Ben and the door. "Gussie, would you mind guarding the rest of our pizza while Ben and I take a little walk?"

"Maggie, are you sure? If that man's lying out there, he may need medical attention."

"Which is why we need to go and see, right now. Did the policeman see you leave, Ben?"

"I don't know. He was talking to someone in a van. Do I have to go back, Aunt Gussie?"

"Ben, you're scared, I know, but you have to keep being brave. You go with Maggie and see how the man is, and get some help for him."

"I want you to go, too, Aunt Gussie."

"Ben, I'd like to go. But my muscles aren't doing too well now, after all we did today. You know how they get. And on that field my scooter would just slow you down, especially at night, when I can't see all the bumps." She turned to Maggie. "Are you sure you want to do this? Ben is my responsibility. Maybe you could just tell the policeman at the entrance and have him take care of it."

"When Ben is the only witness? We can't do that, Gussie; you know it. And I don't mind. I'm sure it will just take a short time."

"The man is dead. I really killed him." Ben leaned against the wall and started to cry.

Chapter 10

———⟋———

The Turning of the Tide, *wood engraving by
Charles Dana Gibson (1867–1944), American
illustrator known for his romantic drawings of
the Ideal American Woman, who became
known as the Gibson Girl. 1901. Elegantly
dressed woman and man kiss on the beach,
ignoring the incoming water covering their legs.
Price: $65.*

Only a few cars and trucks were driving down Oak
Avenue, the two-lane street that separated the small
buildings that were Kosy Kabins from the fairgrounds on the other side of the road. A red neon
sign on the motel office roof flashed NO VACANCY,
and its reflection gave the damp macadam driveway a
surreal feeling. Maggie had a momentary vision of
the pavement glistening with blood and shook her
head. Too much imagination was working overtime.

The ground was wet, but not as muddy as it might
have been. They headed down the motel driveway,
past other cabins and corresponding cars and vans,
and paused at the street.

"Nothing like crossing a dark street at night. Ben, let's make sure we stay together."

"Okay, Maggie."

They carefully looked both ways. "And if we have to talk to anyone, you let me do the talking." People were too quick to blame someone who was retarded. It would be easier for Ben if she could run interference.

Ben nodded.

"Then let's go."

The main gate to the fairgrounds was still open. Tomorrow there would be customers' cars lined up at the entrance, waiting to find parking spaces in the fifteen-acre north field where attendants had already lined up stanchions on the grass to mark rows. The field was so large that Vince usually arranged for a series of minibuses to ferry people from the far parking areas to the main buildings. Better not to exhaust customers before they had even started to walk the aisles.

But tonight there were no cars in the field, and Maggie was relieved to see the gate still open. She glanced at her watch. Ten o'clock. The two policemen guarding the grounds looked as though they were about ready to close and lock the two large swinging, metal fence sections that were the entrance.

"Excuse me, folks, but the fairgrounds are closed." Officer Taggart was still on duty. He looked at them curiously. They made a strange couple. Maggie looked tense and Ben was disheveled and pale. Both were walking too fast for a casual stroll.

"I'm sorry to bother you, but, remember me? I'm Maggie Summer—here's my dealer's identification?" Maggie showed him the badge that had been in her dealer packet earlier in the day, and which all dealers wore to identify themselves on the fairgrounds. "I'm from booth two twenty-three. And this is Ben Allen. He's Gussie White's assistant? Booth two twenty-four." Ben pointed to the badge he had pinned to his white T-shirt.

"I remember you—the college professor who colors her hair."

If looks could have killed, Office Taggart would have stopped breathing right then. Maggie instantly decided not to share the purpose of their errand with these two cops.

"The exhibit buildings are locked for the night and"—Taggart checked the clipboard in his hand—"according to my list, neither of you are sleeping on the grounds." He looked at them both again. "I'm about to close up for the night."

"We're staying across the street," Maggie said. "We just have to see someone. Someone who is staying here. We'll be right back."

"You'd better be quick; I remember you, but I'm going off-duty in about an hour, and the next guy in may not be enthused about having to open these gates again."

"Understood."

Maggie took Ben's arm and steered him down the slightly inclined driveway that led either to the customer parking lot on the left or the dealer parking lot on the right. They turned right, around the side of the exhibit hall that was toward the south field, where the overnight dealers were parked.

"Maggie, you told the policeman we were going to see someone. We're not going to see anyone."

"Oh, Ben, I hope we are. We're going to see that man you knocked down."

"I don't think the policeman understood that."

"It's all right, Ben. It was just a little lie. Sometimes you have to compromise a little."

"I never lie."

"Well, you're right, Ben. That's the way it should be. No one should lie." They were almost to the end of the last building. "Okay, Ben, where do we go from here?"

"Over toward the bathrooms." Two separate, large wooden sheds, one labeled LADIES and one GENTLEMEN, were ahead of them and to the right; the worn white paint and the chipped letters on the signs were clearly visible in the lights over their doorways. They were the only lights in this area, although there had been several high halogen safety lights near the entrance.

The mud was heavier here, in the area around the fair buildings where vans had been parking and unloading. The sneakers Maggie had worn all day had been damp when she'd changed to her heels earlier. Now the replacement loafers she'd slipped on were covered with heavy mud. Almost every other step hit a puddle and splashed her long skirt. There must be a small hole in the seam of her left shoe; she could feel a trickle of water making its way across her toes.

Dealer vans and trucks were parked in three haphazard lines along the field. She could see figures moving near the vans, but it was too dark to make out who they were.

"Hey, you're Maggie Summer, aren't you?" She

jumped as a deep voice came from beside the dark van on her right. "I thought someone told me you were staying in comfort with the motel crowd!"

Will Brewer, the new dealer from across the aisle, stepped out of a shadow.

Kindly women might have called him a teddy bear, complete with beard and slight beer belly.

Maggie hesitated. Lydia had whispered to her that Will was a nice fellow; she'd done shows with him before. Until recently he'd taught woodworking at a private school in western New York State and spent weekends traveling to antiques shows. He was now trying to make the antiques business a full-time job.

Maggie hadn't had time to more than wave at him before the reception started.

But clearly he remembered her.

And she was glad he was there. The more the merrier.

"And this is?" Will looked at Ben. "I got in late this afternoon, but I think I saw you helping to set up."

Ben nodded.

"This is Ben Allen. He's Gussie White's assistant. We are staying in the Kabins across the street, but . . ." Maggie was torn. Will seemed like a nice guy, but she didn't know how this would turn out. On the other hand, if there was a problem, she could probably use some help. Ben was trying hard, but this was a situation far from his normal world, and she wasn't sure how long he'd be able to cope.

He was shaking slightly as they stood in front of the GENTLEMEN sign.

Maggie looked over his shoulder and saw Vince

talking with someone over by the exhibit building.

"Ben was running on the track, in the back of the rest rooms, and he—he left his jacket back there. So we came to see if we could find it."

Maggie hoped Ben wouldn't say anything. She'd just told another falsehood, but she couldn't tell the truth. It sounded too far-fetched.

She took a quick sidelong glance. Will was an attractive man. What was she thinking! This was not the moment to revive hormones best left dormant.

"It's pretty dark back there. Mind if I walk over with you?" Will just naturally turned them toward the track. "Lydia Wyndham told me about your husband, Maggie. Sorry. Must be rough."

Lydia must really have been talking.

"Yes, it's a hard time."

He nodded. "After my wife died, I kept thinking I saw her everywhere, even though I knew, of course, that she was gone. It was as though a big piece of the puzzle of my life was missing." Will paused for a moment, but Maggie remained silent. "So, Ben, where exactly did you leave this jacket of yours?"

Ben looked at Maggie in panic.

"Didn't you say you were just coming off the track when you dropped it?" Maggie said.

Ben half nodded.

"Then it must be somewhere near the entrance to the track." They walked past the rest room buildings, past the picnic tables set up for tomorrow's concession-stand customers, and turned left onto the path to the track.

Tomorrow this area would be full of prospective customers. Tonight it was quiet, despite the sounds of people settling in for the night. Dealers were sitting around two of the picnic tables. Several people were playing cards in the dim light and had tuned in the evening news on a small portable TV, and another group was talking and drinking beer. Between the vans and the cars people stood and talked, and occasionally you'd hear the sound of a laugh, or of a car door closing. A radio. A couple of people looked up and nodded as they walked past.

It's another world, Maggie thought. She had never considered staying on the fairgrounds; a soft bed and a private shower had always been important to her. And women by themselves did not generally stay on the grounds. The atmosphere had changed dramatically from that of an hour or so ago, when everyone was dressed up and entertaining customers. Now it felt more like a late-night neighborhood barbecue.

Except that she and Ben were in search of a body, not an extra bag of chips or ice cubes.

Ben touched Maggie's sleeve. "We have to go behind the buildings, toward the track." The backs of the buildings were vented, but had no doors or windows. The buildings themselves blocked the light.

"That's a funny place to leave a jacket, young man." Will looked doubtful as Ben pointed to their left. "How did you even get onto the track? The gates are shut."

Ben turned around and pointed at the gates. "I'm not very big, and the gates are loose. I squeezed between the doors and the fence. That's how I got on and off the track to practice. I'm a good runner. I ran good tonight. Mud usually slows me down."

"Where was the—jacket?" Maggie looked from

side to side, but in the dim light she couldn't see anything on the ground larger than two crushed soda cans, a partially eaten hot dog roll, and a few pieces of crumpled paper that had blown near the gate.

Ben walked off the pavement across a few yards of grass toward the back of the rest room building.

"Over here." He gestured toward an area where a landscaper had planted some trees and bushes in an obvious attempt to add some country atmosphere to the otherwise treeless fairgrounds. Maggie could identify two or three white pines, at least one sugar maple, and several large azalea bushes whose pink flowers glowed eerily in the half-light.

Michael would have known all of these plants, she thought as she instinctively identified the shrubbery. Michael had loved gardening. But Michael wouldn't have been looking for a body late at night on a New York State fairgrounds.

Ben was a few feet ahead of her, searching the ground.

"I'm sure he was here! I really am sure! I came out of that gate, and I ran about ten or twelve steps, and it was dark here . . ."

"He?" Will came up behind them. "Ben, I don't see a jacket here. Who is 'he'?"

The light from the buildings ended several feet from where the three of them were now standing. No dead or injured bodies were to be seen.

"I'm sure he was here! I'm sure!"

Maggie sighed. Will looked at her, waiting for her response.

"When Ben was leaving the track, he thought he saw two people back here."

"I did! I saw that pretty lady in a green dress, and I saw a man. And they were really yelling!" Ben looked at Will. "I saw them! And I ran up because I thought he was going to hit the lady. And I pushed him. And he fell down. He was lying on the ground. And he didn't get up. I tried to help him." He thrust his hand in front of Will. "See? I have blood on my hand!"

"Whoa, just a minute. Young man, are you telling me you hit someone? And then you two came out here by yourselves to see if a man covered with blood was lying on the ground?"

Maggie and Ben nodded.

"And what did you have in mind to do if you'd found this . . . man?"

"I didn't really lose my jacket, sir. I'm really careful with my jacket."

"I'm sure you are. But not so careful about knocking people down!"

"But he was going to hit the lady! I know he was! And I wanted to help the lady." Ben's face showed his distress. "I'm telling the truth! I wanted to help! I didn't mean to hurt him, really! And Maggie made up the story about the jacket. I didn't lose my jacket."

Will tried hard not to smile as he looked again at Maggie, who was subtly trying to survey the area to see if anything looked disturbed.

"Ladies sometimes say funny things, don't they?"

"Why didn't I think to bring a flashlight?" Maggie bent down and looked at the ground. "Ben, are you sure this is where the man fell?"

"Yes. At least I think so. It had to be here. But he's not here now."

Will shook his head. "I don't believe we're having this conversation. Maggie Summer, are you crazy? What if there *had* been a man here who was injured. Or worse? And just you and Ben to cope."

Maybe Will was being sexist. Or maybe he was just being nice. Well, she could play the game, too.

"But nothing happened. And you're with us, Will. And there are no bodies. In this light, and on this mud and grass, there's no way to see anything clearly now." She turned to Ben. "Maybe whoever it was just fell down. He had the breath knocked out of him, and after you left, he just got up and walked away." She looked again at the area. If there had been a man here, he wasn't here now. She gave Ben's shoulder a squeeze. "He probably just picked himself up and went back to wherever he came from. How long did you stay here after you pushed him?"

"I didn't stay. I was scared. I ran to get you and Aunt Gussie."

"Then he's probably fine. You may not have shoved him as hard as you thought, and he's walking around wondering how he's going to explain a bruised shoulder." Maggie turned to Will for confirmation. "Don't you agree?"

"If anyone fell down here, then he's gone now; that's for sure. Are you certain you didn't fall yourself, Ben? And maybe cut your hand?"

"*No!* There was a man lying there."

"You're sure you don't know who he was?" Maggie asked.

"He just looked ordinary. He had light hair, I think. And he was taller than I am. Just like most of the dealers. And old. Like you and Aunt Gussie."

Will grinned. "Well, that clinches it, Ben. You don't lie."

Maggie glared at him before turning back to Ben.

"Like the dealers? Do you think he was a dealer?"

"He wore one of those tags with his name on it that dealers have. Like the one you have on."

Maggie glanced down at the tag that read RENSSELAER COUNTY SPRING ANTIQUES FAIR—MAGGIE SUMMER—SHADOWS. Everyone who worked at the show had one. Dealers had blue badges; security guards had red badges; Vince and the porters he had hired to set up the booth walls and help customers and dealers load and unload vehicles had green badges.

"Did you notice what color badge he wore?" If the man had a badge on, it meant he had some role in the antiques fair. He wasn't just someone who had wandered onto the grounds. If Ben had noticed the color of the badge, the list of possible suspects would be narrowed.

Ben shook his head. "I don't know. I didn't look at it. I just saw it was there."

Maggie nodded. It was dark enough over here that colors were indistinct. Well, there was one way to know for sure. Maggie hesitated and clicked the dial light on her watch. They had a few minutes left before Officer Taggart would close the gates. And she would rest a lot better tonight if she knew everything was all right. Even more important, so would Ben and Gussie.

"Are you sure the woman you saw was the same woman you saw at the Show Management booth today?"

Ben nodded. "Yes; the pretty woman. She had on a fancy green dress tonight."

It must have been Susan. "Well, let's see if we can find her, and maybe she can explain what happened."

"Aunt Gussie said not to bother her again. I went back too many times for coffee this afternoon."

"We won't bother her. I'll explain it to Gussie. We just want to make sure everything is all right."

Will stepped in. "That sounds like a good idea. Ben, would you mind if I came along with you and Maggie to try to find that pretty woman?"

"No; it's okay with me," Ben responded seriously. "I'd like to find the dead man, too."

Chapter 11

—⁊—

Arabian—Illumination of Manuscripts, German chromolithograph, c. 1880, one of a set displaying modes of decorative arts in various areas of the world. Elaborate maze designs in blues and oranges. Price: $60.

Susan and Harry had sometimes stayed at the motel, sometimes at the fairgrounds. But Maggie was sure she'd seen their van parked near the "overnighters" and hoped Susan was using it, not Harry. Susan seemed to be running the business this weekend, even if Harry was buying out her part of it.

Will answered Ben's look. "I agree with Maggie. If the lady was at Show Management this afternoon and had on a green dress tonight, then I think the lady you saw is Susan Findley."

Maggie nodded. "Her van is blue, with New York license plates."

"Let's see if we can find it."

They walked back toward the parking lot.

Maggie scanned the first row of vans; there was a blue van, but it was from Montana. She remembered

that dealer. He specialized in Native American jewelry and blankets.

They crossed through the line of parked vehicles,
past a red RENTALS ARE US truck and a green, dented
minivan, toward the second line. As she passed the
truck, Maggie almost bumped into Lydia, who was
carrying a flashlight focused on the ground in front
of her, and a towel and toilet kit. "Oh—sorry!"

"Maggie! Are you camping out this show?" Lydia
looked around, as though Maggie's van would mate-
rialize in front of her. "And Will. And Ben!" Lydia
was obviously trying to think of a reason that particular trio would be looking over dealers' vans and
trucks at ten-twenty at night.

Maggie ignored the obvious questions in Lydia's
eyes. "No. I'm across the street at the Kabins.
We're"—Maggie nodded at Ben and Will—"looking
for Susan Findley. Do you know where she's parked?"

"I think I saw her van over toward the far fence. I
haven't seen her. I did see Harry after the show closed,
though. He was over by the entrance to building two,
where we unloaded today. I think he was talking to
Vince." Lydia shook her head sagely. "Strange things
happening, that's for sure. And policemen around. But
better safe than sorry, that's what I always say."

For sure, thought Maggie. "Thanks! We'll head
over toward the fence and see if we can find her." She
looked back at Will, who was following a step or so
behind with a bemused expression on his face.

"Will, you don't have to stay with us, if you have
something to do."

Will just grinned again and caught up with her.
"And miss all this excitement? Here I thought I'd be

cozying up to a cognac and a sleeping bag tonight. And now I'm given the chance to aid a lady and her squire with a quest! How could I turn down an opportunity like that?" He looked at Ben. "We're looking for a pretty lady who had an argument with a light-haired old man. Right?"

Ben nodded.

"Susan Findley is striking, that's for sure."

Maggie remembered seeing Will talking with Susan during the preview. "Do you know the Findleys?"

"I've run into them before. Susan certainly doesn't lack for conversation."

That didn't exactly answer her question. Maggie wondered how well Will did know Susan. She fought back a blush as she realized she'd had an involuntary flash of jealousy. Lady, take it easy.

They passed three men Maggie didn't recognize, all of them wearing dealer's tags.

"When the stock market's up customers buy," the tall man in the windbreaker said, dropping his cigarette on the ground and grinding it into the mud with his heel. "Always."

"Not for me." A man in a blue poncho with long, braided gray hair disagreed. "I figure, when the stock market's down, that's when people invest in antiques. They can't lose money on something with age."

"To a point. I never understood why people pay thousands of dollars for new furniture that's going to be used and worthless tomorrow when they could invest in good eighteenth- or even nineteenth-century furniture that usually becomes more valuable. Built better than the modern stuff, and when you get tired of it, you can call me back and I'll take it off your hands."

"We're the ultimate recyclers, John. Finding value in what other generations have discarded."

"Well, I'd still rather invest in some good Chippendale than in those Barbie dolls your cousin Jack is hawking!" They all laughed.

"But he's making a darn good living. How many pieces of Chippendale have you sold this year?"

Maggie kept going. The perennial debates. Value versus investment. Collectibles versus antiques. Quality versus commercial popularity. It was all part of the business.

"Maggie, isn't it getting late? Aunt Gussie will be worried."

"Ben, you're right. We'll just see if Susan is at her van, and then we'll get back to the motel." She glanced at her watch: 10:25.

Susan's van was the last one in the row over by the fence, as Lydia had said. It was faded sky blue, with a large dent in the left side, and New York license plates. No vanity plates or business logo for Manhattan dwellers. They'd be advertisements for car thieves.

The van looked empty, or as though the person inside had retired for the night. Maggie walked all the way around, listening for voices. She really didn't want to disturb Susan if she was sleeping.

"Okay, Ben, I think we call it a night. All is quiet here. Let's head back and assure your aunt Gussie that you're not a murderer. Will, thanks for your help."

Ben breathed an audible sigh. "And we'll see if the pizza's still warm?"

"I don't have any pizza, warm or otherwise, but I

do have some terrific salami and ham and cheese in a cooler, and there's enough cognac for two, and some soda for you, Ben, if you'd like to visit my home away from home," Will said.

"Thanks! Actually, the cognac sounds nice . . . but Gussie is waiting for us, and the police will be closing the gates. Tomorrow morning and, I hope, customers will arrive faster than we think." Maggie tucked a stray piece of hair behind her ear and smiled up at Will. Maybe he was lonely, too. And he seemed nice enough. But she had other obligations.

"Maybe a rain check, then. But let me be a gentleman of the old school and escort the two of you back to the gate. You have to go through some dark areas to get there." Will fell into step with Maggie. They walked companionably away from the last rows of trailers and vans, headed diagonally toward the entrance.

Maggie wished they'd seen Susan; she would have felt better knowing what had really happened when Ben knocked down whoever it was. Whom could Susan have been arguing with? It could have been anyone.

And Lydia Wyndham had seen Harry and Vince talking. That must have been an interesting conversation.

"That was some rain we had for an hour or so this afternoon. Did you have any trouble getting your prints in?" Will was obviously trying to turn the conversation away from all the questions they hadn't found answers to.

"No; I was fine. I got unloaded before the storm hit."

"I got a late start driving up from my cousin's place in White Plains and then hit bad traffic. Good thing I brought an extra set of clothes for the weekend; the ones I was wearing to set up look like sponges now."

"Lucky your inventory is mostly iron and tin and brass."

"Rust was the biggest worry today. But I got everything dried off."

They had almost reached the end of the exhibit buildings when they heard the screams.

Chapter 12

~~~

Die Abgotts-odoer germeine Baum-
Riesenschlange *(boa constrictor)*. *Large snake
curled around tree limb. German lithograph by
Dr. Leopold Fitzinger, director of the Munich
Zoological Gardens and the first to design a
worldwide nomenclature for reptiles and
amphibians. Price: $60.*

Somewhere a woman was screaming, over and over, a
high-pitched voice without words, as though the
screams had taken over and she had lost control.
Like an animal caught in a high-powered trap.

All over the parking lot flashlights and headlights
turned on, and van and truck doors opened. Maggie
turned and ran back toward the area they had just
left. She stumbled once when her long skirt caught on
a clump of dirt and leaves, but kept going. Both her
feet were now wet; she could feel the cold water ooz-
ing over her toes. Will and Ben ran with her. But at
least a dozen dealers got there ahead of them.

Susan Findley stood with her back against a dark
brown van parked in the middle of the parking lanes.

She looked like an actress in a horror movie. Lights from flashlights everywhere pierced the darkness and focused on her. Her green dress had been replaced by a pink jogging outfit, and the flowered towel and white cosmetic bag she must have been carrying were on the ground at her feet. Her arms covered her face, and she was screaming. The scene was so unreal that it took a few seconds for Maggie to see what was in front of Susan.

The body was on its right side, the face lying in a pool of blood that had already blended into the muddy field. The left side of the skull was caved in.

"Somebody! Help! Get an ambulance!" Susan's voice dropped almost to a whisper as the crowd gathered and her screams became intelligible.

Maggie knelt down in the mud and tried to get a pulse, just in case. No one spoke; only Susan's sobs broke the silence. After a long minute or two, Maggie shook her head, then she stood and reached out to hold Susan and turn her away. Maggie had EMT training, but that wasn't going to help now.

The group of stunned dealers parted to let Officer Taggart through. He took one look at the ground and pulled out his police radio.

"Nine-one-one. We need an ambulance and police out at the Rensselaer County Fairgrounds. Stat!" He gave directions quickly. "Does anyone know who this man is?"

Will was the one to speak: "His name is Harry Findley."

Chapter 13

❦

The Little Brothers, *hand-colored engraving published by Currier & Ives, 1850. Small folio. Two young boys holding hands, dressed in red velvet jackets and long pants, surrounded by rambling roses. Typical C&I mid-Victorian sentimental engraving. Price: $95.*

It took only about three long minutes for the police to arrive, about four minutes for the ambulance, and about four and a half minutes for a detective to announce quietly but decisively that the Rensselaer County Fairgrounds were being sealed as a possible crime site. No one could leave without express permission from the police.

Another antiques dealer had been murdered.

Maggie was still holding Susan, who was weeping quietly. Looking pale, Ben stood to the side, next to Will. Lydia came over and patted Susan on the shoulder and offered tea; a man Maggie didn't know offered something stronger; and Vince had already started arguing with the young detective about how long they would have to seal the site. Vince was expecting eight thousand customers to arrive at 10 A.M. Saturday morning, and by God, those customers had better be able to get in.

Will went up and spoke with Officer Taggart and then came back to Maggie. "I've just asked the officer if it would be all right for both of you to come back to my van. He needs to question Susan, and probably the rest of us as well, but I think we need to get Susan away from this area. I have a cell phone you can use to call Gussie."

Maggie nodded. "Thanks, Will. Come on, Ben."

He stood still, looking at Harry's body.

"Ben, you come with us; we'll call your aunt Gussie."

Ben turned slowly and followed, as Maggie helped Susan toward the row of vehicles nearest to the exhibit building where Will's RV was parked.

Will opened the door, and Maggie helped Susan up the step and into the tiny living space, which included two narrow beds and a small table. The low hum she immediately identified as a small electrical generator. It was powering a ceiling light and a small refrigerator built into a wall of stained-pine, louvered cabinets. The room wasn't much longer than the beds, but it was cozy. The windows even had tiny curtains that matched the spreads on window-seat-type beds and some pillows piled in a corner.

Maggie glanced at Will appreciatively.

He smiled. "I taught woodworking, remember? And the home economics classroom was right next door. I spend a lot of time on the road at shows, so I figured, why not be comfortable?"

She helped Susan down onto one of the beds. Ben sat on the other one.

"Before we forget, we need to call Gussie; she'll be worried, especially after she's heard the police and ambulance sirens."

"Right." Will pulled his phone out of its belt case and handed it to her.

Maggie hadn't realized her hands were shaking until she hit the wrong numbers twice. She took a deep breath and tried again.

"Gussie? Maggie. . . . No, no, Ben and I are fine. The man was gone. But there's been an accident, and the police want everyone to stay on the fairgrounds for a while." She glanced at Will. "It may be all night, so you'd better go ahead and get some sleep. Ben and I will be fine. We're with Will Brewer, in his motor home." Maggie listened for a while. "Gussie, no, really, we're fine. It's—Harry Findley." At the sound of Harry's name, Susan, who had just been sitting quietly, burst out crying again. "Susan's with us, too. . . . Yes, whatever we can. You take care of yourself. Do you want to talk with Ben?" Maggie handed over the phone.

"Aunt Gussie, everything here is very bad. I'm scared. There's a dead man, and the police are here, and an ambulance, and it's not like on TV at all. And I didn't get any pizza."

Will took over the phone. "Gussie, this is Will Brewer. We haven't met, but I have the fireplace equipment down the aisle from you. Don't worry. I'll look after Ben and make sure he has something to eat, even if it's not pizza. Maggie is going to stay with Susan, and we'll all have to talk with the police, so it's going to be a late night. You get some rest, because we're all going to need a lot of energy for tomorrow." He paused and glanced at Susan. "I really can't say just now, but, yes, that's the way it looks." Another pause. "Vince is going to do his darnedest to make sure the show opens on time tomorrow, and you know Vince. It probably will. Okay. Just don't worry. We're all fine." He paused, listening. "Of course. You're welcome."

He put down the phone. "Ben, your aunt is concerned because you're a growing boy and you may be starving. Shall we put some sandwiches together?"

"I wish we had pizza."

"Me, too. But we don't, so how does ham and cheese sound?"

"Do you have mustard?"

"Absolutely. Couldn't have ham and cheese without mustard."

"Okay. Thank you."

Will pulled out a small shelf that was hidden between two of the cabinet doors and reached into the refrigerator for bread, mustard, ham, and cheese. He deftly made a sandwich for Ben, adding a pickle and a handful of potato chips from a bag in one of the cabinets. "Soda?"

Ben nodded.

"Ladies? Mineral water? Beer? Cognac? Soda?"

Maggie glanced at his supply. No diet soda. She thought longingly of the cognac, and then of the police questions to come. "Some mineral water would be good."

Will produced two glasses and the water, then gestured at Ben. "Why don't we leave the women alone?" Susan looked up questioningly from the bed where she was seated next to Maggie. "We'll just be right out-side, sitting at one of the picnic tables, if you should need us."

Maggie nodded. Thank goodness for Will. Some-one would have to be with Ben, and someone should be with Susan. She couldn't handle both of them.

"Susan, do you think you're able to talk about it? I know the police are going to ask questions, but maybe it would help if together we think through what happened."

"Don't ask me what happened! I don't know any-thing! All I know is after the show I talked to Will for a few minutes. But Will really wanted to talk with Harry, not with me, so I took off. Let them cope with each other. I decided to look for Vince, but he was busy talking to his crew, so I started to go back to my van to change into more comfortable clothes. That's when I ran into Harry. He said he needed to talk with me in private. I said, what's the big deal? Privacy was never one of Harry's priorities, you know? But he said it was important, and there were a lot of people around, so I said okay. I asked him if he wanted to come back to our—my—van, but he said no, he didn't have time. So we walked over by the gates to the track to talk."

That must have been when Ben saw them.

"What did Harry want to talk about?"

"Nothing new. He just wanted to make sure every-thing was okay for the divorce to go through. I told him, 'For this you bring me over here for privacy and the mud ruins my shoes?'"

"I thought you said this afternoon the divorce was all arranged."

"It is. No problem. He was just checking. He gets nervous sometimes. Wants to make sure we haven't forgotten anything. Some things we wanted to get straightened out before we signed off on the deal."

"He was going to buy your share of the business?"

"Right. That's what we decided. He was going to give me the money when we met to sign the final papers."

"What are you—were you—going to do then?"

"Nothing different. Work for Art-Effects. Harry was going to pay me a salary, though."

"So instead of being a co-owner you were going to be Harry's employee?"

"Right. I'd have my share of the business now. In cash. That's what I wanted."

But now Susan would have all of the business, not just half. And Ben had said "the pretty lady" and the man were yelling at each other.

"So, did you argue?"

"I guess we yelled a little. We always do. Sometimes Harry can't hear anything unless it's screamed. He wanted me to talk to some people and do some things I didn't want to do. I have my own life, you know? So we had a disagreement. Anyway, we were having this private discussion, and then your pal— the retarded kid? He came racing up like he was going to put out a fire or something. So I took off."

"Did he knock Harry down?"

"He might have. The kid was going full speed."

What if Ben had really hit Harry hard? Hard enough so he hit the ground but was able to get up and get himself over to that line of vans where . . . there were still a lot of questions to be answered.

"Was Harry staying with Joe tonight?" It had just occurred to Maggie that she hadn't seen Joe since the show closed.

"Well, actually Harry helped pack the van and drove up with me. We're still partners, you know. I guess he was going to stay with Joe tonight. I don't know. Joe's van is over there." Susan gestured vaguely toward exhibit building one. "He drove over from Connecticut today."

"Was Harry going to move to Connecticut, then?"

"No, I don't think so. Did Harry tell you that? Doesn't sound like him. Joe has a little studio over on Avenue A, and Harry spends some time there, and some time at the loft. Joe spends most of his time at his house near New Haven. That's where his business is."

"You and Harry are still living together?"

"Some of the time. When one of us isn't somewhere else. But Art-Effects is in the loft. We've lived there for years." Susan was still speaking of Harry in the present tense.

"But you said Harry was gone! Off! With Joe!"

"Yeah. I said that, didn't I? Well, I meant we're getting divorced. You know, legal commitment kaput. I didn't mean Harry and I had stopped working together. Or loving each other." Susan put her head in her hands. "This all doesn't make any sense. Harry dead. It just doesn't make sense."

"Susan, the police are going to ask you all kinds of questions. Do you have any idea who might have killed Harry? Did he have any enemies?"

"That's a joke. I mean, Harry wasn't always the nicest guy. To me he was, of course, and to Joe."

Right. And simultaneously. Why wouldn't everyone love a guy with that much charm?

"Business is business. There were times when Harry had a chance to make a few bucks, and sometimes other people weren't so happy. I mean, everyone has to look out for himself, right? Like—Will." She gestured toward the door. "Will hated Harry. Just because a deal Harry arranged for him didn't work out as great as Will hoped." Susan paused. "Harry was really smart about a lot of deals, and there were people who were jealous sometimes. People are always jealous of success, you know? No real enemies, though. Who would kill someone over a few dollars?"

It would depend on how many dollars were a few, Maggie thought. Harry had been a hustler; that was clear. She wondered how many people Harry had beaten to a buy—or a sale. And was Will one of them? Will didn't seem the type who would hate anyone.

But Harry was dead. Someone had wanted him dead. And that someone could have been anyone. Will had been with Maggie for the past half an hour—but how long ago had Harry been killed? What if Will had killed Harry, then run into Maggie and Ben? Maybe he was establishing an alibi. But what sour deal could make someone angry enough to kill? And could Harry's death have anything to do with John Smithson's death last week?

Maggie's head reeled. There were just too many possibilities to consider. She had to concentrate. On Susan, for instance. Now Susan would own all of Art-Effects, not just have the cash for half of it. Plus, she was Harry's widow. Any insurance would come to her. On

TV crime shows, police always looked at the spouse first.

"Susan, how angry were you with Harry tonight?"

"You think I killed Harry? Me?" Susan broke into shrill laughter. "Me? I loved Harry. Harry taught me everything I know. When I first met Harry, I was just Susan Maria Coletto, a scared eighteen-year-old from Bayonne, New Jersey. One of seven kids in a two-bedroom walk-up. All I knew was that I loved beautiful things, and that someday I wanted to be able to live with those things. I used to take the bus to the city just to walk through all those fake rooms in the big department stores, like Macy's. Everything there was always so planned. All the colors went together, and the decorations matched. It was so clean. So perfect. I used to dream that maybe I could be an interior decorator or something. And someday even live in a place that looked like those rooms. When I got accepted by the School of Visual Arts, I thought I'd really made it."

Maggie could understand that. SVA was a top school.

"That's where I met Harry. He'd grown up in New York, and he knew how to get by. He showed me around. Harry had had a real tough childhood. His dad just disappeared when he was little. And his ma drank too much to hold down a regular job. Harry tried to take care of his ma, even when he was little. Kids in the city have to be tough, especially when they're not exactly prizefighter types, you know?" Susan paused. "You have a cigarette? I could really use a cigarette."

"No. Sorry. I don't smoke."

"Me neither. Just sometimes I like one. Anyway, Harry did what he had to. He got by. And even after his ma died, he kept going to school. He moved in with his uncle for a while, and there was this priest—Father Jim—who let him sleep in St. Jude's sometimes, when his uncle wasn't around, and who bought him the art supplies he needed to put his portfolio together to apply to schools." Susan looked at Maggie. "Having a talent with art wasn't exactly something you bragged about on Ninth Avenue."

Maggie could imagine.

"Anyway, Harry graduated high school. He went to Visual Arts, too, and we met. And then Harry got friendly with Professor Hochman, who taught there. A real smooth guy. Uptown, you know? And handsome. All the kids at SVA had crushes on him. Girls and guys both, you know what I mean?"

She was learning.

"Well, this professor decided to help Harry, and Harry helped me. The professor had friends with big money who were real well-known interior designers and decorators and all that. The Park Avenue kind. And he knew what kind of stuff they liked—sort of unusual and funky and Art Deco, art nouveau, Erté, you know?"

Maggie knew just the kind of art and sculpture on the borderline between great and garish that a type of Upper East Sider would pay big money to display in his off-white, Bloomingdale's-inspired living room.

"Well, the professor told Harry that if he could find the kind of stuff those designers and friends of his were looking for, he'd buy it from Harry. That would help Harry pay his tuition and expenses. Harry and I had met in Introduction to Design, and we were hanging out together, and he told me about the deal, and we decided to do it together. Harry knew how to bargain, and it turned out I had a pretty good eye for what these uptowners liked, so we went to all the flea markets and Lower East Side places, and sometimes even out to Jersey, and we found this stuff. We sold it to Professor Hochman, and then he sold it to his uptown friends."

Susan took a sip of her mineral water. "We got good at it. Real good. Only problem was, we spent so much time together looking for stuff and selling it that we didn't have much time for classes and assignments. But then Harry got the idea that we didn't need the professor; we could sell direct to his pals. We'd met some of them already. And why should the professor be making money when we did the work? He'd made a bundle off us before we caught on to just how much people would pay for all this stuff we were finding. So we got married. Harry said it would look better. My family in Bayonne sure thought so, too, and they're the kind that gives money for wedding gifts, even when they don't have much. We took all the cash we could get our hands on, and we got the loft, and we put all the stuff in it, artistically arranged—sort of like those department-store rooms, you know? Only a little more arty. And then we started to have parties. We invited all those decorator types, and they brought their friends. They thought it was slumming—coming to visit these young artists in their loft who had all this great stuff. But they kept coming. And that's how we got started. That was twelve years ago."

Susan took another sip. "We were partners in everything, Harry and me. We bought, and we sold, and we gave big parties, and we were invited to these really spiffy places where we didn't fit in, but that's why they invited us, so we had fun anyway, and we did what we wanted. We weren't like those people, Maggie. And we knew it. But that's why they liked us. We always were just a little more different than they wanted to be. They thought we were 'amusing.' We didn't care. We worked hard, we had fun, and we got to know all kinds of posh types."

Maggie listened with some amazement. She believed every word Susan was saying, but it certainly wasn't the usual story of "how I became an antiques dealer."

"How did you get started doing antiques shows?"

"Maybe six or eight years ago we met Vince at some big decorator's party. He was with a really rich lady who was looking to decorate her new weekend place up in Connecticut. He was helping her to find people who had the accessories she wanted. Vince liked us; he said, 'Come do my antiques shows, you'll meet some classy people and make some bucks, because no one at antiques shows has the stuff you have,' so we thought, what the hell, we'd try it. We've done all four of Vince's shows each year since then. We've met some new customers at the shows. And it's a nice thing to be able to drop at parties, you know, that you do antiques shows, even though we only do the four. 'Cause some people don't think the kind of stuff we carry is really antique, because it's twentieth century and all. Although that's changing."

Maggie agreed. Even some shows that vetted were now allowing items from up to the 1930s to be displayed. "Susan, what happened after you and Harry argued tonight?"

"Well, your retarded pal there came racing up as

though he were going to save the world, and I took off. I was going to leave anyway. That's what I always do. Lets Harry cool down. I went to my van to change, and then I went to wash up for the night. On the way back I stopped at Joe's van, to see if Harry was there. To keep everything calm. But no one was there.

"So I started walking back to my van. And—I saw him. And I started screaming. Then everyone else came. You were there."

"And that's all? Did you see anyone else nearby?"

"No. And I hadn't seen Harry from the time the kid—Ben—came at us from out of nowhere, until I saw him lying on the ground out there."

"Susan, think for a minute. Did you see Ben knock Harry down?"

"Did he really do that?" She almost chuckled. "Well, good for him. I've tried a couple of times myself. No. I just saw Ben coming and decided to get the hell out of there. I'd let Harry take care of it. Ben's not that big, so I just thought Harry'd cool him off a little."

"About how much time was there between the time you left Harry and the time you—found—him again?"

"I don't know exactly. What time is it now?"

Maggie looked. It was about twelve-thirty.

"Then I'd guess an hour. I took some time in the van, you know, straightening up and figuring out what to wear tomorrow. I had to take some medication. I haven't been feeling so well recently. Maybe an hour. I didn't look at the clock."

They were interrupted by a knock on the side of the trailer.

"Mrs. Findley? Officer Taggart. The detective needs to ask you some questions. Could you come with me?"

Susan took a last sip of mineral water and went to the door. Taggart was there, accompanied by a young policeman with a notebook, metal-rimmed glasses, and a slightly green expression.

"Will this take long, Officer?"

"That depends on how much you know, Mrs. Findley. I realize this is a difficult time, but the more you can tell us, the faster we'll be able to find out what happened to your husband."

Susan hesitated, looking back at Maggie. "Would it be all right if I came back here . . . after? I don't want to spend the night alone." She looked even paler and thinner than usual, and very vulnerable.

"Of course, Susan." Maggie offered Will's hospitality without thinking. "I think it's going to be a long night."

"And you will help me?"

Maggie nodded. Although she couldn't think of anyone who didn't need help right then. She could have used a hug herself. And her husband hadn't just been murdered.

Chapter 14

~~~~~

Hackles, *chromolithograph by Mary Orvis Marbury, published in* Favorite Flies, *1892. Colorful group of fishing lures. Mary Orvis Marbury was the daughter of the founder of the Orvis sporting goods company and now has a line of clothing named after her. Price: $60.*

Maggie stepped down from Will's RV and looked around. It was almost one in the morning. The show was due to open in only nine hours. But no one was sleeping. The field looked as though it were under siege. Groups of dealers had gathered and were talking quietly.

The police had pulled several picnic tables together, and two detectives were questioning Susan and taking notes. Although the sirens had stopped, the area where Harry's body had been discovered was still brightly illuminated. They must be taking pictures or gathering trace evidence, Maggie thought. She hoped they had removed Harry's body. She didn't want to see it again. She did want to find out where Harry had been this evening, and whom he had talked to.

Maggie made a mental list. Harry knew Will and Gussie and Joe, and Lydia and Abe Wyndham, and Vince. If you add me to the list, and Susan, we're probably the ones here who knew Harry best. We're the likely suspects. Ben, of course, would have to be on any list, although he didn't even know who Harry was. Gussie is the only one of us who isn't a possibility. She had no motive and no opportunity. And I didn't do it.

Maggie knew she'd have to talk with Ben again, preferably before the police did, and she wanted to find out why Susan had said Will hated Harry. But right now Ben and Will weren't here.

One person she might be able to find was Lydia Wyndham. Lydia kept her eyes open and was always a good source of gossip. And she had said she'd seen Harry talking to Vince earlier that night.

Abe and Lydia had a motor home that no one could miss. It was not only the oldest vehicle used by any dealer Maggie knew, it was the most dilapidated. The outside must once have been white, or maybe gray; now the paint was totally gone in large areas, particularly near the underside, where patches of rust were fast turning into major holes. One of its windows had been broken and patched by cardboard, duct tape, and a heavy garbage bag, and only the broken pieces of what might once have been a luggage rack were on the roof.

Maggie knocked.

"Yes? Oh, Maggie. I thought you might be the police. Abe is sleeping, and I was afraid someone might wake him up." Lydia answered the door wearing a floor-length flannel nightgown that had once had flowers on it; it was so faded that in the dim light Maggie couldn't tell what color the flowers had been. As Lydia turned to reach for something, Maggie got a glimpse of the inside of the home. It was as cluttered as Will's had been neat: uneven boxes were piled to the ceiling, and garbage bags filled most of the otherwise open space. The bags could have held anything from clothes to bedding; it was hard to see. The odor of azaleas was strong. Lydia must have liberated some blossoms from the bushes surrounding the fairgrounds.

Lydia pulled on a long gray man's sweater that covered two-thirds of her nightgown. Perhaps it was Abe's. It could as easily have been pulled from a rummage-sale bag. There were runs in three or four different places, and as Lydia pushed up the sleeves, Maggie saw a large hole in one elbow. She had items in her own wardrobe that were definitely past even the "comfortable" stage. But she wouldn't have worn them to open the door in the middle of the night. Particularly if she expected the police to drop in.

"Could we talk for a few minutes?"

Lydia nodded as she reached behind herself and shut the door softly. "I couldn't sleep either. Isn't it horrible? And after the murder last week at Westchester. It's almost like fate; all these antiques dealers dying."

Fate? That someone gave the dealer in Westchester a poisoned pill, and that Harry's head was caved in? Maggie shivered. Not what she'd call fate.

"I can't even close my eyes, just thinking about it. Abe was so upset I gave him some chamomile tea.

He's just fallen asleep. Deaths upset him, ever since our son passed away." Lydia looked closely at Maggie. "This must be hard for you, too, dear. Your husband's passing so recently and all."

"It's not easy." Maggie didn't allow herself to think about that; there just wasn't time. She'd be like Scarlett O'Hara: think about it tomorrow. "I didn't know you'd had a son."

"We don't talk much about poor Danny, but never a day goes by that we don't think of him."

Maggie was sorry for Lydia, but they needed to get back to the subject of the evening. She went right to the point.

"Do you think Susan could have done it?"

"Susan's always been a little . . . different. I guess she and Harry had one of those 'open' marriages."

"She may just be flirting."

Lydia looked at her. "Maggie, I may be older than you are, but I'm not daft. Susan's never figured out that the field on the other side of the fence may be greener, but that's because it's full of crabgrass. But she and Harry were getting a divorce. Maybe Harry woke up and smelled the coffee."

"She said she and Harry were still going to be in business together. He was going to buy her out."

"Oh? Everyone knows Susan's been hanging around Vince like a bee to an apple tree in bloom. I thought she might be trying to hang on to him. She wouldn't be the first to try. But no one's tied Vince down yet."

"Earlier, when I was looking for Susan's van? You said you'd seen Harry talking to Vince."

"They were talking real serious like. I saw them

when I was looking for Abe earlier. Wanted to make sure he'd had some supper before he settled in."

"Did you hear what they were talking about?"

"No. They were too far away. And they were talking low. I couldn't hear even when I walked by pretty close."

Maggie contained a smile. Lydia had probably done her best to tune in, too.

"They weren't just chatting. I could tell. Harry kept shaking his head and trying to hand Vince a piece of paper. Vince wouldn't take it. He backed up a few feet, you know, like someone who's trying to get away. But I was just walking past. I didn't get a real chance to see."

She'd done all right for someone who was just walking by. "About what time was that, Lydia?"

"I'd guess about nine-fifteen. The show had just closed. The police were still shooing people out of the buildings."

Before Harry and Susan had talked.

"Maggie, what do you think is going to happen? Will the police ask all of us questions?" Lydia was obviously hoping to be on their list.

"I don't know, but I'd guess so. Harry's dead. Murdered. Someone here must have done it."

"You know, I always thought the antiques business would be a calm, sort of aristocratic, way to make a living." Lydia leaned back against a spot on her trailer that was almost red with rust.

Maggie hoped the side wouldn't cave in.

"When Abe and I lived back in Iowa, we thought it would be a good way to spend our golden years. See the world, meet some nice people, and not have to worry about mowing the lawn and what the neighbors thought."

Maggie had never imagined Abe and Lydia living anywhere but in that trailer. "How long have you been in antiques?"

"Full-time since about 1990. Not too long."

Lydia looked around, as though someone might be listening. "Abe and I, we had a good life in Iowa. We're both university graduates, you know. He had a good job at the First Federal Bank, and I taught botany and zoology at the high school and sometimes at the community college, when they needed someone. We worked hard, too. A penny saved is a penny earned. Both our families were there. I never really thought we'd leave. But, life changes." She looked at Maggie. "Sometimes the Lord hands you problems to deal with that make life pretty difficult."

Maggie wondered. "And so you left your home and your families?"

"It was hard after Danny died."

Maggie looked at her questioningly.

"He was a good boy, but, you know, bad things sometimes happen to good people. The good die young. Anyway, life wasn't the same for Abe and me after that, so one day Abe came home and said he'd just up and retired early from the bank, and we put the house up for sale. I'd been collecting silver flatware and jewelry and such for years, after I inherited some from an aunt in St. Louis. So we took my collection and we started to do some shows. We took the money from selling our home and we got a good deal on a used trailer."

She turned around and looked at her mobile

home. "At first it was fun. After thirty years of fixing supper at six o'clock and going to school meetings and choir practices, it felt great to have no deadlines or schedules, except for the dates we had shows lined up. We've traveled all over the East Coast and the Midwest. Before, I'd only been as far east as Chicago, once, to see Danny."

"You mean you really live out of the trailer all the time? You don't have a home?" Maggie tried to think of all that would mean. "Where do you get mail?"

"We use my brother's address. He collects mail for us. Once a month or so we let him know where we'll be and he sends it on to us. Sometimes in care of the show manager, you know. And we call back to the family every few weeks. We keep in touch. But it's not as easy as we'd thought. When shows go well, we're okay. But if we get a couple of bad shows in a row, well, we don't have that many friends we can stay with. Most of the folks we know live in Iowa, and there aren't that many shows there. We go south in the winter. There are lots of shows along the Gulf, and the weather's warm. Then we come north in the spring and do New England and Ohio and all in the summer. But the trailer's getting a bit of wear on it."

That was a major understatement. Maggie wondered how they even got it to start. And with the rust patches it looked as though it would soon be hard to guarantee that anything in the trailer would still be there after they'd driven over a bump.

"The Lord is there to lead and protect us, isn't he, dear? Beggars can't be choosers. So we're doing all right. Although we're getting a little old to do this all the time." She leaned even closer. "I'm thinking that maybe we should just stay on the circuit six months of the year. You know, find a little place back in Iowa for some of the time. Be better for Abe, as he's getting on and doesn't seem as interested in the traveling as he used to. Maybe it's time we thought about retiring again."

Maggie agreed. "Makes sense to me. By the way, did you see Harry anywhere else tonight?"

"Just talking with Vince, like I said. And then— after Susan started screaming."

"What about Joe? Or Susan?"

"Didn't see Joe. Susan I saw a few minutes after I saw Harry. She was walking at a right fast pace, heading toward her van. She went past Abe and me here; we were having some tea and tuna sandwiches, you know, before bedding down. I don't think she even saw us; we had pulled out our folding chairs and were sitting here in the doorway, where we're standing now. But she looked as though she had something on her mind. She was going along a mile a minute. You'd think she'd be tired after a setup day, and then the reception. My feet were aching like two coals pulled out of a hot stove."

Maggie nodded. Her feet sometimes felt like that, too, after a long day. Although she'd never phrased it quite that way.

"Who do you think killed Harry?"

Lydia looked at her as though she were crazy. "Maggie, the Lord knows. He'll take care of it. You go back and get some rest. We've got a long day tomorrow. I'm going to bed." Lydia turned toward her door. "Leave well enough alone. Whatever will be, will be." The door shut, and Maggie was left in the dark by the trailer.

Well, maybe the Lord knew. But that wasn't going to help her. Or help Ben.

She glanced at her watch. No wonder she was tired. It was close to 2 A.M. Maybe there wasn't much more to be done tonight.

Will's trailer looked like a sanctuary as Maggie made her way back through the now quiet lines of vans and trucks. It had been a long day. Most of the dealers, including Maggie, had been up at dawn or before to pack vans, then drive at least several hours, set up, and get dressed for a reception. Even the excitement and fear of a murder hadn't been enough to keep exhaustion away, and most people had retired to their sleeping bags or cots. A couple of uniformed policemen were still walking the grounds and talking to each other on radios, but no one was being questioned at the picnic tables.

Maggie knocked softly. Will opened the door almost immediately and gestured to her to be quiet as he stepped outside. "Susan's asleep inside. She went back to her van with one of the detectives, so they could search it, and then she came here and collapsed. Where've you been?"

"Talking with Lydia. Remember she said she'd seen Harry talking with Vince earlier? I wanted to know whether she'd overheard what they'd been talking about."

"Well, while you've been playing detective, the police think they've solved the crime."

She looked up quickly. "Who?"

"Ben. They've taken him down to the local police station for questioning."

Already. She'd thought she had some time. What would Gussie think?

"Did they arrest him?"

Will shook his head. "I think they're waiting to see if they can get some more solid information."

Maggie sat down on the nearest picnic-table bench. "When did it happen?"

"About fifteen minutes ago. It seems Susan told the police Ben had come flying at Harry, and she'd run away. Some other dealers saw Susan running from in back of the rest rooms, and then, a few minutes later, Ben running from the same place. Plus, when they asked Ben, he didn't lie."

"He told them he'd knocked Harry down."

"Of course. And the police want this to be simple. A young, retarded boy gets a crush on Susan—several people saw him following her around today—and then kills her husband out of jealousy. He doesn't really understand what he's doing, of course, but Harry is dead."

"Do you believe that, Will?"

"Hell, no. Even if he'd been able to knock Harry down hard, resulting in that gash in Harry's head, it doesn't explain how Harry got from in back of the rest rooms to the middle of the parked vans. Either he walked, or someone carried him, through a lighted area where people were talking. So far no one's come up with a reasonable explanation." Will paused. "I suspect even the police are trying to figure out how Ben moved the body."

Maggie started up. "Gussie—"

"I've already called her. Ben's been told not to say anything more. Gussie said she had a lawyer she was going to call."

"Ben's retarded. Can the police just take him away like that?"

"They're just questioning him. And Gussie did tell him not to talk. Ben probably won't even ask for a glass of water."

Maggie shook her head. "It's all happening too fast. Will, we have to figure out who really killed Harry. We can't let Ben be blamed just because he's young and has Down's syndrome."

"And just happened to knock down someone who was found murdered an hour later? Maggie, the police did the obvious thing."

"Then we have to do something not so obvious. If they've arrested Ben, they're not going to keep looking for the murderer, and he—or she—is going to get away with it!"

"Whoa. I didn't say we wouldn't do anything. But what can we do? For example, you talked with Lydia tonight. What did she know?"

"Not much. She said she'd seen Harry and Vince together after the show closed. Sounded as though she'd gotten as close as she could to try to check it out, too."

"Depend on Lydia! She and Abe are a strange couple. She seems definitely in charge. He never says much except about that mourning stuff he collects. Poor Abe. Henpecked and nowhere to escape in that trailer of theirs!"

"Abe collects mourning things? I didn't know that."

"Well, he did a year ago anyway. I had a mourning

vial of tears—you know, one of those small blown-glass bottles that Victorian women used to collect tears shed for the dearly beloved? It was even filled and sealed. Just the thing for a cheery mantel decoration. Anyway, it was in a box of early iron kitchen utensils I bought at an auction. I was doing a show in Ohio that week, and I put it out just for the novelty, since I don't usually carry that sort of thing. Abe practically grabbed it off the table. I let him have it for a reasonable price, and he told me that he had cartons of the stuff. Mourning jewelry, hair wreaths, jet jewelry, calling cards for those in mourning, mourning samplers—you name it. He even took me inside that trailer of theirs. He has cartons of really terrific stuff. Said he and Lydia argued about it all the time. He feels it's his right to collect, while Lydia wants him to put some of his collection in the business and see if they can make a profit on it. The old guy told me he puts aside the money she gives him to buy sodas and then doesn't tell her when he adds to his collection."

"But in that trailer? Where would they have any room for a collection of anything, between their clothes and the inventory and cases for the business? And they don't look as though they're making a mint in the business." Maggie thought of that crowded, rusting trailer. "I think I'm on Lydia's side."

Will shrugged. "Well, that's their problem. Anyway, I gather she didn't have much information."

"No. Did Susan say anything after the police questioned her?"

"Just that she didn't want to talk to anyone; she wanted to sleep. So I let her."

"Is the fairground still closed?"

"For the duration. I think you're the only one here who hadn't planned to spend the night."

Will failed to squelch a yawn.

"I think it's time for us to collapse. I have one more bed to offer." Will attempted a lewd wink. "But, in case you don't want to share, I also have a sleeping bag I can use."

"Is that a proposition?"

"Hell—I wish I had the energy to make it one!" They climbed into the van as Maggie thought fleetingly of the soft, unreachable bed she was paying for across the street at Kosy Kabins.

But the single bed felt just fine, and with thoughts of Ben and how frightened he must be, Maggie fell into a restless sleep.

Chapter 15

—◦—

Vanda Insignis *(small orchids)*, *German chromolithograph, c. 1880. Price: $85.*

Maggie woke to the sound of the RV door closing. She stretched and felt her muscles resisting. She was going to pay for all the toting and carrying she'd done on Friday, combined with the night of little sleep. She swung her legs over the side of the bed, realizing that she was alone. She looked at her watch: almost seven o'clock. Had Ben been able to sleep at all?

Outside, she made a quick trip to the ladies' room. The mirror reflected a thirty-eight-year-old woman who'd stayed up until 2 A.M. talking murder and then sleeping in her clothes. It wasn't a pretty reflection. A shower and clean clothes would be essential if she was to greet customers civilly at 10 A.M.

Will was at the trailer when she returned.

"Good morning, sleepyhead! Susan's gone to change, and the police have opened the fairgrounds for the show, since they've got their suspect and Vince pressured them to let him open the show on schedule at ten this morning. But I'm told we're all still considered witnesses, so if you want to go back to the motel, you'll have to show identification at the gate, answer a few questions, and leave word where you'll be for the next twenty-four hours."

"'They've got their suspect!' How can they really believe Ben could kill someone?" Maggie thought of Ben's open face and usual grin, and of Gussie, alone at the motel. "Will, have you talked with the police?"

"Briefly, after Susan went back to her van."

"Was she all right?"

"She seemed in pretty good shape. She said she had some telephone calls to make."

Susan had said Harry's father had been missing for years and his mother had died, but he might have other relatives to notify. "What kind of questions are the police asking?"

"Basically just how well we knew Harry, and whether we saw him last night. That sort of thing. Apparently not many people knew him well; most are saying they wouldn't have recognized him. So the questioning is going fast."

"I need to get in line, then." Maggie ran her hand through her hair in an attempt to put it in order. "And I really need to get back to the Kabins to check on Gussie, and then shower and change before the show opens."

"I'm going out for a hot breakfast. There's a diner down the road about a mile. Care to join me?"

"Sure, but seeing Gussie and taking a shower take priority. How would eight-fifteen sound? We'll need to get back here by nine-thirty at the latest; customers start lining up by then."

"It's a deal."

The police were working from the two picnic tables they had pulled together the night before. They, too, looked as though they hadn't had much sleep. Officer Taggart wasn't among them.

"I'm Maggie Summer. I was staying over at the Kosy Kabins and would like to go back to shower and change before the show." One look and they should be able to see that it was a reasonable request.

The same young detective Maggie had seen last night nodded wearily. "Okay. Just a few questions."

He turned the notebook he was carrying to a new page.

"Name?"

"Maggie Summer."

"Occupation?"

"My antiques business is called Shadows. I also teach at a college in New Jersey." Maggie pulled out a business card to give him her address and telephone number.

"Did you know Harry Findley?"

"Yes. He and his wife had the booth next to mine. I've known him for about six years."

"Did you see him last night?"

"Not after the show. Not until Susan started screaming."

"Do you know if Harry Findley had any enemies?"

Maggie thought fast. She knew several people who were not thrilled with Harry, but none of them were really enemies. She wished she knew more. "No."

"Where were you at ten-thirty last night?"

"Here. I came over with Ben Allen to check something. Everything was all right, so we were on our way back to the Kabins when we heard Susan."

"What was Ben Allen checking?"

Maggie took a deep breath. "Ben had been running on the track, and on his way back to the motel he saw a man and a woman arguing. He thought the man was going to hit the woman, so he tried to stop him and pushed him to the ground."

That was what Ben had told her, and Maggie believed him.

"How do you know that?"

"Ben panicked; he thought he might have hurt the man. So he went to his motel room to tell Gussie White, his aunt. I was there. Gussie was very tired so I agreed to go back with Ben to see if the man was hurt."

"Anyone else with you and Ben?"

"Will Brewer was with us most of the time. We also spoke with Lydia Wyndham."

"Did you find anything?"

"No; there was no one near the area where the confrontation occurred."

"What did you do then?"

"From Ben's description, Will and I thought that the woman involved was Susan Findley, so we looked for her. When she wasn't at her van, Ben and I decided to go back to the motel. Will was walking us to the front gate when Susan started screaming."

The officer sighed. "Okay. You're going to the Kabins now?"

Maggie nodded. "I'll be back by nine-thirty to prepare for the show's opening. Then I'll be here all day. I have a reservation for the Kabins again for tonight."

"I may come by to say hello during the show, since you were the victim's neighbor, and you spent part of last evening with Ben Allen. We'll want to verify some of the time periods involved. But I think we have this case pretty well wrapped up. If you think of anything else we might find helpful, get in touch with me."

Maggie resisted a strong desire to tell the young officer he had no idea what he was doing.

"Do you know how Harry died?"

He hesitated. "You saw the body?"

Maggie nodded.

"Then you know someone hit him on the left side of his head from the back."

"The traditional blunt object?"

"Lady, we're conducting a murder investigation here. Not writing a novel." He sighed. "We'll get the results of the autopsy later today. That should fill in some of the details." He looked down at the notes in front of him. "You can go. But don't leave the Kabins or the fairgrounds without telling one of us." He gestured at himself and at the slightly older man who sat to his right, who looked, if possible, even more tired. His eyes were almost as red as the ink he was using.

"Officer, do you think the murderer could have been the same person who murdered John Smithson last week?"

"That's the question of the day. But, no, I don't. Most murderers stick to the same style. Harry Findley was bludgeoned; John Smithson was poisoned. Not the same modus operandi at all. This looks like a separate situation. And, of course, we do have a suspect in this case."

"Ben just couldn't have done it! I've known Ben for years; he's kind, and gentle, and he had no reason to hurt Harry!"

"We'll see. That's why Ben Allen is being questioned. I think that's all we need from you right now."

Maggie glared at him.

"You can go to the motel if you like."

"I was going to have breakfast at the diner."

"You and every other antiques dealer. Yes, you can go to the diner. Just don't disappear."

What she needed was a hot shower, and to get away from this place and think.

An hour later, clean and dressed in a tailored denim shirtwaist dress, a red scarf, gold *M* earrings, and a pair of comfortable shoes, Maggie pushed open the heavy glass door to Marvin's Diner. There had been no answer at Gussie's Kabin, and her van was gone. She was no doubt at the police station with Ben. There would be a lot of catching up to do if and when she saw Gussie at the show.

For a Saturday morning the diner was surprisingly full, and not surprisingly, most of the red vinyl booths were filled with familiar faces. The dealers were getting in a good meal before a long day. Although there were food concession stands at the fairgrounds, dealers had to have someone watch their booth at all times: leaving your booth could mean losing a sale. Most dealers took some food to the show with them or depended on a partner to go and get coffee and sandwiches. Dealers who worked alone, such as Maggie, knew they'd have to ask someone to "booth-sit" at least once or twice during a show.

Will waved from the third booth up on the right.

He'd changed into a sports jacket and slacks. The blue tie he was wearing made his eyes look bluer than she remembered. She shook her head mentally and told herself to keep cool as the waitress stopped to fill their cups with coffee.

"Diet cola, please," Maggie asked, covering her cup. "Will, are the police still all over the fairgrounds?"

"They don't have much more time before the crowds arrive. I saw some cars turning into the customer parking lot."

"I keep trying to think who might have killed Harry. Susan did say that he'd made some enemies. In fact, she said you were on the list."

"I guess it's good that I have an alibi for most of last evening, then, isn't it? Harry wasn't my favorite person. But *enemy* sounds a little strong."

"What problem did you and Harry have?"

"I met Harry through a mutual acquaintance in New York. When I told him I specialized in early fireplace equipment and kitchenware, Harry said he had a new customer, someone who had just bought an old home out in the Hamptons, and who wanted to decorate authentically. He said the guy didn't have much money left after buying the house, and Harry was helping him pick up some quality items to set the decorating tone. The house featured an old fireplace in a part of the house that had once been a kitchen, and he wanted to decorate it with period fireplace furnishings."

"Sounds like a good customer for you."

"I thought so. Harry hinted that when his client had a little more money, he'd be back for more. So I quoted him a low price, on the theory that this was just the beginning." Will paused for a sip of coffee. "Over the next couple of months Harry bought about a dozen really good pieces from me. Again, I gave him a deep discount, so he wouldn't have to mark them up very much higher for his client. You know the drill."

Maggie nodded. Dealers usually gave discounts to each other, and if you bought a group of things, often the discount was higher. It kept merchandise circulating. At some shows, more buying and selling went on between dealers than between dealers and customers.

The waitress stopped at their table to bring Maggie her cola and waited expectantly.

"Three eggs scrambled, with home fries, bacon, waffles, and orange juice. Maggie?"

"Orange juice, two eggs scrambled, and raisin toast, please." Maggie handed her menu to the waitress and hoped she'd ordered enough. She hadn't realized how hungry she was until she'd looked at the menu. "And Harry didn't come back for additional items?"

"No. But that was only part of it. About a year later I was at my dentist's office and I picked up a copy of *House Beautiful*. There was a six-page spread on a home in the Hamptons that had been renovated. There, in living color, was a photo of the kitchen, featuring all the things I'd sold to Harry. Everything was there: the iron crane and kettle, the tin oven, the brass trammel, all the iron spoons and forks, the hand-crafted dough board. Turns out the owner wasn't a real-estate impoverished young man; he was one of those guys who made a mint in Internet stocks and sold them at the right time. I asked around. Seems

Harry had been bragging about what a bargain he'd gotten on the fireplace stuff, and how he'd really soaked the client, charging him ten times what the stuff was worth." Will's large hands on the cup of coffee grew tense. "What would you have thought?"

There was nothing illegal in what Harry had done; dealers sometimes lucked out and made large profits. But in a case where he knew he could make a bundle, Harry shouldn't have asked Will to increase the discount he was giving. The fair thing would have been to pay Will's asking price, or slightly below it.

Maggie grimaced. "All's fair in love and commerce. But you're right. I'd have been plenty aggravated if that had happened to me."

"Well, it got to me. It was right about the time when I was trying to turn my business into a full-time occupation, and every dollar was important. I decided if he ever wanted anything else from me, he'd have to pay full price. But"—Will looked up as the waitress slipped his breakfast in front of him—"I never had the chance. He avoided me after that." He raised his fork toward the eggs. "Probably just as well."

They both concentrated on food for the next few minutes; breakfast never tastes as good as when you're not sure when you'll have lunch.

Maggie took a sip of juice. "Do you know anyone else at the show who might have had similar dealings with Harry?"

"Could have been anyone, I guess. Although Harry wasn't really into antiques shows. Most of his contacts were with decorators or auction houses. I suspect the reason he came to me was that he didn't know anyone else who specialized in early kitchen gear and tools." Will paused. "I don't like to think it was also because I lived in Buffalo, so he wouldn't be running into me very often. I'm doing a lot more shows now, but, as it's turned out, this is the first show I've done with him."

"I think he and Susan only do Vince's shows. You were lucky to get in. You must have called at just the right moment."

"I was at the show in Westchester last week, when John Smithson died. I'd seen discount cards for this show in his booth, so I took a chance and called Vince. This is a show I've been wanting to get into."

"Don't you feel a little like a grave robber?"

"Someone had to fill the space; John wasn't going to be here, and Vince wouldn't have left the space empty. I figured I might as well be the one." Will took a bite of his waffles. "Am I still on your list of possible murderers?"

"Susan told me you were looking for Harry after the show closed last night. Did you find him?"

"I saw Harry leaving right after the show-closing announcement. I did want to talk with him to tell him what I thought of him, so I tried to follow him. But I saw him with Vince, and I had second thoughts. I went back to my RV and made myself a sandwich. After dinner I went for a walk around the fields and didn't speak with anyone until I saw you and Ben."

"Do you think all the dealers will be at the show today? Surely Susan won't."

"She told me this morning that she was staying; certainly she could pack up if she wanted to. Even Vince wouldn't make her remain under the circumstances. But the police wanted her to stick around, and she said she needed any money the show might bring in."

"Not acting the grieving widow role."

Will shrugged. "Looked to me like she and Harry just had a marriage of convenience anyway. From what I saw when I met them in New York, marriage didn't appear to be slowing down her social life. And Harry didn't seem to mind; he always had his own agenda."

"And what about Joe? I wonder if he'll be there today."

"I'd guess, yes. Besides, even if the police think they've got the killer, they're certainly not encouraging anyone to pack up and leave."

"I didn't see Joe anywhere around last night. But I'm assuming he was there."

"I don't know him well, but I have run into him at a couple of shows. He doesn't seem to socialize a lot. Probably last night he was just minding his own business. And he really seemed to like Harry. He may be the really bereaved person in this scenario."

"I wonder if he has an alibi."

"Maggie, leave the detecting to the police. You have a show to do today. Think of all those prints you're going to sell."

"I haven't forgotten them. But I'm so worried about Ben. Harry was no angel, but I just can't imagine anyone hating Harry enough to kill him. And I know for sure that Ben didn't do it."

"What about Susan? She had a motive—I heard Harry was divorcing her for Joe."

"Jealousy? It's possible. But, as you said, Susan always seemed to have other interests of her own.

Vince, for instance. I'm thinking more about the money involved. She told you she was staying at the show to make money? Married to Harry, she had a half interest in the business; divorced from Harry she would have cash for her share of Art-Effects; widowed, she'd have all of the business and any insurance Harry might have had."

"You're right, Maggie. It sounds strange. But maybe money is a problem. It could be anything. Gambling? Maybe she borrowed some money and is under pressure to return it. Maybe she made some investments that went sour. Maybe she wants a month at a spa. She looks as though she could use some rest."

"What about Vince? He knew them both well."

"What would be his motive? Jealousy? Vince seems to have had Susan. Business? He and Harry didn't compete, so far as I know. Different interests. Doesn't add up."

"Someone has to have a motive. Could you keep an eye on my booth if I do a little wandering today? I'll ask Gussie, too, assuming she even comes to the show. She must be frantic about Ben."

"Okay. I'll help. But I think you're crazy to play amateur detective." He picked up the check that lay on the table. "Tell you what—if you figure out the murderer, I'll buy you dinner."

"And if I don't?"

"Well, you'd better stay by your booth long enough to make some big sales. Because I plan on being very hungry."

Maggie smiled. "Then I guess it's a date."

Chapter 16

———&———

City of New York from Brooklyn Heights,
*hand-colored steel engraving by A. G. Warren,
New York, 1872. Scene includes many sailing
vessels and one steamboat as well as the
Brooklyn Bridge, which was then under
construction. Price: $125.*

By 10 A.M. the line of customers waiting to pay the
$8 admission charge was already snaking around the
exhibit buildings. Maggie heard Vince Thompson
wondering whether the murder had encouraged
curiosity seekers. Although it had happened too late
to make the local papers, radio stations had picked
up the news and were headlining, "Second Antiques
Dealer Murder." Customers who hadn't heard of the
grisly events must have been puzzled by the presence
of so many police.

As Maggie was straightening prints that had gone
off-kilter the night before, Gussie arrived. Her scooter
practically left skid marks as she stopped right in front
of Maggie. "What a night! I can't believe this nightmare! They're still holding Ben. Jim arrived two hours

ago. He's making sure Ben doesn't say anything and is hunting down a local criminal attorney just in case we need one." She took a deep breath. "Where have *you* been all this time?"

"Whoa! They were keeping all potential witnesses on the grounds, so, as I told you last night, I slept in Will's RV. I stopped in to see you when I got off the grounds this morning, but you weren't there."

"Sorry. I was having breakfast with my sister and her husband. They told me I should go ahead and manage my booth; they don't hold me responsible. But I can't help thinking, Why didn't I keep Ben with me all the time? Why did I think he'd be all right by himself, in a new place?"

"Gussie, it wasn't your fault. Ben was just in that classic wrong place at the wrong time." Maggie reached over and touched Gussie's hand. "If you need help with anything, I'm here. I've just about finished checking my booth."

"Thank you, Maggie. I just need someone to reassure me that I'm going to wake up any minute and find it's all a mistake and Ben is back helping me put miniature furniture on the high shelves." Gussie turned and took a deep breath. "I will be all right; really I will be. Be my friend today and keep me sane?"

Maggie nodded. "I'll do everything I can, Gussie. To help you, and to try to figure out what really happened last night."

Gussie looked over at Will's booth, where he was adjusting a wooden fireplace frame he was using as a background for his Colonial kitchen equipment.

"And I must thank Will! He was with Ben when

the police picked him up for questioning . . . and he's the one who called me." Gussie moved up the aisle to Will's booth. She was back in a moment. "He is really a nice man. You spent the night with him?"

"Go dust your dolls and your dirty mind!" Maggie grinned. "Yes, we spent the night together. Will and I and Susan. It was a wild time, Gussie!"

"Give me five minutes, and then you've got to tell me everything." Gussie arched her eyebrows. "And I mean everything. Maybe it'll get my mind off Ben." She turned into her booth and started uncovering her tables.

Maggie sat down and checked once more that her prints were straightened, business cards out, magnifying glass and tape measure handy. Diet cola. To hold sold merchandise, plastic bags stashed optimistically near her chair, but hidden by the table covers. She really did hope it would be a good show. She wasn't as desperate for money as Susan appeared to be, but she could certainly use some extra cash flow. Just being away from home this weekend meant she'd had to hire a neighbor boy to mow her grass. One more $40 expense to have someone else do something Michael had always taken care of.

She looked around. Susan was in her booth, as Will had predicted, nibbling on what looked like fast-food scrambled eggs and a bagel. She looked less like the grieving widow. She was talking to a dealer Maggie didn't know, although he looked familiar. Maybe he was the one selling embroideries and laces over in building one. Will was gulping another cup of coffee he'd clearly picked up from one of the concession stands on his way in. Lydia and Abe were unlocking their glass cases of jewelry and sterling flatware. And Joe was in his booth, straightening shelves of leather-bound books.

The show must go on, Maggie thought, as Vince's voice boomed over the intercom.

"All dealers in their booths. Welcome to the Twenty-third Annual Rensselaer County Spring Antiques Fair. The show is now open. Concession stands are on the south side of the grounds. If you plan to leave the show grounds and return, please take your stamped admittance ticket with you. Porters are available to help you take your purchases to your vehicles, and shipping arrangements can be made in the Show Management booth. Enjoy the show!"

Gussie motored around the side of the booth. "All right; now, before the onslaught begins, tell me everything you know. Anything that will help Ben. I don't even know exactly what happened. When I saw Ben at the station, he was in a daze, crying and scared."

"I don't think anyone knows exactly what happened, Gussie. But I can tell you what Ben and I did."

Gussie nodded when Maggie finally ended her account of the evening's events.

"It all happened too quickly," Maggie added. "We ran back and there was Susan, standing over Harry's body. He'd been hit on the head."

Gussie paled. "Could Ben . . . ?"

"I don't think so. But the police apparently think he did, so they're not looking very hard at other possibilities. They're just trying to tie Ben to the time and place. They've got his virtual confession that he hit

Harry, and they have the blood on his hand. Chances are, it's Harry's blood. That's why we've got to figure out who is responsible. They have a long list of everyone who was here last night, including Ben and me, but the murderer most likely is one of us who knew Harry well enough to want him dead."

"No signs of robbery?"

"I didn't ask. But anyone wanting to steal last night would have hit the exhibit area. There are hundreds of thousands of dollars' worth of antiques in here. Why kill someone in the parking lot?" Maggie paused. "No, I think it had to be someone who knew Harry well, and who was very angry."

"What about the John Smithson murder?" Gussie shivered. "This is the second antiques dealer to die in two weeks. Is anyone looking at that?"

Maggie shook her head. "I asked the detective who interviewed me. He said most killers with more than one victim use the same method all the time. John Smithson was poisoned; Harry was hit on the head."

"How is Susan taking it?" They both looked toward Susan's booth. She was laughing with an overweight gentleman who seemed to share her amusement.

"Right now, she seems to be taking it well," Maggie replied dryly. "But last night she was hysterical. She and Harry may have had an untraditional relationship, but I think they really cared for each other. All those years we thought they were the ideal couple! But I guess each couple defines its own relationship. Harry and Susan shared their business. And apparently, they shared a belief in open marriage."

"Until now, when Harry left her for Joe."

"Even that situation doesn't seem clear to me. Last night she described the divorce as basically a financial rearrangement. She needed cash, and Harry was buying out her share of the business. It didn't sound as though either of them planned to move out of their loft, for instance."

"Harry was always charming to me, but I've heard he was really manipulative. He took care of Harry first, Susan second, and anyone else a far third, depending on how valuable the relationship was to Harry."

Maggie nodded. "That's what Will told me. He was involved in a deal with Harry where nothing illegal happened, but Will felt Harry had used him."

"That sounds like Harry. There are always rumors about dealers, but I never heard any about Harry being involved in anything illegal. Just that he was good at maneuvering people. That you had to watch him. And that Susan was a bit of a sycophant. But they always seemed close."

Maggie turned to smile at the young couple looking through her Maxfield Parrish prints. "That's a good example of Parrish blue," she pointed out. "He loved pure colors and seldom blended them; he was so known for his use of cobalt blue that his contemporaries named it after him."

"I like the print, but I've never heard of him."

"Parrish, N. C. Wyeth, and Jessie Willcox Smith were the three best-known students of the Brandywine School. They all worked in the early part of the twentieth century."

"That was Howard Pyle's group, wasn't it?"

Maggie nodded.

"All his people look the same." The young woman, red sunglasses perched precariously on her blonde hair, had lined up several of the Parrish prints. "Men and women; old and young. There's something similar about them all."

Maggie peeked over her shoulder. "All those prints were taken from oil paintings Parrish did, and for years he only used one model—Susan Lewin. He would pose her in various costumes and roles. Sometimes he photographed her in different positions and then painted from the photograph."

"And then did he marry her and live happily ever after?"

Maggie smiled. "Actually, no. He was already married. Lewin was a young woman he had hired to help his wife with the housework and to care for their four children. As you guessed, she became his mistress. She lived in an apartment over his studio, which was only a few feet from his house in Cornish, New Hampshire. Certainly an interesting arrangement for the early twentieth century. The three of them—Parrish, his wife, and his mistress—lived that way for almost forty years."

The young man spoke up. "I think I've seen prints like this at the Westchester Mall. Are these really from the early twentieth century?"

"Absolutely," Maggie assured him, pointing at the "1904" penciled below the price on the print. "All my prints are guaranteed to be the age I've indicated. In Parrish's case, they are the first printing of the illustration: usually a book plate or a magazine cover or illustration. Parrish has become popular recently, and you can find modern copies of his work in almost any poster store today. But these are originals."

The couple conferred a bit before deciding to purchase *The Lantern Bearers*, a print showing Susan Lewin in six different overlapping poses, each figure identically dressed as a clown holding a large moon-like glowing ball reflecting the moon in a navy blue night sky, done for *Collier's Magazine* in 1912.

"I just love the real thing, don't you?" bubbled the blonde.

Maggie nodded as she wrote up the sales slip. What was even nicer was the real money she was now adding to her cash box.

She made two other, smaller sales, after that—a Denton salmon, and a late-nineteenth-century lithograph of girls playing with a hoop. An unusually large number of customers were at the show, and a good percentage of them seemed to be carrying bags. Even if they weren't interested in prints today, they had to be finding something they liked. That's what kept people coming back to this show.

Maggie noticed Lydia Wyndham wrapping up several good-sized pieces of Victorian sterling, and Will attempting to find a bag strong enough to support a copper kettle. So far so good, for all of them.

"Gussie, would you like some diet soda? I picked up some extra cans this morning and put them in my cooler."

"Thanks, Maggie; that sounds great. I'm just not focused today. I have iced tea in my van, but I forgot to bring it in." Gussie took a can of cola.

"How are you doing?"

"Fine. I had to ask one of the customers to lift

down a doll he wanted to look at, but there was no problem. In fact"—she raised her can in the general direction of the crowd—"he bought it."

"Not bad for the first couple of hours."

"How about you?"

"I've made a couple of sales, including one Parrish print. And the usual number of people who say they're interested but want to see the whole show before they make a decision."

Gussie nodded. "The 'be backs.' Well, sometimes they do come back."

"Sometimes," Maggie agreed. "But I wouldn't take their interest to the bank. And while we're waiting for them to make up their minds, we have to figure out who wanted Harry dead." Maggie stood in the aisle just outside both of their booths so she could talk with Gussie and still keep an eye on her own merchandise. She wouldn't want to miss a sale or encourage someone to walk off with a print. At some city shows theft was a major problem, but at all shows it was a possibility.

"Gussie, I've been thinking." Maggie lowered her voice and glanced around at the J. COUSINS, BOOK-SELLER sign in back of her. "There are at least two people I haven't talked to who might know something about Harry—Vince and Joe. Would you mind keeping an eye on my booth while I try to find Vince? I've already asked Will, but I'd rather have two people do it, in case one of you gets a customer."

"Okay. As long as you booth-sit for me later, when I need to take a break."

"It's a deal. And if things slow down a bit, maybe you could talk with Joe."

"I'll try. He's right across the aisle. I just don't know him that well. He's always kept pretty much to himself."

"But he must have seen us talking with Susan yesterday. And certainly you, of all people, want to know as much as you can. It's Ben they're holding!"

"You're right. I'll try to talk with Joe."

"See if you can find out where he was last night. I didn't see him at all. I would expect him to be pretty upset. He and Harry obviously had a close relationship. And maybe he knows more about the situation between Harry and Susan. I'm really not as clear about that as I'd like to be."

"Excuse me, but is this your booth?" A woman in yellow shorts pushed a stroller containing two-year-old twins (also wearing yellow shorts) into Gussie's booth, blocking the entrance. "I'm collecting 'twin things.' You see—I have twins! Do you have anything that is twinnish?"

Gussie began telling her about a Dionne-quintuplets book she had, but Mother of Twins was not to be distracted. "No. I'm just interested in twins. No supertwins."

"Sorry, I don't think so. Unless you count Raggedy Ann and Raggedy Andy?"

The twin lady didn't think so.

"Why don't you ask across the aisle?" Gussie suggested. "There are several groups of twin books—*The Bobbsey Twins, The Twins of Different Nations* series, the . . . ," but the twin lady had already turned and blocked Joe's booth with her stroller.

"Well done!" Maggie congratulated. "If he makes a sale, he owes you one. And even if not, you tried—at least he owes you a thank-you!"

"Unless, of course, that double stroller blocks his booth and keeps out customers looking for autographed Hemingway first editions," said Gussie.

Maggie's search for Vince was further delayed by the arrival of a large man wearing bright blue slacks and a knit shirt embroidered with a yachting club logo. He was searching for a print to give his son to commemorate his graduation from dental school, a print his son could hang in his first office. Maggie was happy to show him a selection of several plates of cross sections of teeth, and of jaws with teeth, all originally produced as plates for nineteenth-century medical books.

That sale was immediately followed by one of an 1867 wood engraving of women dressed in full-skirted dresses, heeled kid shoes, and mandatory hats and men in suits (and hats) playing croquet in a pastoral setting overlooking a river. Older couples chatted and children romped in surrounding areas, ensuring that the young couples remained well chaperoned.

"Did you know," Maggie explained, "that croquet was the first sport in which it was acceptable for women to compete with men?" She read a line from the article accompanying the engraving, which she had attached to the back of the mat that now framed it. "'To the interest of the game is added the relish of out-of-doors, and, possibly the strongest charm of all, the little coquetries and gay flirtations which summer pastimes may innocently include.'"

The woman who bought the print, a croquet enthusiast, was thrilled with both the print and the information. "I can't wait until I tell my husband! I've finally convinced him to buy us a new croquet set for our summer place. We can hang this print right above the rack I'm having built to hold the mallets!"

Often Maggie sat at a show and twiddled her thumbs for long minutes at a time between customers. Today, when she wanted to leave her booth, customers kept buying. Nice, but ironic.

She finally drained her soda can and motioned to Gussie that she was going for a short walk. Gussie nodded back as she continued her discussion of toy stuffing with an earnest-looking man holding three teddy bears. On her way up the aisle, Maggie also nodded at Will, who was trying hard not to get in the middle of a disagreement between two people, presumably husband and wife, about what size their fireplace was.

Across from Will's booth Susan was sipping a cup of tea. A half-eaten bagel sat next to her cash box. That was good. Susan should eat something. And Lydia would know the right kind of tea to help Susan get through the day.

Vince's Show Management booth was quiet. A couple of porters waited behind the desk for requests to carry newly purchased Queen Anne bureaus or mahogany sideboards to a buyer's car or truck. A representative of a local trucking company was also present, so customers could arrange to ship furniture or anything else to the far corners of the country.

"Can I help you?" one of the porters asked, glancing at her dealer's badge. "Do you need a porter at your booth?"

"No, thanks. I was just looking for Vince."

"And here he is." Vince came up in back of her, his arms full of brochures for future shows and subscription forms for antiques magazines and journals. "What can I help you with, Maggie?" He dropped the piles on the desk and started re-sorting and straightening them. "We had too many materials for the information tables between the buildings, so I thought I'd leave some piles here, in case anyone was interested." Maggie noted that brochures for his future buying trips to Europe and the Far East were on top.

"I just wanted an update on the investigation. We're all pretty upset, you know." Maggie fluttered her eyelashes a little. It wasn't her usual style, but maybe Vince would think she was just a concerned and silly woman. "Harry and Susan had the booth next to mine. And, of course, with Ben being arrested, we're very concerned."

"Yes. The police are right on top of the situation, aren't they? It's all so very unfortunate. A mentally disabled young man, confused, and poor Harry a victim."

Maggie took a deep breath. "Vince, I'm sure Ben didn't do it. He's a very kind and friendly young man, and he had no reason to hurt Harry."

"Well, the police don't seem to agree with you, Maggie, and they're the experts." Vince rearranged another pile of brochures. "I heard Susan spent the night with you and Will last night. That was good of you. Susan and I are friends, you know, and I was concerned about her. And I had so many things to take care of, with the police here, and the show opening today and everything." He looked at Maggie as though he were waiting for her to say something else. "How is she taking it?"

"Having her husband murdered at an antiques show where she thought she was among friends and colleagues was obviously upsetting. But she's tougher than some people think. You know, she's working her booth today."

"First thing this morning I told her she could go home; forget the show contract, I told her. This is a unique, a tragic, situation. A couple of other dealers volunteered to fill her space, and I could have gotten porters to help her pack up and get out before the show opened." Vince shook his head a little. "I wouldn't have held it against her. I would have offered her a contract next year."

"You're a generous man, Vince," Maggie said dryly.

"I try to be," he agreed. "Susan's a special lady. And she and Harry were a special couple."

"Maybe. But, after all, they were getting divorced, so I guess their relationship wasn't quite what it used to be."

Vince started slightly. "Getting a divorce? I didn't know. Who told you that?" He had turned visibly paler behind his gray and black mustache. Clearly, Susan and Harry's divorce was news to him.

"Susan told me yesterday. She said they were signing the final papers next week, and that Harry was buying out her share of Art-Effects. She was going to stay on as an employee, though." Maggie looked carefully at Vince to see if any of this meant anything to him. Something did; he looked like a pigeon who had plumped himself up and was ready to sputter.

"I'm sure Susan mentioned it to me; I just must have forgotten."

Sure he had. But why hadn't Susan told him if she'd told everyone else?

"Lydia Wyndham saw you and Harry talking last night."

Vince looked straight back at Maggie. "As I told the police, Harry and I had a short discussion after the show. Harry was going out to the Coast for a while, and he asked me to keep an eye on Susan. He said she hadn't been feeling too well."

"Really? Did you agree to do that?"

"Well, normally, of course, I would have been glad to help out. I told him I was sorry about Susan. She'd have gotten a little faint several times when we were in the Far East last month. Once I had to hold up the tour for her. Luckily, not too many people complained. But I can't keep watching out for her. I have other commitments in the near future. A tour to the UK and Paris, for one. She was his wife, not mine. I told him she was his problem. He'd have to find someone else to help out."

"Does Susan know you'll be away soon?"

"I'm sure she knows about the tour; there are brochures all over, and some of the people who went on the Far East tour are going. The trip's been fully booked for almost a year."

"Why was Harry going to California?" Susan hadn't said anything about Harry's planning to go out of town.

"He didn't say. Something about business. Said he'd be leaving soon."

Instead, he was killed.

"Did you talk with Susan last night?"

Vince looked around impatiently. "Listen. I'm not on trial here." He paused for a moment. "But I have no secrets. Susan and I talked off and on all day. She helped me with dealer registration. After Harry's body was found I was with the police most of the time. At first they actually wanted to cancel the show for today! Can you imagine what the dealers—and the customers—would have said? It took me most of the night to convince them that none of the dealers would leave today. The best way to keep us all in town was to open the show. They had us all imprisoned by economics. Right, Maggie?" Vince shook his head. "But then, luckily, they found their prime suspect, your friend Gussie's nephew. That made them feel better about the show's opening, and there was no real reason to hold everyone else up."

"But they don't have good evidence against Ben," Maggie said. "No one actually saw Ben knock Harry down."

"I think several people mentioned his behavior to the police. He spent a lot of time yesterday hanging around here, staring at Susan. And then, last night, a couple of us saw him running around the field. He was sweaty, and he looked very anxious." Vince shrugged. "And I understand he confessed."

"He said he'd run into Harry and Susan last night. He certainly didn't say he'd murdered anyone."

"That's not what I heard."

Maggie changed the subject. "Then you didn't talk with Susan after the show closed last night?"

"I don't think so." Vince shook his head and touched his mustache. "I talked briefly to a lot of people. It's a lot of work to make sure a show this large runs smoothly, Maggie." He looked thoughtful. "No, I'm pretty sure I didn't. She was working at her booth last night; I had to play host and organizer. After the show closed, I locked the area and then walked around the buildings with Officer Taggart to make sure everyone had left and the buildings were locked for the night. We had just finished doing that when . . . we all heard Susan."

Maggie frowned. She was missing something, but she couldn't think what it was. "If you think of anything that might help, Vince, would you let me know?"

"Maggie, there are police investigating Harry's murder. You have a beautiful booth, where dozens of people are probably standing with their checkbooks open right now. You had a rough winter, but this is spring."

Vince put his arm around Maggie and headed her back in the direction of her booth. "You go and make lots of money, and then come back and tell me what a wonderful show this is, and what a wonderful promoter I am, and by that time the police should have had this totally wrapped up." He looked at Maggie as she started to say something. "I know this is difficult for Susan. I want to help. I even went out this morning and got her some fresh-squeezed orange juice, the way she likes it."

Orange juice would certainly make a difference when your husband had just been murdered.

"You're a caring person, Maggie, and Gussie is your friend. But Harry Findley is dead. And the police have found his killer. Just leave well enough alone. After all—the show must go on."

Maggie headed back to her booth. Vince knew something. But what? And why would Harry ask Vince to take care of Susan?

Maggie wove through the crowds of customers who filled the aisles and most of the booths. Vince was right. It was silly to leave her booth. She needed the sales. Gussie and Will would both try to keep an eye on her booth, but no dealer could speak for another, and neither Gussie nor Will knew much about prints. The antiques business was so specialized that everyone in the business, dealer or collector, spent sizable chunks of money and time on buying and studying reference books that helped to separate the old from the new, the desirable from the merely interesting, the popular from the trite. To know more than a few areas of antiques in depth was rare. Auctioneers tried; appraisers tried; but even they depended on specialists for advice and counsel. There was simply too much to learn about antiques.

And not enough to learn about Harry's murder. How could it have happened so fast, with all of them so close by? Vince's reporting of his conversation with Harry didn't really give any clues, other than that Harry had been concerned about Susan's health. Well, maybe if she ate more than vitamins and vegetables, she'd be healthier, Maggie thought. What a problem! Susan was too skinny. True. But a good talking to and maybe a dietitian would solve that problem. It wasn't a matter of life and death. Or, was it?

Maggie stopped at the concession stand to get a couple of tuna sandwiches to share with Susan and Gussie, then headed back to her booth.

Chapter 17

—◇—

The First Day of the Season, a hand-colored wood engraving by John Leech, who was known for his humorous sporting illustrations, published in The Illustrated London News *on November 22, 1856. Group of elegant gentlemen on horses in hunting attire greeting each other before the fox hunt begins. Price: $75.*

The minister and her husband were thrilled when they saw Maggie's N. Currier (the company originally founded by Nathaniel Currier in 1835, before he formed a partnership with his brother-in-law, James Ives, in 1857), *The Tree of Intemperance* (1849). Originally part of a pair (the other half of which was, of course, *The Tree of Temperance*), the print was of a dark green tree emerging from roots labeled "Wine," "Beer," "Cider," "Rum," "Gin," and "Brandy," its trunk encircled by the snake named "Alcohol." Its branches, labeled "Disease," "Misery," "Poverty"— and Maggie's personal favorite—"Insanity," were broken and yielded fruits ranging from "Degradation,"

"Ignorance," and "The Wrath of God," to "The Alms House," "Robbery," "Murder," and "The Gallows." On the right side of the tree were a sobbing woman and her three children. On the left side were two men brawling in front of a tavern.

"I love it!" the minister said as she read yet another "fruit": "'A Feeble Body.' 'Blasphemy.' 'Failure in Business.' My husband and I have been collecting temperance materials—posters, books, political buttons. We hang them on the walls around our bar. This is perfect!"

Her husband agreed. They left their names in case Maggie found a copy of the matching print. "It would be lovely to have the pair," the young minister said, smiling. "And if you ever have any other temperance or Prohibition materials, please, give us a call!"

Maggie filed their names with her list of customers looking for specific materials, then turned the sales book to a clean page.

Her booth had been busy since she'd returned; both Will and Gussie were no doubt glad she was back. Sales, after all, were why they were all here. Being asked to watch a friend's booth was not an unusual request, but it could mean having to choose between your own customers and those in another booth. Not an easy choice.

Maggie glanced around. The early steady stream of customers had abated, but a good number of people were still browsing through the aisles.

Gussie was talking with an elderly couple who had brought two dolls to the show, hoping to sell them to a dealer. Will was reading a book in between customers. Maggie couldn't see Susan, but occasionally her voice rose above the partition separating her booth from Maggie's. Abe Wyndham must have gone for a walk; Lydia was showing berry forks to a young woman.

Maggie straightened her cash box and reorganized a few prints that customers had left in the wrong piles. It was hard to concentrate on keeping her booth arranged and smiling for customers when she knew a killer was nearby. A killer who was no doubt relaxing, since he— or she—knew the police had a suspect. She wondered if Gussie's friend Jim had been able to get Ben out of jail. Could a young man with Down's syndrome be held legally responsible for a crime? In many ways he was a child. But he did know right from wrong. It was lucky that Gussie's friend was a lawyer.

Gussie had told her stories about Ben years ago. He was always the gentlest of children, the child who cried when the boy next door made a game of stepping on ants or throwing stones at herring gulls. Ben had never understood that some people couldn't be trusted; Gussie often mentioned his wandering off and befriending anyone he met until his anxious family could find him. His parents were always scared for him; Ben was never scared for himself.

Ben could never have murdered anyone; he couldn't have. Thank goodness his parents had driven the five hours from the Cape last night. At least he must know they were here, and Jim was here, doing their best to help him.

"Maggie!" Gussie backed her scooter so she could see into both their booths and not block the wide aisle. "Did you find out anything? What did Vince say?"

"Not a lot. He was pleased the police have caught Harry's killer quickly so nothing will disturb the workings of the show."

Gussie's face fell. "I really hoped he might know something helpful."

"Well, I did learn a few interesting facts. Seems Vince

and Harry had a little talk after the show last night during which Harry asked Vince to keep an eye on Susan because she wasn't well, and he had to go out to the Coast for some business reason."

"That is interesting. The husband asking the lover . . . strange."

"I agree. Especially since Vince denied knowing anything about the divorce. He also did not agree to watch over Susan; he told Harry that was his job."

"Well, that rings true. I can't imagine Vince taking responsibility for someone else unless the situation was very temporary and he was going to make some money out of it."

"Vince focuses on business; not on people. Harry focused on business, too. But Harry did make commitments to Susan, and, Susan says, to Joe." Maggie paused a moment. "Speaking of Joe . . . ?"

Gussie glanced over her shoulder at the J. COUSINS, BOOKSELLER sign. Joe was in the rear of his booth, discussing something with a tall, thin man with very little hair. Gussie and Maggie moved in unison so their backs were discreetly turned away from Joe's booth.

"He's obviously very upset about Harry's death. In fact, he started to tear up a little when I said he must have been close to Harry. He's obviously not coping well, but I talked to him for quite a while. I was glad when a customer interrupted us."

"What did you learn?"

"Well, Joe kept rambling; I couldn't get many direct answers."

"Was he avoiding the questions?"

"He seemed just too upset to concentrate."

Maggie looked over her shoulder at him. "He seems to be making sales. If he's upset, he's not showing it from this distance. But who knows? Maybe he's giving terrific bargains."

"Or maybe he's able to block all this out when he's dealing with books. He always seemed more comfortable with books than with people anyway, Maggie. You know he never talked much at the shows. Smiled, nodded, but never chatted the way the rest of us did."

"True. I remember someone's once telling me that Joe pretty much grew up in the business. His shop was his father's before it was his."

"That's what he told me. His father had the shop, and Joe did shows. He inherited the whole business when his father died three years ago. Harry met him here and went to him a couple of years ago looking for books that were beautifully leather-bound. It didn't matter what the books were. They would be sold by the foot, to line studies and offices with the look of old money and education."

Maggie smiled. "Like buying ancestors."

"Right. Anyway, it seems Joe's clients had always been other dealers, whom he would see at his shop or at antiquarian-book fairs, or collectors. He had never thought of some of the more commercial properties of books—such as books purchased as decoration. So when Harry explained what he could sell to interior decorators, it was a whole new look at the world of bookselling."

"Wouldn't all book dealers know about that kind of purchase?"

"Apparently not Joe. Maybe he'd spent too much time in New Haven. In any case, he started to look for decorator books and sold them through Harry."

Just as Will had sold fireplace equipment, Maggie thought. Only Will didn't think working with Harry was such a terrific deal.

"He seemed really impressed by Harry. He kept talking about how kind Harry was, and how intelligent, and how he always treated Susan well."

"For two people about to get a divorce, everyone seems to agree they were a great couple."

"Well, add Joe to the list. Harry and Susan started inviting him to their parties a year or so ago, and for a while he stayed with them when he was in New York City."

"That must have been cozy. Did he mention that Harry was going to divorce Susan to be with him?"

"Not exactly. He did say that Harry had seemed distracted recently, but he assumed it was because of everything that had to be done before the divorce." Gussie paused. "He did say one interesting thing. He said the paperwork was finished last Wednesday."

"For the divorce? Susan said it wouldn't be complete until next week."

"No. Not for the divorce. We knew that Harry was going to buy out Susan's share of Art-Effects, right?"

"Right."

"Well, guess where he was going to get the cash?"

Maggie took a deep breath. "You're serious? From Joe?"

"Seems Joe inherited something over half a million from his father's life insurance three years ago. He hadn't decided what to do with it yet. He had it in a savings account."

"Three years ago! At least he could have put some of it in a bond fund!"

"I don't think Joe is a financial genius. He may know books, but not financial markets. In any case, Harry suggested Joe lend him the money so he could buy out Susan."

"So, in effect, Joe was paying for Harry's divorce! Was he going to become a half owner in Art-Effects?"

"That's what I thought at first, but apparently not. Harry just wanted a personal loan. He told Joe he'd pay him back within a year—maybe sooner—since he had a big deal brewing."

"And Joe just handed him the money?"

"Sounded that way. He said his father's lawyer had drawn up some IOU papers, but that he trusted Harry, so he just wrote him a check. Last Wednesday."

"So Harry already had the money."

Gussie nodded. "According to Joe he deposited it on Wednesday. The check should have cleared by now."

"If there's not even an IOU in Harry's estate, Joe has no claim on the money." Maggie paused. It sounded as though Joe hadn't just lost a lover; he'd lost part of his inheritance. "But Susan is—was—still Harry's wife. She'll inherit his estate. Maybe Joe thinks she'll just hand him back the money."

"I don't know. Joe was funny about it. He kept saying he needed to talk with Susan. That he wanted Susan to have the money anyway. Of course, I asked him why."

"And?"

"He just kept saying Harry would have wanted it that way."

"Did Joe say where he was last night?"

"He said he left right after the show with a local collector who wanted him to see a collection of transcendentalist first editions—you know, Emerson, Hawthorne, Bronson Alcott—that might be for sale soon. The guy met him here and drove him in his own car, so Joe wouldn't have to find the place."

"When did he get back?"

"About midnight; by that time the fairgrounds were covered with police, who wouldn't let him in. They just told him there'd been an accident, and no one could come in. I take it the collector wasn't thrilled, but drove him back to his place for the night, and then dropped him at the entrance about nine this morning. Joe didn't find out about Harry until then."

"Sounds like a pretty tight alibi for last night. There'd be no reason to invent a story like that. And no doubt the collector would vouch for him."

"That's what I think, too." Gussie paused. "He seemed genuinely upset that Ben had been arrested. Said the police always blame the wrong people."

"Well, he's right in this case, anyway."

"Agreed. But it seemed like a strange remark. I was going to ask him who he thought might have murdered Harry, but we were interrupted. And it's not an easy question to raise in a casual conversation with someone who's just lost his dearest friend. That's what he called Harry. Several times."

"I'm sorry for him. He always seemed like a loner; the stereotype of the traditional quiet little man in the patched tweed jacket who spends his time with old books instead of new people."

"I felt the same way. I almost invited him to dinner with Jim and me and my family tonight, but then thought better of it. We need to concentrate on Ben. I keep wondering what is happening in the world outside the antiques show today."

"No one got much sleep last night."

"That's for sure. I did go to bed, but I kept wondering what was happening, and when Will called to tell me about Ben at two, I was still awake. And then, of course, I had to call the Cape and wake everyone there.

By the time they were on the road, it was almost four, and I was much too worried to get much sleep." Gussie looked at her watch. "It's almost ninety minutes to go until closing. I hope I make it!"

Lydia crossed the aisle, her perpetual cup of tea in hand. "Abe is going to make a stop at the concession stand. Can he get anything for either of you? A late-afternoon snack? Life must go on, you know."

"That would be great, Lydia. I think I need a triple espresso."

Lydia hesitated. "Do they have that at the concession stand?"

Gussie shook her head. "No; that was a joke. Just wishful thinking. But a couple of chocolate chip cookies would be great."

Maggie added, "Double the order and get me some?" She reached into her cash box for some money.

"No problem. Anything to drink? I know you two aren't tea people. Susan and I have been sharing blends all day." Lydia glanced at Gussie. "Most without caffeine, though. Caffeine is bad for the heart, you know."

"No drink; thanks. I still have some cola left. Gussie?"

"Actually, plain coffee would be good just now. Heart problems or not. Thanks." Gussie waved a thank-you to Abe, who was back in Silver in Mind's booth.

As a young woman approached Gussie to ask about turn-of-the-century paper dolls, Lydia touched Maggie's arm and gestured for her to move down the aisle, out of Gussie's hearing range. "I know you're fond of that poor retarded boy, Maggie, but sometimes people like that are unpredictable, you know. Don't know their own strength. Don't understand how serious things are."

"Ben may be slow about some things, but he understands right and wrong. And he's not violent!"

"You just never know, Maggie. Why, back in Iowa there was a boy like Ben. His parents lived about four farms down from where my folks lived. They kept people at home in those days, you know. They couldn't afford one of those institutions, and no boys like that went to regular schools until very recently. Not that they get that much out of it, anyway, but that's what the federal government says people have to do. This boy—his name was Alfred, as I remember—well, Alfred helped around the farm, feeding the chickens and doing other chores and such. One of his jobs was chopping firewood. Back when I was a girl, you know, a lot of people still used wood-burning stoves, and that's what his folks had. Well, one day he was out chopping wood, and his mother, dear soul that she was, the very definition of patience, she came out and asked him, was he almost finished? And, nice as could be, he just turned about and started chopping at her. And then, when there was no point in doing that anymore, he finished chopping the wood, and was sitting there, all covered with his poor mother's blood, when his father came home from the fields."

Maggie just looked at Lydia. "Well, I don't think Ben would do that. Or anything even close to that."

"That's just my point, dear. With those people you never really know, do you?" Lydia patted Maggie on the arm. "Now, just you relax. I'm sure the police are doing everything they can. That nice detective was over here this morning, and I've seen him wandering about during the day. I'm sure he'll do the right thing. I just wish Susan would eat something. She's looking paler all the time. I've been giving her a lot of honey in her tea, for energy, you know? But I'm not sure she can hold up for the rest of the afternoon." Lydia shook her head. "Such a horrible situation. Poor Harry. And now Susan, left to cope with everything."

"You're right. I think I'll ask if she'd like someone to watch her booth for a while. My booth is the closest to hers." Maggie got up. "Customers are quiet at the moment, anyway." And helping Susan would get her away from Lydia and her stories.

As Abe headed toward the concession stands with a list of orders, Maggie walked around the corner of Susan's booth. Lydia was right; Susan didn't look well. Everything that had happened during the last twenty-four hours must have been hitting her. She was slumped in her chair, her head on her hand. Next to her was a half-empty cup, and three prescription bottles: one held white capsules with a blue band around the middle; one tablets; and one small, round white pills. "Susan, are you all right?"

Susan looked up slowly and seemed to have trouble focusing. "No, not really. I took my medication." She waved toward the pills. "It usually helps me. And I've been drinking teas that should help, too. But I'm so tired. And I guess I'm too nervous to eat anything. My stomach is really upset." She hesitated. "Maggie, I can't believe that Harry's gone." One tear dripped down the side of her nose and she didn't even bother to wipe it away. "I just don't know what I'm going to do without him."

Maggie put her hand on Susan's shoulder in sympathy.

"At least your husband died in an ordinary way. No one murdered him!"

That was a strange thing to say, but Susan was under

stress. Vince had said she had felt faint several times on the Far East tour. Maggie wondered if she was going to faint now. "Do you feel light-headed? Do you want to put your head down?"

"No. I don't think so. I just feel so foggy. And nauseated." Susan looked up. "How can I feel nauseated when I haven't had much to eat? I had some breakfast, and you brought me that tuna fish for lunch, but I couldn't get much of it down."

"Maybe that's the problem. Can we get you something else to eat? Abe just went out for some snacks for us; he could get something for you, too."

Susan shook her head listlessly. "Lydia already asked me. I told her I didn't think I could keep any food down. All I want to do is sleep."

"Susan, if that's what you need, then let me take you back to your van. I'll ask Will to look after your booth, and Gussie to look after mine. Then I'll come back here, and between Gussie and me we'll take care of everything for the rest of the afternoon." Maggie glanced at her watch. "It's almost four-thirty; the last hour and a half are always the slowest anyway." Susan really didn't look well. "Let me take you back to your van to rest. Please."

"Maybe that would be good. I do think I need to lie down." Susan reached under one of her tables for her small soft-sided cooler.

"Just give me a minute." Maggie made hurried stops to talk with Will, Gussie, and Lydia, who all agreed to help. She then came back and helped Susan find her pocketbook, put most of the cash from her cash box in it, picked up the cooler, and put her arm around Susan as they headed out the building, dodging a few customers. Susan stumbled as though she'd had a little too much wine for lunch.

"I don't know why I feel so awful," Susan said as they walked slowly toward her van. "Sometimes I get faint and tired, but not this bad. I guess it's the shock. All I want to do is sleep."

"You've been doing too much," Maggie said. "Harry's dead, and you've been trying to carry on as if nothing had happened. You need to take care of yourself. You're just exhausted, physically and emotionally."

Susan's van was farther off than Maggie had remembered. It was a relief when they finally got there, and Susan lay down on a cot.

"You'll feel better soon." Maggie covered her with a blanket.

But Susan was already asleep. She looked dead to the world.

Chapter 18

—◦—

An Auction Sale, *wood engraving by W. L.
Sheppard, published in* Harper's Weekly,
*April 30, 1870. Elegantly dressed auctioneer,
standing on a chair, trying to sell a painting to
a group of elegant, but uninterested, viewers.
Price: $65.*

Maggie realized her hands were shaking.

Harry's death had been so sudden; like Michael's.
Maggie concentrated on the steps she was taking, the
vans she was walking around, the people milling
around the food stands. Anything but remembering
the pain of coming home to an empty house after
Michael's funeral.

She had walked in, exhausted, and relieved that
finally everything was over.

But Michael was everywhere she looked. The oil
painting of the Duomo he had bought for her on
their honeymoon to Florence, the houseplants he had
carefully moved outdoors to the patio every spring,
the chair where he always put his feet up to read the
Sunday *Times*.

She had walked from one room to another, seeing Michael in the choice of colors and furniture; the lavender and magenta vase his parents had given them that both of them hated. The Civil War histories he read, the jazz he listened to, the burgundies he had preferred in the wine rack.

She'd felt smothered by physical possessions that represented whole years of memories. Michael would never be really gone from her life; he would just not be present.

Now Susan would have to live through the same realization. Being a widow meant starting down a new road, but it also meant carrying the weight of what was, and what might have been.

But what had to be focused on today was the Rensselaer County Spring Antiques Fair. Maggie had spent long hours in March and April preparing for this show, as she did every year. She'd checked the inventory and replaced prints sold in last year's shows and matted new ones. She'd have to decide what categories to feature this year. Sporting prints? Botanicals? Perhaps the work of one person—Maxfield Parrish or Winslow Homer?

Maggie had made the decisions for this year with difficulty. It was so hard to concentrate on anything, and with Michael gone this year's antiques shows seemed more important than ever. The money was important; the independence was important; coming home to an empty house after a full weekend was important. They were all steps toward the freedom Maggie had always assumed she had, but in which she now felt isolated.

Maggie had chosen Currier & Ives prints to feature this year because sorting through them had been familiar and reassuring. Her first antiques print purchase had been *Maggie,* one of a series of Currier & Ives prints depicting women with popular nineteenth-century names. At the time Maggie hadn't realized it was one of a series. She was just a starving college student on her way to join friends for pizza at a small shop on Bloomfield Avenue in Montclair, New Jersey, where she was a history major at Montclair State. She had turned a corner and was stopped by the portrait of a smiling woman in the window. When she got close enough to see that the print was titled *Maggie,* she knew it was meant for her.

The elderly antiques dealer, pleased at a young woman's interest, let her make a deposit on it and agreed to accept the money in ten weekly payments. Although at $35 ($3 a week) the print was certainly not the most expensive that Maggie had ever bought, it remained one of her favorites. It had always hung in the room she used for her inventory and study, reminding her of the young woman who had seen herself, around a corner, in the past. Earlier this spring she had moved it to a prominent place in her living room.

That print had led to her investigation of other prints, especially American prints. As a graduate history student, Maggie had written a series of papers on American prints as reflections of American life and culture, and for her doctoral dissertation she had written about Thomas Nast's influence on the American political conscience.

Collecting prints for her own enjoyment and for her research had led Maggie down the road that had brought her to the Rensselaer County Spring Antiques

Fair this warm Saturday May afternoon. But she had never moved totally away from seeing prints as illustrations of America's intellectual and social history, and she often shared prints with her students, as illustrations for her lectures. Over the years she had also created a small following of young people interested in prints—some from a historical perspective, and others just for the joy of bringing a little of the past into their lives.

The rest of the afternoon was a blur: Maggie and Will watched Susan's booth and made a few minor sales for her, although neither of them were experts in the early-twentieth-century items Susan and Harry stocked.

Maggie herself sold several botanical lithographs and four prints of different varieties of New York State apples to someone who planned to frame and hang them in a kitchen overlooking an orchard. And she spent about twenty minutes with a woman who was interested in herbs, and who, in addition to looking through the group of prints Maggie had labeled "herbs," also looked through the rest of the botanical prints to find plants that could be used in cooking. Nasturtiums, the woman swore, made a delicious and colorful addition to any tossed salad.

Maggie smiled and nodded and tried to pay attention to her booth and to Susan's. The abbreviated sleep she'd had the night before was showing. She hoped Susan was getting some good rest.

"You're trying to do too much, dear," counseled Lydia from across the aisle. "Too many irons in the fire. Just take some deep breaths. It's almost five-thirty; we only have to get through another half hour. Why don't you try some chamomile tea?"

Maggie smiled. She had just sold a chamomile lithograph.

"Sorry. I think I need a little caffeine. In fact"—she yawned—"maybe a lot of caffeine."

Before Lydia could make another comment about caffeine's effect on the heart, Joe stepped across the aisle, now only partially filled with customers. "I need a break, and I was going to bring back coffee. I'll get one for you, if you'd like."

"Thanks, Joe. But I think I'll just open another can of cola."

"Are you sure I can't get you something? We've all had a rough weekend." Joe looked as exhausted as Maggie felt.

"No, I'm fine. It seems incredible that it's only Saturday afternoon. We have tomorrow yet to go. It feels as though we've been here a lifetime."

Joe nodded and headed out toward the rest rooms and concession stands.

Maggie stood midway between her booth and Susan's so she could keep an eye on both of them. A white-haired woman in a tailored pink pantsuit had just leaned her gold-headed cane against one of Susan's tables and was looking closely at some Japanese porcelains. She had better not leave that cane for long; it was a beauty, and canes were becoming more collectible every year, with baby boomers approaching the age at which canes became a necessity. If the baby boomers started using them, canes would become the fashion accessory of 2010, and antique canes with gold heads would shoot up in value.

Maggie thought of the antiquarian-book sale she'd been to recently. She often looked for "breakers"—

books with tattered bindings and missing pages that were not of great value to a book dealer or collector, but, especially when their plates were hand-colored, might be valuable to a print dealer. First editions of Little Golden Books—those inexpensive little books everyone's mother had bought for him or her in groceries and dime stores in the 1950s—were selling for $30 and more!

The most valuable were the original 1940s editions with blue bindings complete with dustcovers encouraging the purchase of U.S. Savings Stamps. Other titles escalating in price were those that had not been reprinted many times, such as *Little Black Sambo,* published in 1948 and later viewed as racist; or books that still included the puzzles or gimmicks they had come with, such as *Dr. Dan the Bandage Man* (which had come with bandages), or that featured television characters of the fifties, such as Howdy Doody, Hopalong Cassidy, or Rootie Kazootie. First editions featuring Disney characters were among the most valuable.

Any parent who had tried hard but had never actually got Johnny to read should check the attic. If Johnny's books were in pristine condition, they might now be minor treasures.

You're getting old when your childhood memories turn into someone else's antique, Maggie, she told herself. She wished she had a child to share those memories with, and to help create a few for the next generation.

Ever since Michael's death Maggie had found herself thinking more and more about being a parent. She wasn't too old. There were ways, with or without a husband. Or maybe she'd adopt. If parenthood was something she wanted, then she would have to do something about it. In the near future. She and Michael had put off too many decisions too long. She didn't want to make the same mistake again.

On the other hand, how would she ever be able to cope with being an antiques dealer and having a child? Day care centers would help with teaching hours, but she would never be able to just pop a baby into a carrier and hustle off to a two- or three-day antiques show. Reality, Maggie, she thought to herself. Get real. You're thirty-eight years old.

"Lady, you're looking depressed as well as exhausted. Let me keep an eye on Susan's booth while you sit down in yours for the last half hour and talk with Gussie. She looks as though she could use some company."

Will's voice brought Maggie back to today.

"Thanks, Will. I've just about had it."

"Figured out whodunit yet?"

"No way. Actually," Maggie admitted as she looked around Susan's booth, "I keep coming back to Susan. She had both motive and opportunity. She was the one who found Harry. They'd had an argument that night. He was leaving her for someone else; she needed money for some reason, and now she'll get not only the business, but also any insurance he might have had."

Will nodded. "It's hard to believe, but you're right. A lot of people weren't thrilled with Harry, but I can't think of anyone else who had a strong motive. And"—he glanced down the aisle at Joe's booth—"who was here last night."

"I hope it wasn't Susan. But I'm sure it wasn't Ben, and he's the one the police have in custody."

"Has Gussie's friend gotten him out?"

"I don't know. I've been so busy here I haven't even talked with her in the last hour."

"Well, why don't you do that? I think she needs a friend."

Maggie nodded as Joe stopped on his way back from the concession stand. "We've got just a short time left, and then I'm going to go check on Susan and see if I can take her out for some dinner."

It might look strange to others, but Joe had been a friend to both Susan and Harry. He seemed sad as he went to his booth.

"You'll need to eat, too, Maggie, and we do have a deal. I'm not letting you out of the agreement, although I won't hold you to paying," Will said. "What if I give you an hour or so to collapse, and then I come over and we find someplace with wine and peace?"

Maggie looked at him. The top three buttons of his blue tailored shirt were now open, revealing smooth skin dotted with five small, dark spots. She had to resist the urge to connect the dots. "Wine and peace sound wonderful. Thank you."

He nodded. "I'll see you at about seven-thirty, then?"

"I'm in Kabin A twenty-three. First row on the left as you drive in to the Kabins."

Maggie tried to remember whether she'd brought anything more interesting to wear than the pantsuit she'd planned on putting on tomorrow.

"I'll find you." Will winked, and Maggie returned

to her booth, wondering how she was going to cope simultaneously with a suddenly attractive man, a murder, and exhaustion. Life didn't play fair. That was for sure.

Gussie grinned at her. "Great news! One of the dealers came forward and told the police he saw Harry walking out from in back of the rest room about quarter to ten Friday night. And the autopsy results show Harry had a bruise and small cut on the opposite side of his head from the blow that killed him. They've released Ben, although they still want him close by. Jim went back to the motel to make some calls. He's still trying to find a decent local criminal attorney, just in case. But it looks as though Ben is off the hook!"

"Gussie, that's wonderful! But why can't Jim be his lawyer?"

Gussie shook her head. "He's great at small-town wills and mortgages, not criminal law in another state. But he knows people who know other people, so he's playing his networks."

"How's Ben holding up?"

"All right, I guess. He told my sister that the policemen were really nice, and the food wasn't bad, but that he was missing his practice times on the track." She paused. "He also asked whether he was going to be hanged or put in an electric chair."

Maggie winced. "Not good."

"No. But it's hard for him to focus on everything. Right now I suspect he's back in the motel taking a nap."

Maggie shook her head. "There's an answer to all of this. An answer that does not involve Ben."

"Have you found out anything new?"

"Not since I talked with you last."

"You got Susan to rest?"

Maggie nodded. "I took her back to her van. She really didn't look well. I think the shock of the whole situation was beginning to get to her. Joe's going to check on her after the show and make sure she gets something to eat."

"Good for him." Gussie nodded approvingly. "He's not exactly had a terrific day himself, but he's thinking about other people. And that's the first step in getting your own life in order."

"I just keep thinking there's a piece of the puzzle I haven't found yet. Unless . . ." Maggie hesitated.

"Yes? What?" Gussie leaned back in her scooter. "Out with it, Maggie. What?"

"The only person who seems to have both motive and opportunity is Susan."

"Do you really think she could have killed Harry?"

"I can't seem to come up with any other suspects."

Gussie shook her head. "Much as I'd like someone to be responsible other than Ben, I can't believe it's Susan. She just isn't that strong a person—mentally, or even physically. She looks as though she could hardly lift a pocketbook, much less something that would crush the skull of the man she says she loved."

"She certainly looks weak. But yesterday she was carrying a pedestal that looked pretty heavy."

"The one in her booth?"

Maggie nodded.

"I'd bet it's at least partially hollow. She didn't pick it up, lift it over her head, and hit someone with it."

"No, Gussie, I don't think she did. Although that would have been some blunt object!"

They both smiled slightly.

"Ben saw Harry last night. Susan talked with Harry. Vince talked with Harry. Joe did not talk with Harry. Who else was around?"

"Lydia and Abe; she saw Harry. Will. Me. Lots of other dealers, too, but I think we can rule them out as murder suspects; they didn't even know who Harry was when the police arrived. Harry wasn't as well known on the antiques show circuit as he was in other circles."

"Maybe it wasn't someone he knew. Harry was hit on the back of the head, right? Doesn't sound as though he was having a serious discussion with anyone at that precise moment."

"Well, it certainly turned serious enough."

They both thought for a few seconds.

"There were people in the south field while that was happening; you and Will and Ben were there, and so were at least a couple of dozen other dealers."

"Right."

"I know several people identified Ben as someone who was running around just after nine-thirty looking disheveled and scared."

Maggie nodded. "No doubt that he was. Now if just one person remembers seeing Harry talking with someone who might have killed him . . ." She paused. "I still think we're missing something. But my mind isn't coming up with anything right now."

Gussie glanced at her watch and started closing her cash box. "Right now we've all got too much information on our minds and too much exhaustion on our bodies."

The public address system broke the silence as Vince's

voice filled the four exhibit buildings. "Good evening, dealers and customers of the Rensselaer County Spring Antiques Fair. The show is closing for the evening. Please conclude your purchases. If you wish to return to the antiques fair tomorrow, please get a readmission ticket as you exit. Dealers, please close your booths. The show will be open to dealers at ten-thirty Sunday morning and will open to the public at eleven. Please drive carefully, and have a relaxing evening."

Maggie gave the nearest speaker in the ceiling an ironic glance. "Just like last night, Vince? A nice, relaxing evening."

"Well, I'm heading back to the Kabins." Gussie fit her cash box and receipts into a wide canvas bag imprinted with a lighthouse and VISIT THE CAPE! "I'm going to join the family for a celebration dinner." She hesitated as she turned her scooter toward the door. "Want to come?"

Maggie shook her head. "Thanks, but no. Family time is important." She threw a large sheet over her tables and pulled a chair across the entrance, adding a red-and-white BOOTH CLOSED sign. "And, if I have the energy, I have a date." She gestured toward Will's booth, which was already empty.

"Fast work!" Gussie smiled. "Have a great time. And remember all the good details for tomorrow."

"Only if you do the same." Maggie hoisted the bag holding her cash box and her pocketbook to her shoulder. "I'm too exhausted for an X rating; I definitely predict a PG-rated evening."

"Well, at least try for an R," Gussie said, grinning, as she turned and waved on her way to the side door.

Joe had also finished putting chairs in front of

his booth. "Thanks again for helping Susan this afternoon, Maggie."

"No problem. I really hope she's been able to get some rest."

"I'm going to drop my stuff at my van and then go and check on her. There may be some calls I can help her with, or at least maybe I can get her to go out and have something to eat."

Maggie nodded. "If there's anything I can do to help, I'll be across the street. Will and I are going to have dinner somewhere, but we won't be late."

"I'm sure Susan will be fine." Joe shifted one of the canvas bags he was carrying to his other hand. "She's been through rough times before. She's stronger than she sometimes appears."

"I think most of us are," said Maggie. "No one is ever prepared for what life delivers . . . but, somehow, we get through it."

Joe nodded and started up the aisle. As Maggie started to follow him toward the parking lot, he turned toward her. "At least nothing can be worse than last night. And we all got through that."

"You're right," Maggie said. "Nothing could be that bad."

Chapter 19

Pheasants à la Finauciere, pheasants garnished with crayfish, surrounded by other elegant dishes. Hand-colored engraving from the famous Book of Household Management *by Mrs. Beeton, published in London, 1861, which covered everything from wages for domestics to how to wash butter freshly removed from the churn. It was the first widely used recipe book in England and went through many editions. Price: $65.*

Maggie turned her room radio loud enough so she could hear the local news (Harry's death wasn't mentioned) while she was in the shower. It was loud enough so she didn't hear the red-and-white ambulance screaming up to the Rensselaer County Fairgrounds for the second time in under twenty-four hours. It moved rapidly around the last few customers' cars leaving the parking lots, heading toward the same section of dealers' vehicles it had visited the night before. Within minutes it was on its way back to Rensselaer Hospital.

This time the lights and siren were still on as it left the fairgrounds.

Maggie dressed carefully, putting on a skirt and silk sleeveless blouse she'd packed as extras, in case the temperatures soared, as they sometimes did at the end of May. It had been a long time since she'd dressed for a dinner with someone she hardly knew. Although, she thought ironically, I've already spent one night with Will. The new order in relationships: spend the night, then have dinner. She spent more time than usual on her makeup, using foundation, which she rarely bothered with, along with her usual blush and gray eye shadow.

She considered herself in the mirror, then decided not to wear her hair down. Instead, she braided it and pinned it up, circling her head in an old-fashioned crown that suited her and added a little to her five feet five inches. No jewelry tonight, she decided, after looking over the few pieces she'd brought for the weekend. Somehow life was too complicated right now; she wanted to feel uncomplicated and look undesigned. And she shouldn't make so much of this dinner, which was an informal, spur-of-the-moment occasion.

She was ready ten minutes before Will knocked on her door.

As soon as she saw him, she knew something was wrong. Very wrong.

He put up his hand. "Maggie, I don't know how bad it is. But Susan's in the hospital."

Maggie's mind ran in a spiderweb of directions. But before she could say anything, Will reached out to her, and the tweed on his jacket felt familiar and safe against her cheek.

"Joe found her. The guy in the ambulance said she's in a coma."

They decided to go ahead and have dinner since they could do nothing for Susan that the hospital wasn't already doing, but the relaxation spiced by touches of sexual tension that they had both anticipated was gone, despite the dusky candlelit country inn Will had found. Will ordered a steak, rare, and Maggie decided on chicken breast in white wine with herbs.

"What could have happened?" Maggie hesitated as she put down her glass of chablis. "She said she was exhausted and light-headed when I left her, but she seemed all right."

"She was pale when you helped her out to her van," Will agreed. "Pale, but certainly not unconscious." He waited a moment. "I spoke to Joe briefly; he said he knocked on the door of her van and then went in, thinking Susan was asleep. She must have thrown up, choked, and then passed out. When he couldn't wake her, he called the ambulance on his cell phone." Will put down his knife and fork. "Joe said she'd been ill for a long time, but he didn't realize she was that weak."

"Vince told me she'd fainted several times on his Asia tour last month." Maggie thought for a moment. "He didn't say why."

"Whatever her medical problem is, the stress of having your husband killed—even your almost divorced husband—certainly would make it worse. Plus, Susan didn't get much sleep last night."

Maggie pushed some chicken around on the plate in front of her. "But stress and lack of sleep don't put someone in a coma, Will."

"Maybe she took the wrong combination of pills or the wrong pill. She had a little cooler under her table, and every hour or two she'd take a bottle out and swallow a pill."

"That must be the cooler I carried back to the van for her. She said she had to have it with her."

"It went to the hospital with her, too. Joe seemed to know about it and said the doctors would want to know what she'd been taking. What she had in her stomach."

"That makes sense. But she'd been eating a little, too. Joe got her some eggs for breakfast."

"And you got her a tuna sandwich for lunch. I don't know how much of it she ate, but I know she took a few bites. She complained it had too much mayonnaise on it."

Maggie took another sip of wine. "The last twenty-four hours seem like a surrealistic nightmare. The show went on; some customers bought. And at the same time, Harry was killed, Ben was held for questioning, and now Susan is in a coma."

"How is Ben taking everything?"

"Surprisingly well, according to Gussie. He's with his family now, so that's a tremendous relief. I was hoping that when the police questioned Susan again, she would have been able to provide some more insights into who might have killed Harry."

"She may be fine, Maggie; some comas are very brief."

"You're right; I'm just feeling a bit morbid."

"What about some dessert? They say chocolate is a tranquilizer and has minor aphrodisiac qualities."

Maggie gave him a serious look. "Under the circumstances, perhaps some apple pie would be more in order?"

"Each to his own. But I'm going for the chocolate cheesecake. With strawberries."

"A man after my own stomach," Maggie responded with a groan. "I'm sticking with the pie."

"And a little cognac?"

"Not tonight, Will. There's too much happening."

He sighed. "You're a tough lady, Maggie Summer. But I can handle it." He gestured to the waitress. "One decaf, an apple pie, and a chocolate cheesecake with strawberries."

She nodded and headed toward the kitchen.

"It's been a long day." As Will looked at Maggie, she felt his eyes seeing more than she was sure she wanted him to see.

"I really appreciate all the help you've been during the past two days."

"I hate to say it, because the situation is obviously an awful one, but I'm glad it gave me an opportunity to get to know you."

"Most antiques dealers are good people." Maggie steered the conversation into safer waters. She couldn't help liking Will, but, after all, he had been at the Westchester show last weekend when John Smithson was murdered and had even taken Smithson's place at this show. It was probably a coincidence, but it was a curious one. How many other people had been at both shows?

"I really am glad to get to know you." Will reached over and put his large hand over hers. "You're a very special lady, Maggie Summer."

"Here's the decaf and the desserts," said the waitress.

Maggie withdrew her hand and made room for the plates. She smiled back. "I'm glad, too, Will. But too much is happening for me to think about it."

"You don't have to think about it. You just have to enjoy it."

"I'd like to be your friend. Right now I can't cope with anything else."

"I don't expect anything else right now. Except a lovely evening with a lovely lady." He picked up his fork. "And, of course, a totally evil piece of cheesecake."

Maggie toasted him with her water glass. "To a memorable evening."

"To a memorable evening."

It was almost ten-thirty when Will drove Maggie up to her Kosy Kabins unit. The high lights illuminating the motel's driveway shone directly on a dark van parked in front of her door. There was no mistaking the van; the J. COUSINS, BOOKSELLER logo on the side was clear. They both jumped out of Will's RV and walked over to the van, peering inside.

Joe was slumped over the wheel.

Chapter 20

~s~

Present State of the Capitol at Washington,
hand-colored wood engraving published in The
London Illustrated News *in 1853. Showing*
construction at the U.S. Capitol. The U.S.
Capitol was initially completed in 1839, but
was greatly enlarged from 1851 to 1865, when
the House and Senate wings and the dome were
added. Price: $60.

Will reached in through the open window and tentatively touched Joe's shoulder. Joe's head lurched up as he realized someone was there.

His face was swollen with tears; his eyes bloodshot. "I didn't know what to do. I didn't know who to call." Joe's voice was low, but desperate. His words came out distinctly, one at a time, like bullets fired consecutively. "It's Susan. She's gone. They couldn't do anything to bring her out of the coma, and she just died." Joe reached out for Maggie's hand. "You were good to Susan; you tried to help. I don't know what to do."

Maggie felt as though someone had just hit her so

hard she couldn't breathe. For a moment none of them said anything; they just looked at one another. Joe sat in the driver's seat of his van, holding on to Maggie's hand, while Will put his arm around her shoulders.

"Why?" She finally managed to get out. "What happened?"

Joe shook his head. "They're not sure. She was ill, of course, and we weren't sure how long she had to live. But she had been taking new medications and was doing so much better. None of us thought it would be this soon."

"Why don't we go inside?" Maggie reached inside her bag for her door key. Long forgotten were any thoughts of sleep or romance. Joe nodded and climbed down, and the two of them followed Maggie into her small room. She sat on the bed and let Joe and Will take the two chairs the motel had arranged companionably near a small round table at the end of the room.

"What was Susan's illness, Joe?"

He looked surprised. "You didn't know? She didn't tell many people; she was never sure how people would react. But I thought people would figure it out." He looked directly at Will, and then at Maggie. "Susan had AIDS."

Maggie felt as though she were unsuccessfully trying to swim against a strong current. "AIDS?"

"She'd known she was HIV-positive for three or four years, but about a year ago her T-cell count really started to drop. She was trying all the protease inhibitors along with her AZT and antibiotics, and at first they seemed to be making a difference. Not a big difference, like they have in some people, but her T-cell count was going up."

"That's why she was taking all those pills." Maggie thought of the small cooler. "I just thought she was a health nut, taking vitamins."

"She always was a bit fanatical about vitamins, too." Joe almost smiled. "She's been taking something to cure some part of her ever since I've known her. But they weren't all vitamins."

Maggie thought quickly. Susan, Harry, Joe. "Are you all HIV-positive?"

Joe forced a smile. "As in, are all you gay people sick?"

Maggie turned red. "I didn't mean it that way. I just thought, with Susan being infected and all, that probably she got it from Harry, and . . ."

"And Harry and I were lovers, so I must have it, too?"

She nodded.

"Well, actually, that's not the way it was. Susan had AIDS. Harry wasn't HIV-positive, and neither am I."

"Then?" Will was catching up, fast.

"Susan was married to Harry, but she didn't get HIV from him. In fact, Harry was pretty obsessive about a number of things."

Maggie thought back to some of her conversations with Harry about business and silently agreed.

"Well, one of the things Harry was insistent on was safe sex. With anyone. Susan and Harry had a pretty open marriage, and they both had a lot of— friends—over the years. I don't think Susan knew where she'd picked up HIV."

"What did Harry think about it?"

"He was very upset; very sad. He made her go to different doctors, try different treatments. That's why they were getting divorced."

Will shook his head. "Sorry, Joe; I'm not following. I thought Harry and Susan were getting divorced because Harry wanted to be with you."

"He already had me, when he wanted me. I loved Harry." Joe's eyes began to fill again, and Maggie quickly walked to the bathroom and brought back a box of tissues. Joe blew his nose and started again.

"Harry's the only man I ever loved. But Harry always did what Harry wanted to do. He said he loved me, but he loved Susan, too. I don't think they would have gotten divorced if they hadn't needed the money."

Maggie remembered Susan had said she'd needed money. "For what?"

"For her medications. Harry and Susan were self-employed; they'd never been able to afford health insurance, and no company wants to insure someone who is HIV-positive. The medications Susan was taking cost almost twenty thousand dollars a year. And that didn't include the cost of hospitalizations or doctors. As long as they were married, Susan couldn't get help from Medicaid unless they destroyed the business and went into bankruptcy. They both loved that business. They didn't want to do that. And they didn't want to go on welfare. Harry had grown up on welfare. He would have done anything not to go back on it."

Maggie nodded. "I'm beginning to get it. Susan and Harry were going to get divorced; Susan would get enough money to pay for her medical treatments so she wouldn't need Medicaid, and she and Harry could still keep the business, even if legally it was now all Harry's."

"Exactly."

"That's why Susan was so unclear about where she and Harry were going to live after the divorce; they were going to continue living together."

Joe nodded. "As much as they had before; maybe more, since Susan would probably need more care in the future."

They all sat, trying to put the whole situation in focus.

"And now Harry is dead, and Susan is dead."

"She was getting better, too. The T-cell count had improved." Joe slumped back. "I had decided to take care of her; to try to take Harry's place. He would have wanted that. I was going to tell her tonight."

Will said softly, "She knew you cared about her, Joe."

"She did, Joe," Maggie added. "When she told Gussie and me about Harry leaving her for you, I kept thinking she would be angry or jealous or have some other strong, negative, emotion. But she didn't."

Joe nodded. "She knew I didn't threaten her relationship with Harry. He'd loved her from the beginning. He was bisexual; she wasn't. But it didn't seem to matter to either of them." He blew his nose again. "And, of course, I was helping by loaning Harry the money."

Will looked at him. "What money?"

"The money to buy out Susan's part of the business. Harry didn't have enough cash to do that, and I inherited some money from my father when he died three years ago."

Will looked at Maggie, and then back at Joe. "How much did you loan him, Joe?"

"Five hundred thousand dollars."

Will swallowed a gasp. "Art-Effects is worth a million dollars?" Will looked at Joe in amazement. "Susan and Harry weren't even staying in the motel. They were sleeping in vans to save expenses!"

"Art-Effects is doing all right. But it isn't just the antiques. Art-Effects owns Harry and Susan's loft in New York. That's worth close to a million by itself. It owns their van. It owns just about everything, except their clothes. And they have a heavy inventory."

Maggie and Will nodded. Most antiques dealers had huge investments in inventory. It was not unusual for an antiques dealer to be inventory-poor.

"Art-Effects is a solid business. Harry and Susan had it figured so almost everything except their toilet paper was deductible. But the cash flow was slim." Joe nodded at Maggie's incredulous expression. "The business is worth at least the million dollars."

"When did the loan go through?" Will hadn't talked with Gussie that afternoon, so he hadn't known about the money. He was still trying to comprehend what Joe was saying.

"I gave him the money last Wednesday, before we started packing up for the show. He wanted to deposit the check so it would clear before he had to make out a check to Susan next week."

"Did your lawyer draw up the agreement?"

Joe shook his head. "I loved Harry. I trusted him. We didn't need anything on paper."

Maggie and Will exchanged looks, and Maggie changed the topic of conversation quickly.

"Joe, wasn't it hard for you that Harry was still so involved with Susan? I don't think I could handle someone I loved having other relationships." Maggie looked at both of them. "And Susan had other relationships, too. Harry had to cope with that."

Joe shrugged. "Harry and Susan didn't seem to care about each other's casual sexual interests. I've known them both for several years, although I wasn't really involved with them until the last year or so. By that time Susan was already ill. I've never heard Harry say anything about Susan's male friends, other than that she was stupid not to have been smarter about them." He paused. "Harry was really angry about that sometimes. He and Susan had many friends who died of AIDS. They both knew better than to ignore taking obvious precautions. But Susan didn't want to be bothered. She didn't think she was in danger." Joe swallowed hard. "Lots of women think that, you know. They think they won't get infected as easily as a man—especially a gay man—would."

"But I've read about HIV; even practicing safe sex doesn't guarantee that you won't get it."

"True enough, Maggie. But, according to Harry, Susan never practiced safe sex. She never even tried. Sometimes, after he'd had a few drinks, he would talk about it. About the characters she'd gone off with that they'd hardly met. About the weekends she'd disappear. Harry wasn't an easy guy, but he was really careful about sex. I don't think he had that many partners. He had a lot of control in his life."

Maggie thought about it. Harry had always been the decision maker; the leader. Susan had been the weaker partner. Joe made sense.

"She was involved with Vince?"

Joe nodded. "She had been off and on. During the last couple of months she spent a lot of time with him. She even went on his Asia buying trip without Harry. That was unusual. She seldom left Harry for more than a couple of days."

"Was Vince serious about her?"

"Who knows? She seemed to think so. But she thought that about a lot of men. She was sometimes like a teenager with a crush. But she always came back to Harry. And—now." Joe started crying again.

Maggie put her hand on his arm. "Is there anything we can do to help? Is there anyone you'd like us to call? Or maybe we could help with the arrangements?"

Joe shook his head. "No. I can do it. But thank you. I don't think Harry has any family, but Susan has relatives in Jersey. I'll call them. And they have a lot of friends. With everything happening so close together, I guess the funerals will be at the same time. It will depend on the medical examiner, too."

"The medical examiner? Hasn't he finished with Harry?" Maggie's mind revolted at the images her words implied.

"Harry? I guess so. But he's going to have to do an autopsy on Susan." Joe's tears were still flowing. "I tried to say that Susan wouldn't want that; that we all knew she had AIDS. She was so upset when the police told her they'd have to autopsy Harry. But the doctor said there's a state law requiring anyone who dies within twenty-four hours of being admitted to a hospital to be autopsied unless they're under the continual care of their own doctor. And the doctors aren't sure why she went into a coma. I never thought so many awful things could happen in two days. We were just packing up on Thursday night, and now it's Saturday, and they're gone." Joe stood up, looking distractedly around the room. "I have to call Susan's family. I have to get things organized. I have to do something, or I'll go crazy." He headed toward the door.

Will got up. "I'll go with you." He looked at Maggie. "I'll make sure he's all right."

Maggie nodded as the door closed.

She would have to tell Gussie. But right now all she could think about was the $500,000 in Harry Findley's checking account. If Joe hadn't made any legal agreements about it, then his money was now in Harry's estate. Which would be inherited by Susan. But now Susan was dead, too. Her relatives in New Jersey would probably get the New York loft, the business, and the money.

Someone had killed Harry. Joe had lost $500,000. Now Susan was dead. What more could happen?

Chapter 21

—⁓—

Bloedhond (bloodhound), Dutch, 1911, by
Kleurendr, printed at Leiden, The Netherlands.
Originally published in an agricultural journal,
there are two fold marks. Price: $38.

Officer Taggart and Joe were deep in conversation
when Maggie arrived at the show the next morning.
Exhaustion had caught up with her; she'd slept later
than she'd planned and had just had time to pick up a
diet cola and a bagel and get to her booth before the
doors opened to the Sunday morning crowd. Gussie
motored up immediately.

"Maggie! Where have you been? Have you heard?"

"After I called you last night I went to bed, and
that's where I've been, like any sane person on a Sunday morning." Maggie put her can of soda on the
corner of the table, balanced the bagel on top, and
pulled her cash box, sales book, and calculator out of
her red canvas bag. "Heard what?" As she talked,
she reached around her neck and twisted her long
hair into a knot, securing it with two ivory hairpins,

and pulled off the sheets that had covered her prints for the night.

"The police think Susan was murdered."

Maggie dropped the sheet she'd been folding and sat down heavily.

"Murdered! She had AIDS; she was under stress; it's horrible enough that she died so soon after Harry. Why would they think she was murdered?"

"You don't die just from HIV; you die from another type of infection that your immune system can't fight. The doctors didn't see any signs of the usual infections, like pneumonia. And you don't go into a coma as a result of stress." Gussie paused. "They think she was poisoned. Her throat was burned."

Officer Taggart appeared next to Maggie. "I'd like to talk with you for a few minutes, Dr. Summer." He turned to Gussie. "Would you excuse us?"

Gussie nodded and headed back toward her booth.

The officer reached inside his suit jacket and pulled out a small spiral notebook and a pen. "I assume Ms. White"—he gestured toward Gussie's booth—"has informed you that some questions have come up regarding Mrs. Susan Findley's death?"

Maggie nodded.

"And I understand you were the last person to speak with Mrs. Findley."

"I may have been. She wasn't feeling well yesterday afternoon, so I helped her back to her van so she could get some rest."

Maggie frantically thought back over the last time she'd been with Susan. "Her stomach was upset; she said she was nauseated and faint. She wanted to lie down." Maggie paused. "Gussie said you think Susan was poisoned."

"We'll have to wait for results of the toxicology tests, of course, but Mrs. Findley's throat appeared to be swollen and slightly burned. She may have ingested poison."

Maggie tried to think back to Saturday afternoon.

"Susan was taking a lot of medications, and vitamins. They were in a cooler she had with her."

"We have the cooler. Mr. Cousins brought it to the hospital when the ambulance picked up Mrs. Findley." Taggart paused and pushed his glasses back up onto his nose. "We're confirming that the medications contain what they appear to. But nothing in that cooler, taken as prescribed, could have caused Mrs. Findley to react as she did." He flipped his notebook to another page.

"Did Mrs. Findley appear despondent in any way?"

"Of course she was despondent! Her husband had just been killed. She had AIDS. She didn't have enough money to buy medication. Yesterday wasn't exactly a time for celebration." Maggie forced herself to slow down a bit. "But if you're asking if Susan seemed about to commit suicide, then the answer is no. She was tired; she was discouraged; she was having trouble focusing on what she would do next. But she was trying remarkably hard to pull everything together."

"So you don't think she would have intentionally taken an overdose of anything?"

"No!"

"How upset was she? Upset enough to have taken incorrect dosages of her medications?"

Maggie thought a moment. "I don't think so. She

knew her medications. Actually, she was somewhat of a health nut. I can't see Susan making a mistake about medication, even if she was upset." Maggie thought of the dishes of radishes Susan had been almost obsessive about last year. "She was exhausted when she left here. I helped her to her van so she could lie down because I was afraid she might faint; she said she felt light-headed."

"Did you stay with her all the way to her van?"

"Yes." Susan had seemed so fragile; her skin had been so white, and she had been so vulnerable. "I was afraid she might collapse; she was very pale." Maggie reached up and tucked an escaping strand of hair into the knot at the nape of her neck. "I carried the cooler; she had it with her during the show, and I had seen her taking some pills from it."

"Did she take anything while you were with her at her van?"

"No. She lay down, and I covered her with a blanket. I just thought she was exhausted from stress. After all, her husband had just been murdered."

"Did you know she had AIDS?"

"Not until Joe—Mr. Cousins—told me last night."

"Was anyone else near Mrs. Findley's van?"

"There were customers near the refreshment stands in the south field, but no one near the vans." Maggie thought carefully. "No, no one was nearby. All the dealers were in the show, of course."

"So no one knew you had taken Maggie to her van?"

"The dealers here knew: Will Brewer, and the Wyndhams, and Joe, and Gussie. Oh, and we passed Vince; he knew."

"That's Vince Thompson, the show manager?"

"Yes." Maggie tried to remember the details of that walk to the van. "Other people must have seen us, but no one spoke to us, and I was concentrating on Susan. I didn't notice anyone else."

Officer Taggart nodded and made some notes. "And what time was that?"

"About four-thirty. I remember because Abe Wyndham had just left to get us some snacks and we were joking that we had to keep going for another hour and a half." Maggie looked at the policeman. His hair was thinning, and he had combed it over his forehead in an attempt to look less like Humpty-Dumpty. The attempt had failed.

"We were all tired, of course; we had been up late Friday night, after . . . after Susan found Harry's body."

"You said that Mr. Wyndham brought you all snacks; did that include Mrs. Findley?"

"No; she didn't want anything." Some customers were looking at Maggie's anatomy prints. She nodded toward them, and Officer Taggart shrugged agreement.

"May I help you?"

The young woman was holding a print of the torso of a woman.

"This is quite special," Maggie said, taking it from her. "Unusual because"—Maggie slipped the print out from the plastic envelope protecting it—"the print was designed to show the relation of different internal organs to one another." She carefully began to fold the print back, revealing a series of three-dimensional foldouts of internal anatomy. "In this case, the print shows the progression of a pregnancy; each sequential fold shows the baby in another month." Maggie demonstrated. "The final drawing is of the child descending during birth."

The young woman was intrigued. "Are there many foldout prints like this?"

"Very few; I've seen four or five different foldouts of the torso, but only two different ones showing pregnancy. Of course, at that time most doctors were men, and the emphasis was on the male body." Maggie carefully reinserted the print into the plastic. "I have a similar large print of a tooth, showing the different layers, from a French anatomy book, if you're interested. I also have a few three-dimensional prints of horses or cows, from veterinary textbooks."

"I want to show these to my father; he's a physiology professor." The young woman looked around. "He and my mother are here someplace."

Maggie smiled. "Well, you'll know where the prints are when you see him." She handed the young woman her card. "If you're interested in a print of a particular part of the body, I could check my inventory and send you a print on approval. Just give me a call, anytime."

As the young woman left the booth, Officer Taggart pushed his glasses up. It was getting warm, and his nose looked slippery.

Maggie looked over Taggart's shoulder. Vince was near Susan's booth. His jacket was draped over his arm, and he was, almost too casually, carrying something under the jacket. As Maggie watched, he disappeared into Susan's booth.

"So Mr. Wyndham didn't bring Mrs. Findley anything to eat."

"No."

"Did you see Mrs. Findley eating anything yesterday?"

Maggie thought back. "I brought her a tuna sandwich for lunch, from the concession stand."

Taggart was taking notes.

"Joe brought her something for breakfast: scrambled eggs on a bagel, I think. I remember thinking that Susan didn't usually eat anything that wasn't natural and cooked without fat, but yesterday she was overwhelmed, of course, and I think she ate some food just because people were trying to be kind and were bringing her things."

Vince was standing in the aisle now, speaking with Will. He didn't seem to have whatever it was he had been carrying. What had it been? Had he left it in Susan's booth? The booth had been closed off by placing several straight chairs across the entrance. As she watched, Vince turned and headed back down the aisle.

"Do you remember anyone else bringing her anything to eat?"

"Vince brought Susan some orange juice in the morning. And, of course, she was drinking tea most of the day. Some she made, some Lydia Wyndham made. They always shared herbal teas. Susan said she hadn't eaten too much, though; I think she just nibbled at what people brought for her." Maggie looked at him. "Do you think something she ate yesterday was poisoned?"

"It's possible. There's no way to test the food. It's gone."

"Was anyone else at the show ill? What she ate

came from the concession stand, or from one of the local fast-food places."

"We have no reports of anyone else being ill. We are, of course, checking every possibility." He closed his notebook and put it back in his inside jacket pocket. "Dr. Summer, will you be staying after the show closes tonight?"

"I was going to pack up and drive back to Jersey late today." Right now New Jersey seemed a long way from the Rensselaer County Fairgrounds.

"I'd like you to check in with me before you leave. I have your address and telephone number"—he picked up one of her Shadows cards from her table—"and until this issue is solved, you'll need to be available."

"Do you mean I can't go back to Jersey tonight?"

"Right now we have no reason to hold you. Or anyone else. But if Susan Findley didn't leave her booth from ten A.M. until four-thirty P.M. yesterday, then sometime during that period, while she was here, in the booth next to yours, or after she went back to her van, she was poisoned. Until we can identify what the poison was, we won't be able to guess at how long it took for her to go into the coma, and then to die. Anyone who might have witnessed any irregular situation could help us immensely if they would tell us about it. And, of course, we need to identify anyone who might have given Mrs. Findley something to eat yesterday."

Maggie winced. Damn the tuna sandwich. She was a suspect, too.

"Do you have any idea of anyone who might have had a reason to think they would to benefit from Mrs. Findley's death?"

Maggie thought of Joe's lost money, and of the estate. But she didn't know who would inherit. She shook her head. "No."

"Is there anyone you know of who would have wanted Mrs. Findley to die?"

Vince was fed up with Susan. Joe was concerned about her. Harry had loved her, according to Joe.

"I can't think of any reason anyone would have had to murder her."

"What about Mr. Findley? During the past thirty-six hours have you thought of anything that might help us to know who might have wanted him dead?"

She shook her head. Harry had been vastly less popular that Susan, but, despite Maggie's best efforts, she hadn't been able to figure out who might have killed him.

"Well, if you think of anything, keep in touch. I'm going to be spending the entire day here at the show. We were never enthused about having all of these out-of-towners arriving twice a year to begin with. And two murders in two days? We're going to have every detective we can pull in from the county here to help today." He looked her straight in the eye. "And to make sure everyone leaves a forwarding address before they leave tonight."

Officer Taggart headed up the aisle toward Will's booth.

The enthusiasm and excitement of Friday afternoon's setup seemed months ago.

Chapter 22

_Trout-Fishing—the First Cast of the Season,
wood engraving of elegantly dressed fisherman
standing by a rural stream in early spring
putting a lure on his hook. Published in a
Harper's Weekly supplement, August 24, 1878.
Double page. Price: $110._

"Is your family going back to Massachusetts today?"
Maggie asked Gussie, turning toward her friend's
booth. Maggie had to focus on the job at hand. It was
Sunday morning, customers were browsing along the
aisles, and everything was as it should be on the closing day of the Rensselaer County Spring Antiques Fair.

Except that Harry and Susan were dead.

"Jim has to get back, so he's leaving this morning.
But the family decided they'd tour the area for the day
and then come back tonight and help me pack up
before we all head home. We all have to leave reach
numbers, of course, but we'll be off for the Cape early
tomorrow morning." Gussie paused. "The police
seem in a quandary. I think Susan's death caught them
short. It seemed such an easy case when they had Ben

as a suspect in Harry's death. But now Ben isn't the only possible suspect. And with Susan's dying, there are all kinds of other questions."

Susan might have died of poison. John Smithson had died of poison last week.

Maggie nodded. "The charming and sweaty Officer Taggart certainly didn't look thrilled at being here to begin with. I think he's sure we all intentionally arranged two murders in his territory to ruin his Memorial Day weekend."

"Makes sense to me," Gussie agreed. "Did he ask you what Susan had eaten yesterday?"

"Yes; I assume he's checking everyone's story against everyone else's."

"Before you got here, he talked with Joe, and the Wyndhams, and then with me. And"—Gussie gestured down the aisle—"it looks as though he's chatting with Will now." The rotund officer looked like Tweedledee standing next to Will, who towered at least eight inches over him. "And, if he hasn't already, I guess he'll talk with Vince."

"Speaking of Vince, did you notice him near Susan's booth a few minutes ago? I could have sworn he was carrying something under his jacket."

Gussie shook her head. "I was busy with a customer. That's the third person this weekend who's asked me about twins memorabilia! All of these multiple births resulting from fertility pills seem to have brought back the market for anything to do with twins or supertwins."

"An interesting marketing angle."

"Unfortunately, I don't have anything left in those categories to market at the moment!" Gussie rolled her eyes. "A few years ago those items were so specialized only a few collectors were interested. Where was my crystal ball then? I should have been picking things like that up when the prices were lower."

Maggie nodded. Hindsight was always easy. "Joe's been on his cell phone for the past half hour." She looked across the aisle to where Joe's telephone was balanced between his cheek and his shoulder as he took notes on a pad.

Gussie glanced over. "He's called a lot of Susan's and Harry's friends in New York, to let them know." She paused. "Although I'd guess the newspapers are doing a pretty good job at communicating the story, too. And I'm pretty sure I overheard him trying to reach his lawyer."

"Lawyer?" Maggie looked across at him.

"Maybe we should all have them, the way those detectives are checking up on what we've been doing this weekend. Didn't you get Susan some lunch yesterday?"

"Tuna sandwich."

"Well?"

"I am not going to call a lawyer. Yet. There's no word of a solution to John Smithson's murder. That's three antiques dealers dead in one week. It doesn't make sense to think there'd be three different murderers. But nothing is making sense. The big question is motivation. Who would have wanted Harry and Susan—and John Smithson—dead?"

"It could be more than one killer. Maybe someone is taking advantage of the situation to make everyone think there's only one person involved. There could be two—or even three—separate killers."

Maggie shuddered. "But why?" She twisted an escaped strand of hair around a finger. "Why here, at the show? If someone really wanted to kill Harry or Susan, why not do it far away from a large crowd of people; here someone was bound to see something."

"What about John Smithson last weekend? Maybe there's some pervert around who's preying on antiques dealers."

"What connection could there have been between Harry and Susan and John Smithson?"

Gussie shook her head. "I don't know. I don't even think they knew each other, other than seeing each other at this show."

"That's why I keep thinking we're missing something. There's a piece of this puzzle we're not seeing."

"Isn't it dreadful? That awful detective is saying that someone killed poor Susan!" Lydia Wyndham's voice was higher than usual. "I feel like a pig in a paper bag! Dark corners everywhere you turn. There's just no way to explain this. Susan was a little silly, of course, but such a dear, sweet person. And so careful of her health."

Gussie and Maggie looked at each other.

"It just goes to show: you never know what tomorrow will bring. Just yesterday Susan was so sad about Harry. I made her a cup of chamomile tea, because that's calming you know, and she said it truly helped. Susan always liked my teas, although she always added too much honey for my taste, and here it's one day later, and she's gone to the Lord. Mr. Wyndham is just awfully upset, too, you know."

Maggie glanced over at Silver in Mind. Abe was sitting in his customary chair at the side of the booth, reading the same book he'd been reading since Friday. If he'd been any more upset, he might have blinked.

"In any case, though, dears, life does go on, doesn't it, and, Maggie, have you had a chance, and I know you certainly have had your mind full, what with Harry, and Susan, and customers, and all, but have you had a chance to look for those herb prints you said you might have?" Lydia turned to Gussie. "You know, tomorrow is another day, and my niece will still be getting married, and I just had it all planned that I could give her and her husband-to-be those prints of coffee and tea plants."

Gussie smiled sweetly at her. "Well, certainly, priorities are priorities, Lydia." Gussie almost winked at Maggie. "Maggie, you have looked for those prints, haven't you?"

"Actually, no, I haven't, Lydia. But I was just about to do that." Maggie patted Lydia on her shoulder. "I know they'd have to be in one of a couple of portfolios, so it won't take long for me to look."

"Thank you so much, dear. I do hope you'll be able to find them for me."

Lydia smiled at Joe, who was still talking earnestly into his cell phone and ignoring two customers who were looking through his Hemingways and Faulkners, and returned to her booth. Her perennial cup of tea was waiting, as was a woman looking for a sardine fork in the Chantilly pattern. Sundays weren't usually heavy customer days, but you could still make some good sales.

No customers were in Maggie's booth, however, so she resolved to put aside thoughts of murder and concentrate on prints. She had several portfolios of prints from classic British herbals. Collections of drawings and descriptions of plants that had practical uses, whether for food, medicine, scent, or flavor, were particularly popular in the seventeenth and eighteenth centuries. Many of the plants and flowers in the prints were considered only decorative today, such as the rose or the lily. Their popularity in medieval gardens was based on their "virtues," or religious associations or their edibility. Some of the earliest herbals were beautifully hand-drawn and colored and had carefully scripted Latin descriptions of what the plant could be used for.

But none of those would contain coffee or tea, Maggie realized as she interrupted her search to sell two astrological prints to a gentleman wearing a Hawaiian shirt just short enough to reveal a rolling stomach.

Chamomile or sage or dandelions or poppies or tobacco or marijuana she could find, but not coffee or tea. She thought a few minutes. Coffee and tea were both evergreen trees, or large bushes. She did have a portfolio full of prints of trees, with full descriptions of the uses of their berries, leaves, or bark, and their pharmaceutical uses. Some, like the willow, the source for aspirin, had been used in Native American medicine. Some, like coffee and tea, had found their way into mainstream contemporary life. That was the portfolio she needed.

As part of her marketing and presentation strategy, Maggie always researched the subjects of her prints. That meant digging up historical details about the subject of the print, or particularly interesting information about the artist or engraver who had produced it. For some of her botanical prints Maggie had researched the uses of the plants. She often shared them with her social history classes to illustrate changing cultural perceptions of the environment.

She pulled out a portfolio labeled "Misc. Trees & Plants, with Historical and Current Uses" and quickly thumbed through it. Some were trees whose fruits or nuts had dual uses, some whose bark was used for medicines, some, like coffee and tea, whose berries or leaves were used. Willows, hickories, elms, azaleas, spruce—and here were coffee and tea. Luckily for Lydia Wyndham's niece they would make a nice matching pair.

Maggie tucked the portfolio under the table and took the prints over to Lydia. "This is the only pair I have. Look them over, and if you're still interested, I'll quote you a dealers' price." Lydia nodded eagerly and then was distracted by a customer.

There were no customers in Maggie's area. She walked up the aisle a little and looked at Susan's booth. It was closed; chairs blocked the entrance. Someone had put two lilies of the valley on the center chair.

A nice gesture. Although Susan wasn't exactly the lilies type, Maggie thought ironically. She focused on what was displayed in the booth. Vince had been carrying something under his coat this morning, and he had left it here. She was sure of it. Why would he have had something that belonged to Susan? And if he did have something, why return it today?

Nothing was noticeably different from yesterday afternoon. There were four Japanese wood-block prints; the pedestal was still in place; the embroidered hangings were still all here.

Suddenly she sensed someone near her. She whirled around, coming almost face-to-chest with Will.

"Whoa!" He took a step backward. "Sorry to crowd you!" Will's green-and-blue tie was crooked; Maggie resisted the urge to reach up and straighten it.

"Sorry. I'm a little jumpy. You've talked with the friendly local policeman?"

He nodded. "Pretty awful, isn't it?"

"Especially for those of us who brought Susan tuna salad for lunch yesterday."

"At least you didn't go home and whip up your own special mayonnaise to mix in it."

Maggie made a face at him. "Will, do you remember talking with Vince this morning?"

"Sure. He came by to make sure Susan's booth was closed off. He's going to get some porters to help repack her stuff in the Art-Effects van tonight once the police have finished going over it."

Her van. The last place I saw Susan, Maggie thought. She tried to erase the picture of Susan lying on her cot, pale and exhausted.

"Vince and Joe are going to make sure all Harry and Susan's stuff gets back to their loft."

Maggie nodded. For disposition by whoever was their beneficiary. She shuddered a bit. She knew all too well just how complicated dealing with estate laws and lawyers could be. And she hadn't had to handle anything as remotely complicated as the Findleys' estate would be.

"Will, I'm pretty sure I saw Vince hiding something under his jacket when he was here this morning, and then, later, when he was talking with you, whatever he was carrying had disappeared."

"Dr. Summer, your eyes are not failing you. But your intuition may be turned on high. Vince wasn't hiding anything. He was just returning a temple lion he had borrowed from Susan." Will gestured toward the back table in Susan's booth, where a pair of bronze Chinese chimeras, each standing about a foot tall, were facing each other.

"Of course." Maggie looked at the lions. "There was only one here yesterday, and they almost always come in pairs. You know, I admired that lion on Vince's desk Friday; it was with a couple of other Asian antiques. He said they weren't his, but I didn't connect it with the one Susan had."

"Well, the lion is now back where it should be. He said he'd borrowed it from Susan so a photographer could take some pictures of it for his next brochure advertising dealers' trips to Asia. He wanted to make sure it was back with her things before they were packed up and sent back to New York."

"That makes sense." There were often photographers from the antiques trade papers at the Rensselaer County Fair, and one of them might have volunteered to do a special job for a few extra dollars.

She looked at the lions. "They are handsome. Do you think anyone would mind if I took a closer look?"

"I'll fight off the hordes. No one said anything about not touching her booth; it's just closed to the public."

"And we're not public—right?"

Will smiled. "I'll stand guard."

Temple lions traditionally guarded the entrances to important tombs in southern China. These appeared identically and elaborately molded in bronze; every surface was etched or sculpted, from their large, clawed feet to their traditionally fierce faces. The bronze was slightly worn by time, and perhaps weather. Maggie lifted one. It was heavy. About the weight of the ten-month-old baby one of her students had brought with her to class a week ago—perhaps eighteen pounds. She examined the lion carefully.

No polish had disturbed the patina that showed its age, which was probably at least one hundred years. She wished she knew more about Asian art.

Maggie picked up the second lion and turned it over. She pulled her magnifying glass out of her pocket and checked all four feet carefully, then did the same with the first lion.

As Will watched, she replaced the lions on the table and moved the chairs back to block the booth.

"Well? I'm learning more about you every day. I didn't realize you were so interested in Asian art."

"Do you know which of those lions was the one Vince returned this morning?"

"No. I didn't pay attention." Will looked back over her shoulder at the table. "From here they look identical. Does it matter?"

"It could." Maggie took a deep breath. "I'm going to go and have a chat with Vince." She glanced around. "It's pretty quiet anyway. Would you keep an eye on my booth for me?"

"No problem. But what do you need to talk with Vince about in such a hurry?"

"I just need to know where those lions were all weekend." Maggie hesitated. "Maybe I'm crazy, but I have a hunch, and I need to check it out."

"A hunch?"

"A hunch that the foot of one of those lions was the blunt object that killed Harry."

Chapter 23

A Distinguished Fisherman Enjoying His Well-Earned Vacation, *wood engraving published in* Harper's Weekly, *August 16, 1884. Citified and serious man with elaborate rod and reel sits in a small rowboat while rural guide with beard and fishing net awaits the catching of a fish.* Price: $50.

Vince was getting his own coffee. A bit of his carefully coiffed hair slipped over his forehead as he bent forward and carefully added artificial sweetener to his cup.

Goodness, thought Maggie, here we've all been concerned about Harry's death, and Susan's, and we never thought to worry about Vince. There's been no one to get his coffee for him since Friday night. She shook her head as she approached his Show Management tables. How could we all have forgotten?

"Vince, I really need to talk with you."

There were dark lines under his eyes, and the hands holding the coffee were shaking slightly. "Of course, Maggie. I know this has been an upsetting weekend for all of us. I certainly hope it hasn't discouraged you from continuing to participate in our spring and fall shows? In fact"—Vince patted a carton of files on the table in back of him—"I have your fall contract right here. If you'd like to sign it and put your deposit down now, it would save you the bother of having to send it in later."

"Vince, I need to talk to you about this weekend."

He gestured toward the carton.

"You can send me my fall contract later. I'll sign it."

He looked visibly relieved. Maggie wondered how many dealers had changed their minds about participating in a show during which two dealers had been murdered.

"You know the police have released Ben Allen. They're opening questioning about both Harry's and Susan's deaths."

Vince nodded and took a sip of his coffee. The knuckles on his hand holding the cup were white. "I know they say they have no proof. But they have no proof for anyone else either. Ben could have killed Harry."

"He didn't do it, Vince. I know he didn't do it."

"He's retarded, Maggie. Sometimes those people don't know what they're doing."

"And sometimes"—Maggie's fingernails made a pattern in her palm—"sometimes they know exactly what they're doing. And what is right and wrong. Ben knows those things."

Vince shrugged. "Maybe. The police didn't seem to think so yesterday."

"That was before they found someone who'd seen

Harry alive after the time Ben was supposed to have killed him. And if the murderer wasn't Ben, chances are it was someone connected to the show. Someone who is here this afternoon. And who could be gone tonight."

"It's possible. But that's the police's job, Maggie, not yours or mine. You're a beautiful woman, Maggie, and you should be thinking about your future, and about your prints. Not bothering about all this nasty murder business." The words were there, but they were obviously an effort.

"You knew Harry and Susan well."

"I know all my dealers."

"Some you know better than others."

Vince looked over her shoulder, speaking at her instead of to her. "They were friends of a friend. That's how I met them. I asked them to do some of my shows." He paused. "That was several years ago."

"And you and Susan were lovers."

The paper coffee cup in his hand crumbled and the remaining coffee dripped down the side of his immaculately pressed slacks.

"Half the downtown art community had slept with Susan."

"But you'd spent a lot of time with her recently."

"Yes."

"Yesterday you told me Harry came to you Friday night and asked you to take care of Susan; to help her if she had any problems."

"Yes. He did that."

"And you told him no."

"I don't have time to pick up his pieces for him. She was his wife, not mine."

"But they were getting divorced."

"I didn't know that until you told me, yesterday."

"So, Harry just came up to you and said, 'Hey, Vince, old pal, do me a favor and look after Susan?'"

"Basically, yes. He was going out of town. Sounded like an extended trip. He asked me to be available."

Maggie thought back quickly through all the conversations she'd had with Susan, and with Joe. Neither of them had mentioned Harry's planning a trip. "Where was he going? Who was going to take care of his business?"

"He said Susan would, and that Joe might help her. But that she was pretty sick, and they'd need help." Vince looked at her. "Maggie, I have a pretty good idea of what it's like when a man doesn't want to make a commitment to a person, or to a situation."

That was probably true.

"Harry wanted out. He was ready to travel, soon, and I don't think he was planning to come back. And when a man's ready to travel like that, he doesn't usually leave a forwarding address."

If Vince was right, then maybe neither Joe nor Susan knew Harry was leaving. And Harry had Joe's $500,000 in his bank account for airfare.

"You knew Susan was very ill."

"Hell, Maggie, I'm not stupid and I'm not naive. But I don't like being lied to." Vince's usually calm and professional veneer had broken. His face looked pale, and then it reddened. Vince was terrified. "Susan had lost a lot of weight, and she had fainting spells. She told me she was anemic, and I figured she was a bit of a hypochondriac." He looked at her. "Have you seen all the vitamins and stuff she took?"

Maggie nodded. Susan had fooled a lot of people.

Vince's voice lowered, and he glanced around, making sure no one overheard. "Well, I sure as hell didn't know she had AIDS. I've known people who had AIDS. In this business you can't avoid it. I've gone to hospitals, and I've gone to funerals. Do you think I'm stupid enough to sleep with someone who has AIDS?"

Maggie reached out and put her hand on his arm. "You didn't know?"

"How could she not have told me?" His voice weakened. "How could she have done that to someone?"

No wonder Vince was terrified.

"You didn't—take precautions?"

"I had no reason to think she was sick. She used to joke about people who practiced safe sex. She called them paranoid cellophane collectors."

Vince looked down at his trembling hands and reached out to pour another cup of coffee from the carafe. "She said Harry wasn't HIV-positive, and that she wasn't stupid. And I should trust her, and not invest in a conspiracy by the condom companies. She never told me she was HIV-positive."

"When did you find out?"

"Harry told me. Friday night, when he asked me to take care of her. At first, I was in shock. I didn't know what to say. All I could think was that I was going to die."

"And then?"

"The more I thought about it, the angrier I got. I

wanted to kill Susan. To strangle her or pound her head into a wall. I just couldn't think straight."

"What did you do?"

"Everyone needed to talk with me. One dealer had a problem with his booth size. One of the detectives I'd hired to watch the fairgrounds needed to check on the status of some of the cars. Ellen Stuart over in building one had broken her glasses and needed to find an optician. I was angry, and panicked, but I didn't have time to even think about it. There was one minor crisis after another to take care of." Vince took a deep breath. "I can't believe I'm telling you all this. I haven't told anyone."

"You must have been really angry."

"I was. But I kept doing what had to be done, and by the time I saw Susan, it was nine-twenty or so. And when I saw her, I just couldn't say anything. I just didn't know where to begin. We were out there." Vince gestured toward the parking lot. "Near her van. She looked as though she was on her way to clean up before going to bed. I said Harry had told me she had AIDS and asked her why she hadn't told me herself."

"What did she say?"

"She said Harry had a big mouth, and that she was a person, not just a person with a disease. That it was her business whom she told. I couldn't believe she was so selfish. I told her so." Vince paused. "I told her she deserved to burn in hell."

"Not a pretty scene."

"It wasn't a long one. Both of our voices were rising, and I didn't want anyone to hear. I didn't want anyone to know how stupid I'd been. Because when I saw her, Maggie, I realized that I should have known. AIDS explained all the physical problems I knew she'd had. I was angry. I was confused. I felt sorry for her. I hated her. And I felt sorry for myself. It was all a nightmare. So I just walked away. I walked around the far side of the exhibit building and just kept walking around the parking lot over on the north side where no dealers were parked. I didn't want to see anyone. I didn't want to think."

"When did you come back?"

"When everyone else did; when Susan started screaming."

"Vince, did you kill Harry or Susan?"

"No! Maggie, I was angry, and that evening I hated them both—Susan for not telling me the truth, and Harry for not volunteering the information earlier. My mind was still reeling. I didn't know what to think. I didn't have time to think. And I had the show to manage. People were depending on me. Everything was confused. I was trying to get control. And after Susan found Harry, I had to work with the police. I had to make sure the show opened on Saturday." Vince brushed a piece of hair back from his forehead. "Maybe that was good. I was able to concentrate on something I could do. I could keep people calm; I could protect our investments in this show."

"And Susan?"

"You were with her. I certainly didn't want to be. I was sorry Harry was dead, but not sorry enough to be incredibly sympathetic to someone who might have killed me. Maggie, she may have given me AIDS!"

"There are treatments. Susan was on protease inhibitors. They're supposed to delay the disease."

"Maybe. But right now I can't focus on anything except death. Hell, Maggie, I jog in the morning. I don't drink much. I've always been careful about the way I lived. How could I have been so stupid as to have gotten involved with someone like Susan?" There were tears in Vince's eyes; he shook his head to hide them, and Maggie pretended they weren't there.

"You hated her; you said you wanted to kill her."

"I did. And I meant it. But I didn't do it, Maggie."

Maggie looked carefully at him. She wanted very much to believe him. Vince was not known for having a caring heart, but he was known to be fair, and she'd never heard anyone accuse him of lying.

"You have to believe me, Maggie. I didn't do it!"

"Someone did, Vince. And I need to ask you one more question."

He nodded.

"On Friday, you had a bronze temple lion on your table. When I admired it, you said it wasn't yours."

"It was Susan's. She bought a pair of them when we were in Hong Kong earlier this month. When we got home, I borrowed one to use as an illustration in my pamphlet for next year's tour. Susan said that was fine, as long as she could have it back for this show. She knew someone who was coming in who collected temple lions." Vince paused. "The photographer I usually use in New York had been sick for the past two weeks, so I asked the cameraman for the local antiques paper if he'd do a fast shoot for me. I told Susan I'd give it back to her before the show Friday, but the photographer was late. He didn't arrive until after the show started. Susan was furious. We had an argument about it before the show opened."

The argument Maggie had heard late Friday afternoon.

"I wanted to return it to her Friday night. In fact, I went and got it before I went for my walk. I didn't want to have anything more to do with anything of hers. I couldn't find her, so I left it just outside her van door. It was dark enough, and her van was far away from other people's, so I figured it would be safe, and she'd see it when she got back."

"Did she?"

"I guess she didn't get back to her van then. Anyway, later, after the detectives were here, I was walking around, checking on things, and I saw it there. It's a pretty valuable piece, and I knew then that Susan was with you and Will—remember?"

Maggie nodded. That was only about thirty-eight hours ago. It seemed a century.

"So I picked it up and stuck it in my van for safekeeping."

"Why didn't you give it back to Susan yesterday?"

"I forgot. And Susan didn't remind me. Although, except for bringing her some orange juice in the morning, I didn't go out of my way to see her."

Vince ran his fingers through his hair, brushing it upward in a sort of tall Mohawk. "What a weekend. Harry murdered, Susan dead. I may have AIDS. Detectives all over the place. Reporters are beginning to interview dealers. This is my premier show, Maggie. I can't believe this is all happening. And I guess I'm sorry about Harry and Susan—but I can't say I'm crying over them." He looked straight at her. "Please, don't tell anyone I was so stupid. Don't tell them about Susan."

"Vince, I'm not going to blab. But half the people at this show know now that Susan had AIDS, and a fairly high percentage of those people know you were sleeping with her." But most of them, Maggie thought, will assume that as two intelligent adults they were having safe sex.

Vince was with Harry and with Susan just before Harry's death, and he had argued with them both. If Maggie was right, and the temple lion was the weapon that killed Harry, then Vince was the only one who knew where it was. And he certainly had a motive.

Chapter 24

---~~~---

Atropa Belladonna L. *(also called deadly nightshade, a member of the potato family), German lithograph, from* Kohler's Medizinal Pflanzen, *1882. Belladonna was used in ancient times as a poison and sedative; in medieval Europe, devil-worship cults used it to produce hallucinogenic effects. Price: $55.*

"Maggie, these prints are perfect. My niece will love them. I'll mat them in navy, I think, and frame them in gold, and they'll be elegant. She's going to have a dark blue kitchen, and prints of coffee and tea plants will be just right, don't you think?" Lydia was rhapsodizing almost as soon as Maggie turned the corner of the aisle into her booth. "So how much to a dealer? You'll give me a good price, I know."

Maggie focused on the prints. "Usually they'd be thirty-eight dollars each. I usually give twenty percent off to dealers. That would be"—she did the math in her head—"that would be sixty dollars and eighty cents. Why don't I even it a bit and say sixty dollars?"

"That's fair; that's fair." Lydia nodded. "Now, I

usually give at least thirty percent off, especially with something like this, where I will have to replace the mats and buy frames, so it isn't really complete, but"—she looked over at Maggie, who was about to say something she would regret later—"but these are special prints, and I know some of us operate on a tighter margin than others, so I think sixty dollars will be just fine. I'll write you a check." She scurried back to her booth.

Maggie shook her head and walked over to see Will. He had just finished selling a bed warmer to a young couple. "Sell anything major for me while I was talking with Vince?"

"Are you going to offer me a commission? One 1914 print of a Pekingese, and the Wilson print you had on the wall." Will grinned as Maggie turned and looked at the empty spot on her wall in delight.

"You sold the Wilson?" Alexander Wilson, the Scotsman who'd come to America in 1784 and painted the first major portfolio of North American birds twenty years before John James Audubon, had never received the acclaim Audubon had, but was beginning to be valued. Maggie had put a price of $700 on the large folio framed print of eider and ruddy ducks. "That's wonderful! I should leave you in charge of my booth more often!"

"Please don't. I was so busy with your sale I almost missed one of mine. So far today I've only sold two awls. Oh, and one nice brass trammel and the bed warmer, so it hasn't been a total loss. How's the search for the perfect lion coming?"

"Here's your check, Maggie dear." Lydia pressed it on her. "Did I hear you were interested in lions?"

"I was admiring the bronze Chinese lions in Susan's booth."

"Very nice. I noticed them, too. But a little clumsy for my taste."

Maggie looked at her. "I didn't know you were interested in Chinese sculpture."

"Well, actually not. I mean, they aren't what I would want in my living room, you know?"

Maggie thought of Lydia's van and couldn't help but agree.

"I spoke to Vince about them; he said Susan had gotten them on his Asia tour. He's using a photograph of one in his advertising brochure for next year's tour."

"Susan did show one to me Friday and said she'd bought them recently. She didn't say where. It's so sad that she is gone now, isn't it? But that's all water under the bridge, as they say." Lydia beamed at Will and Maggie. "I was just about to pour some energizing tea. A new mixture I'm trying out. Would either of you like to try some?"

"I'm a coffee man, myself." Will looked down at the top of her head. "But, thank you, Lydia."

Maggie shook her head. "Cola woman here. You'll miss having Susan to share your teas."

"Nothing lasts forever, that's for sure, Maggie." Lydia sighed deeply and glanced over at Abe, who was going to have a stiff neck if he woke up suddenly. "Abe has been so upset this weekend. It's brought it all back . . . when our poor Danny died, you know. Abe has been quite frantic."

Abe sighed and let out a low-tremored snore.

"I can see that," Will said, winking at Maggie. "Well, I'm off for some of that coffee, since both of you ladies are here to watch your own booths, and mine."

"No problem, Will." This might not be a banner day for sales, but Maggie's mind was full of details. She glanced across the aisle to where Lydia was pouring hot water out of a thermos onto a tea ball in a cup.

Maggie looked down at the check in her hand from Silver in Mind. A few more dollars toward the motel cost, in any case. She tucked it into her cash box and took the couple of steps to Gussie's area. "I'm back. How are you doing?"

"I'd feel a lot more comfortable if the police had at least figured out another serious suspect or two."

Maggie nodded. "They're still wandering around the show asking questions, but they don't seem very focused."

"The real question is motive. Who would have benefited from Harry's death?"

Or from both Harry's and Susan's, Maggie thought.

"Did your meandering turn up any information?"

"I'm not sure. I think I need to talk to Joe." Maggie wished she could tell Gussie about Vince's anger and fear, but she had promised not to tell anyone. There was no reason to share what she was privately classifying as his sexual stupidity. Still, that stupidity meant Vince had a motive to kill Susan: anger, and perhaps revenge. And he was one of the people who had brought Susan food yesterday, so there had been opportunity.

But what about Harry's death? Vince had had access to the chimera, but so had anyone else walking near the Art-Effects van Friday night. It could have been coincidence. And she might be mistaken about the lion. Maybe it wasn't the murder weapon. Vince hadn't wanted the responsibility for Susan that Harry had tried to hand him, but that certainly hadn't meant he had a motive to kill Harry. So in Harry's case there had been opportunity, but, so far, no motive that she could discern.

"Joe was closer to both Harry and Susan than anyone else. There might be something else he knows about Vince's relationship to Harry."

"Did I hear my name?"

Joe left his cell phone in his booth and walked across the aisle to join them. "I feel as though I've lived this whole day in a haze. I don't even remember helping a customer. I've just spent the past two hours trying to reach everyone I know who was a friend of Susan's or Harry's. I didn't want to leave a message about their deaths on an answering machine, so I just keep redialing. Everyone in New York must be sleeping in or away for the long weekend. No one's picking up the telephone. I hate just leaving a message for people to call me; most of them are not close friends of mine."

Joe's skin looked even paler than usual, and his tie was listing to the left. "The police told Susan's parents. I talked with them just now. They're going to make most of the arrangements. All they kept saying was they'd never approved of Harry in the first place, and Susan should have never left Bayonne. Actually, they're lucky. They're blaming Harry." He swallowed hard. "I wish I could blame someone else. I just keep thinking there must have been something I could have done. What if I hadn't gone to look at those books Friday night? What if I'd left the show earlier and found Susan before she'd gone into a coma?"

They were all quiet.

"You did the best you could. We don't know why

this all happened, but no good will come out of wishing." Gussie shook her head. "I keep thinking, too. Why wasn't I realistic about my own capabilities—or lack of them? Why did I even attempt to do this show? If I hadn't done the show, it might not have helped Harry or Susan, but at least Ben wouldn't have been blamed, because he would have been safely back on Cape Cod, running errands for his mother and me, and jogging in the morning on the high school track. Instead of spending a day in jail being accused of murder."

"Okay, okay. Let's not have a pity party. None of us is perfect." Maggie took a deep breath as she stood with hands on her hips, looking from Joe to Gussie and back again. "And remember, I was the one who gave her the tuna sandwich. Anything could be hidden in tuna fish salad. What if it turns out she died of mercury poisoning?"

Joe smiled feebly.

Maggie checked her watch. "It's almost two. We have four hours before this show closes, the customers go away poor and happy, and we have to pack up and head back to wherever. And the killer goes, too."

"That policeman was around a little while ago. He didn't look as though he had any good leads. He did say they checked out the concession area," Gussie said, "so I guess they're investigating your tuna fish. But he said no one else who ate here yesterday had even reported a tummy ache, so they were assuming that if the killer bought food here, he or she added something to it. They're not investigating the concession stand people."

Joe smiled weakly. "Well, that rules out about seven people who probably never even met Susan."

"Joe, I know this is hard, but I'm trying to pull some loose ends together. Do you mind my asking you some more questions? Maybe you know something that would tie this all together."

He shrugged. "Ask away. At the moment I wouldn't guarantee my own sanity, but I'll try." A tear fell down his cheek and he dabbed at it with a linen handkerchief. "I don't know what I could know that would help anyone just now."

"Was there any reason Vince would have wanted Harry dead?"

Joe just looked at Maggie. "Vince?" He shook his head. "I can't think of any."

"Did Harry know anything about Vince that he wouldn't have wanted anyone else to find out?" Other than what I just found out, Maggie added silently to herself.

"He knew Harry was bisexual; they had a lot of the same friends. But lots of people knew Harry was bisexual."

Maggie had a sudden thought. "Is Vince bi, too?"

"Not as far as I know. He was always with women, and I never saw him come on to any guy."

"And Harry knew about Susan and Vince."

Joe nodded. "That had been going on and off for years. This time Susan was taking it a bit more seriously." He paused and pushed his wire-rimmed glasses farther up on his nose. "But she'd been taking everything more seriously since she'd been getting more and more ill."

"Did you ever go on any of Vince's tours?"

"Nope. I go to London once or twice a year by myself, and I'm not interested in the other places he goes. His tours are more for people looking for general antiques and conviviality; not for specialists like me." Joe paused. "I think Harry and Susan both went with him to Europe a couple of years ago, though. And did you know Susan went on the Asia trip this spring?"

"She told me."

"She really held that over Harry, that she was going without him. They'd never been apart for more than a weekend, even if they were both involved with people. And he didn't want her to go because of her illness."

"He thought she might get worse?"

"People with AIDS need to avoid germs because their immune systems make them so vulnerable to any infection, and that means avoiding swarms of people. Not only was she going to expose herself to any number of horrible diseases—that's what Harry said—traveling would exhaust her and weaken her further. Plus, of course, she'd be far from doctors who knew her."

"Then why did she go?"

Joe shrugged. "Women! I think she was trying to prove she was independent. And, of course, Vince said he'd look out for her."

"He knew she had AIDS?"

Joe looked surprised. "Of course. He'd visited her a couple of times when she was in the hospital and once called to recommend a new cure someone he'd met swore by."

Vince had known! Then what was all the talk and great trauma this morning? "You're sure he knew?"

"Absolutely." Joe looked at Maggie as though she hadn't heard him the first time. "I was with Harry and Susan and Vince just before the Asia trip when they were checking to make sure he knew about all of Susan's medications, and her doctors' numbers, should anything happen while they were gone." Joe thought back a moment. "He seemed to take it all in stride. He didn't seem worried that there would be any problem, because Susan kept saying she felt fine. Harry was the one who was worried."

Maggie suddenly thought of something else Vince had said.

"I guess, despite everything, Harry was really devoted to Susan." Maggie said the words casually, then sipped her diet cola.

"Absolutely."

"That must have been difficult for you."

Joe flushed a little. "No, not really. We all got along well. And his love for Susan was different."

"Different from his love for you?"

Joe nodded. "There was no one like Harry." His eyes started to fill again.

"Then Harry would never have left either of you."

As Joe looked at her, the flush on his cheeks paled. "That's right. He wouldn't have."

Gussie looked from one of them to the other. "So, Harry was the perfect husband and the perfect lover. But somebody must not have thought he was so perfect, or he wouldn't be dead. I'm tired of listening to everyone talk about just how wonderful Harry and Susan were. People who were that wonderful don't have other people murdering them."

"Gussie, we're not saying they were perfect." Maggie looked down at the angry face of her friend.

"I'm tired of hearing all of it. I'm taking a break. And then I'm going to talk with someone who still has some perspective on this whole horrible situation."

She motored toward the rest rooms as Joe and Maggie looked after her.

"They weren't perfect," Joe said softly.

"Joe, was Harry going on a trip?"

Joe looked at her in amazement. "How did you know?"

"Vince told me. Where was he going?"

"To California. He had a one-way ticket." Joe's pain was obvious. "A one-way ticket! And he didn't tell me he was going. He didn't even trust me." He looked at Maggie. "How did Vince know?"

Maggie watched him carefully. "On Friday night Harry asked Vince to look after Susan while he was away."

"Did he say how long he'd be gone?"

"No. Vince said it sounded—pretty permanent."

Joe's fist held his soaked handkerchief tightly.

"When was he leaving?"

"Tuesday morning. He had a ten A.M. flight to Los Angeles."

"The signing of the final divorce papers was scheduled for Tuesday afternoon, wasn't it?"

Joe nodded.

"When did he tell you about his trip?"

Joe moved back a little toward his booth and sat down heavily in the folding chair he'd left there near his cash box. His voice was low; Maggie moved toward him and bent a little to make sure she heard him. "He didn't tell me." Joe looked up at her. "He didn't even have the guts to tell me."

Or Susan, thought Maggie silently. What a wonderful and caring man he was. He was leaving his wife and, no doubt, taking with him the $500,000 his lover had loaned him that was to pay for Susan's medical treatments. A terrific guy: he was going to clean his lover out of all his savings and leave his wife, who was dying of AIDS, without money.

She looked at Joe. "If he didn't tell you, then how did you know?"

"On Friday morning, right before I left home to drive over here from Connecticut, I checked my answering machine and caller ID. There was a message for Harry from a woman named Julie, confirming his reservations." Joe hesitated. "When Harry stayed with me, he often used my telephone. At some time I guess he'd given his travel agent my number. Anyway, I called her back to check the details of the message, so I could tell Harry when I saw him. She told me he had a one-way ticket to Los Angeles, and he could pick it up at her office Monday morning; she was working over the holiday weekend."

"Did you give him the message?"

"No. I gave her Harry's number in the city; I told her to call him there." Joe looked at Maggie. "If he hadn't wanted me to know, then I didn't want him to think I did know. Maybe he was going to tell me this weekend."

Or maybe Harry was just taking Joe's money and running. Leaving Joe holding an empty bankbook.

Joe looked down. "And then he was dead. We never got to talk about it. Maybe he had a really good explanation."

Maggie nodded. "Maybe." But no one had heard it; that was for sure.

If anyone was adding up motives, Joe's had just increased dramatically. His lover had just borrowed an unsecured half million from him and was taking off without saying good-bye. Sounded like grounds for a lot of actions. Murder would only be the simplest.

"Joe, you must have been pretty angry Friday."

Joe just nodded and didn't look at her. "I wanted to die. I thought everything was so perfect. I kept thinking, Harry's going to tell me any minute what this is all about. Maybe there's a really good reason for his trip. Maybe he's going to postpone the signing for a day or so." Joe looked over at the wall of his booth covered with books on travel and history. "But then he would have bought a round-trip ticket, wouldn't he? Or at least a ticket with an open return. I may not have had a lot of relationships in my life. But I'm not stupid, Maggie." There was a blaze in his eyes, and in the tilt of his neck as he stood up suddenly, knocking his cash box and three pencils on the floor. "I'm not stupid."

"No, Joe, you're not stupid at all."

Just a little naive, and really paying for it.

"It must have been pretty awful, knowing that about Harry. Maybe you confronted him—asked him about the ticket—asked him about your money? Maybe he laughed; maybe he lied. I don't know. But you were very angry."

Joe looked at her. "I was furious at Harry. I was hurt. I was angry at myself for having fallen for him and his lines. But I didn't kill him, Maggie. How could I kill him? I loved him!"

Maggie nodded and patted his arm. "I know, Joe, I know." But she had loved Michael, too, and although she had never killed him, there were moments when she knew she was not thinking straight.

Scenes flashed in front her. The microwave oven

he'd given her for her birthday when she'd asked for a romantic evening on the town in New York. The new silk underwear he'd bought—for himself. The local hotel bill for a weekend he'd told her he had to be out of town on business.

She remembered anger. She remembered what she wanted to slice up and put in that microwave oven.

There was no anger like the kind she had felt and Joe had just described. Betrayal, combined with hurt and anger at yourself for not having seen what was happening until it was too late.

Although when you were involved with a man who would do those things, it was always too late.

Maggie realized with a start that she had walked back to her booth. A slight woman in a dress printed with red poppies was asking, "Do you have one?"

"What? I'm sorry."

"Those charming botanicals in the corner. Do you have a tape measure so I can check whether they'd fit in the frames I just inherited?"

"Of course." Maggie pulled the tape measure out of her pocket.

She focused on the poppies on the woman's dress. She had prints of poppies . . . in her botanical files and, because of their drug connection, in her herb files. She even had a print of Dorothy in *The Wizard of Oz,* lying down and falling asleep in the field of poppies, the flowers overwhelming her with their color and scent. No one would really sleep forever because they took a nap in a field of poppies, but L. Frank Baum had known the power of the flowers, and in Oz, that's just what might happen. A deep, deep sleep. A sleep you might never wake up from.

"I think they'll work. I'll take these two." The blonde in the poppy dress handed back the tape measure. "I've chosen two dark red roses. The frames I'm going to put them in are gold, and about an inch and a half wide. They'll go beautifully in my downstairs powder room because the wallpaper is all roses, and I put in brass fixtures—they look so much more stylish than the ordinary silver kind, don't you think? And I'm going to put a brass bowl full of rose potpourri over the toilet. Won't that be spectacular?"

Maggie nodded as she wrote up the order. "Spectacular, for sure." She hoped none of this woman's friends were allergic to roses or felt claustrophobic. The bathroom would certainly be memorable, though. And she was happy to do her part. "That'll be one hundred twenty-seven dollars and eighteen cents, including tax."

As the rose lady was happily writing out a check to "Shadows," Maggie looked across the aisle. Lydia nodded at her, and Abe was, as usual, nodding off in another direction. Maggie wondered how he managed to stay awake when they had to drive all day between shows or buying opportunities. "Thank you; enjoy your prints."

"Oh, I'm going to!" The poppies headed farther down the aisle.

"Gussie! What time is it?"

"Almost four-thirty—an hour and a half left to go."

"Then we only have a little time. You said you weren't leaving until tomorrow. So you haven't checked out of your motel room?"

"No, I was able to extend the reservation."

"When we were having pizza Friday night, did I notice a laptop computer in your room?"

Gussie looked at her. "I always think I'm going to have more energy than I do and think I'll do some accounting after the show. And when I'm too tired to do anything else, I'm becoming a Web addict. It's a way to have contact with the world even if Massachusetts is iced over and I'm too tired to socialize in person. Why?"

Maggie quickly wrote something down on the pad of paper next to her cash box and handed it to Gussie. "If I promise, on my honor, to watch your booth, would you go back to your room and log on and see if you can find the answer to this question?"

Gussie looked down. "Do you really think this is possible?"

"I don't know. I don't want to talk about it until I'm sure. If it's true, then we may be able to identify the real killer or killers. But we have to do it fast—the show closes soon, and people will be packing up and getting out of here."

Gussie nodded. "I have no idea whether you know what you're doing, but I'm willing to try anything. I'll see you as soon as I get some sort of an answer." She looked down at the question. "It should be out there somewhere." She tucked the piece of paper into the waist pouch she used as a cash box during the show. "What are you going to do?"

"I still have a couple of other things to check out, but I can do that here. There's almost no one left in the show anyway. Hurry, Gussie. I have to think about what to do if you bring me the answer I think you will."

Chapter 25

~~~

*The First of September—Partridge Shooting,
hand-colored wood engraving from a drawing
by Harrison Weir, noted English painter of
sporting scenes. Published in* The Illustrated
London News *on September 3, 1859. Three
men with guns and two hunting dogs
approaching a group of partridges. Price: $50.*

Vince tapped Maggie on her shoulder.

"Still asking questions, Detective Summer?"

"Still curious, Mr. Thompson." She turned so that
her back was to Joe. "You said earlier you didn't know
Susan had AIDS. Joe says you did. Why did you lie to
me?"

"I didn't lie. I knew she was very sick. She told me she
was afraid of AIDS. I didn't know she had it! Why in
hell would I pretend something like that? And even if I
had, why would I kill one of my own dealers at one of
my shows? What kind of publicity do you think that
would be?"

"Any publicity helps the gate. You always said
that. Yesterday, after the news got out about Harry's

death, the gate was larger than ever, wasn't it?"

"Lookers, maybe. I haven't heard of any new customers coming just because Harry got himself knocked on the head Friday night."

"But lookers add to the gate receipts. Receipts that go into your pocket, Vince."

He shook his head. "You're headed in the wrong direction, Maggie. I know you're trying to help, but you've got the wrong person. I'm a victim, too. This whole show has been a nightmare and disaster. Can you imagine what the *Maine Antique Digest* is going to print about all of this?"

Maggie could. Tributes to Harry and Susan, and an indictment of security at the Rensselaer County Spring Antiques Fair. At least. And the *MAD* was the bible for East Coast antiques dealers. Vince's revenues might well be affected.

"I'll buy that you think I had a motive to kill Susan. Okay. I did. I had a damned good motive. But what kind of a motive do you think I had to kill Harry? That he was taking off for the West Coast? That had no effect on me. I wished him well in his new business."

"Vince, what's going to happen to his old business? Do you know?"

The Art-Effects booth stood quiet.

"Well, I've committed to Joe that we'll help get the booth packed up and I'll get one of my people to drive it down to Manhattan, probably tomorrow morning."

She looked back at Joe, who was talking to two men in his booth. "Joe mentioned he would help out. It's kind of him to want to, under the circumstances."

"Circumstances?" Vince looked at her quizzically.

"Well, he loved Harry, but Harry was leaving him. I think he cared about Susan, too. And he'd loaned Harry money that's gone now. If I were Joe, I don't think I'd ever want to see anything connected with Art-Effects ever again."

"Well, detective, you may have asked a lot of questions, but I think you've skipped a major one."

"What?"

"Joe's going to have to be pretty involved with the Art-Effects inventory, and fast." Vince watched Maggie's reaction as he continued. "At least, as soon as the estates are settled."

"Joe—"

"Susan told me, after a few drinks in Hong Kong, that she was Harry's beneficiary, and Harry was hers. But Joe was next in line for both of them. Joe just inherited all of Art-Effects—the inventory, the real estate—everything. I guess that van parked out in the lot will be his, too."

"Does Joe know that?"

"Sure. He came to my van last night to tell me about Susan and said he'd be taking charge of her booth. He asked for my help."

"Last night? Right after she died?" Joe had seemed so upset before he'd left the motel. He'd said he was coming back to make some telephone calls. Will even went with him to make sure he was all right.

"Was Will with him?"

"Will Brewer? No; no one was with him. Joe was stressed-out, but he was definitely coherent. He was concerned about the logistics of getting both his van and Susan's out of here. I told him, no problem. I'd get one of the guys who works the shows for me to drive the van down to New York tomorrow and meet him at the Findleys' loft. Joe's going to drive his own stuff back to his place in Connecticut tonight."

Joe. Inheriting everything. "I can see Harry leaving his estate to Joe . . . but Susan? Why?"

Vince shrugged. "Who ever understood Susan? I asked her the same question. She just said she was leaving everything to Joe because of all his help during her illness, and because Harry loved him. But, of course, she didn't expect Harry to die first." Vince patted Maggie on the shoulder. "So, you never know, do you?" He turned a little toward Joe's booth, then back to Maggie. "I came over to ask Joe when he'll be at the loft tomorrow. He said he'd already talked with Harry's lawyer and got his agreement to put the stuff in there. He just can't take anything out until after the estate gets through probate."

Maggie took a deep breath. "Thanks for telling me."

"Well, I didn't want to leave a bad impression, my dear. After all, I am going to have that"—he looked around carefully—"that test we discussed earlier? And I'm probably going to be fine. The more I think about it, the more I'm not worried. And, as a single lady yourself, and with me left pretty much on my own now . . . if you ever want to have a nice dinner—or—whatever—in the city, now, you just give me a call." Vince winked at her. "I hear Jersey can be lonely for a single person sometimes."

"I'll keep the offer in mind, Vince."

"Never close an option, Maggie."

She shook her head in amazement as he turned to consult with Joe.

Never close an option. That sounded like something Lydia might say.

But options were getting narrower. Joe! Poor, bereaved Joe. She had been assuming he was destitute and without friends. She glanced over at him. He seemed to be talking to Vince about the Art-Effects inventory without its causing him any undue stress. Harry had left Joe. Joe was angry. Joe might have lost some friends, but he'd gained a million-dollar business. People had killed for considerably less.

She looked at him again. It probably hadn't been planned, but this weekend had sure worked out in his favor. She felt her sympathy for poor, grieving Joe melting away.

"Maggie?" Lydia Wyndham stood so close to her she could smell Lydia's perfume. It was a showy floral of some sort. Maggie wrinkled her nose. She wasn't much for fragrance. Especially scent that strong.

"Maggie, I couldn't help watching you this afternoon. You've been as busy as a bunny, walking around and chatting like a magpie with just everyone." Lydia was buzzing like a persistent little bee. "This has all been so very upsetting for all of us, hasn't it? Harry's murder was bad enough, and then for that poor, dear Susan. Not exactly a lady, but she was always friendly. I know this is awful to think about, Maggie, but I have been thinking that at least her end was a peaceful one. She just went to sleep and never woke up."

Went to sleep with a burned throat and fell into a coma.

"You know, she was very sick."

Maggie nodded. "Yes."

"Dying of AIDS is not pretty, Maggie. This horrible experience may have just been a blessing in disguise for poor Susan."

"You knew she had AIDS, Lydia?"

Did everyone except Maggie and Gussie know?

"She never told me, dear, but I saw all those pills she took. You saw those capsules she had that were white, with a blue stripe around the middle?"

"I didn't pay any attention. Susan was always taking pills. I thought they were all vitamins." Naive me, Maggie added to herself.

"Well, they weren't. She did take vitamins, of course, as we all should. But those capsules were AZT. And no one takes AZT unless they're HIV-positive."

Maggie just looked at Lydia. "How do you know what AZT looks like? I wouldn't know it if I ran into it."

Lydia looked suddenly uncomfortable. "I knew someone who had AIDS once, Maggie. It was very sad. And those pills were always on his table." She refocused. "So, what have you found out? You've been trying to figure out who did it, haven't you?"

"We all have to do what we can. After all, someone is murdering antiques dealers."

"Don't you worry, Maggie. That's not your job or my job. Those nice policemen will figure it all out."

"I hope you're right, Lydia. I really hope you're right."

Maggie wondered if those nice policemen knew about Vince's fear of AIDS. Or Joe's sudden inheritance. Or even if anyone'd checked to see if Will was still resenting the deal Harry had got him into.

Will. She looked over; he wasn't in his booth. He'd probably made a last trip to the coffee stand. By this time of day on the last day of a show, almost no customers were left, but contracts forbid packing anything up until the show was officially declared closed. And that would be another thirty minutes. Would that be enough time?

She looked at her booth. Friday's setup seemed years ago. She didn't even know how much she'd sold at this show. At most shows she recalculated that figure hourly. I hope I didn't lose money, she thought to herself. Here I have to depend more and more on the print business for financial support, and instead, I've spent the weekend investigating two murders. Life never turns out the way you think it will; that's for sure.

She busied herself straightening prints, rearranging those that customers had examined and carelessly left in the wrong place. Usually she straightened the prints frequently, but at this show there had been no time for fussing. Not with Ben under suspicion and one, or even two, killers in the area.

Gussie rounded the corner and almost ran into her. "I found it! The Web came through!"

"And?" Maggie took a deep breath.

"You were right. Here, I took a few short notes." Gussie pulled a small spiral notebook out of her skirt pocket and handed it to Maggie. "Now—what can we do?"

Maggie skimmed the notes. "Gussie, this is terrific. You got it."

"But does it all make sense?" Gussie's voice was low, partially because she was whispering, and partially because she was out of breath.

"I'm not sure, but we don't have any choices, if anything is going to happen today. We have to risk it." Maggie brushed back her hair and tried consciously to think calm thoughts.

"We have"—she checked her watch—"about twenty minutes before the show closes. I have to talk with one more person. Then I'll be here to move my van and start packing up." She started to leave. "Gussie, I'm not thinking straight. Do you need someone to help you pack up?"

Gussie shook her head. "My sister and brother-in-law and Ben are all going to meet me in about half an hour and do the actual packing." She looked around her booth. "I just wouldn't have the strength tonight."

"Of course. Well, I'll pull my van next to yours, and if I can help in any way, you let me know."

Chapter 26

~⌒~

Moving Wigwams—Comanche, *hand-colored steel engraving by George Catlin (1796–1872), American traveler and artist, who was the first white man to realistically portray forty-eight nations of Native Americans. This engraving is from* Manners, Customs and Conditions of the North American Indians, *1841, published by Catlin in England because there was no interest in the United States. His original drawings are now in the Catlin Gallery at the National Museum in Washington, D.C. Price: $85.*

The Rensselaer County Spring Antiques Fair was over, and 7,324 customers had paid their admission, looked over the wares of almost 250 dealers, and perhaps purchased a souvenir of their Memorial Day weekend in the country.

But to look at the fairgrounds now, at six-thirty Sunday night, an observer might think that no one had sold anything. Dollies laden with cartons, tables, and bookcases filled the aisles, as vans and trucks lined up two rows deep outside the buildings. The end walls of the exhibit buildings were opened to the late-spring evening, and all 250 dealers were trying to get inventories packed up and stacked in their vehicles before driving back to wherever home was. Few dealers could afford the time or money to stay an extra night and start for home Monday morning; most knew they'd have at least a four-to-six-hour drive after they'd loaded their vans or trucks.

Prints, books, and jewelry were three of the easiest inventories to pack. Fine crystal and china dealers were at the other end of the spectrum; each piece had to be carefully wrapped and cushioned before cartons could be loaded in vans.

True to their promise, Gussie's sister and brother-in-law were packing out her booth, while Ben, seemingly none the worse for emotional wear, was beginning to load her van, under Gussie's careful direction. Will was meandering about, keeping an eye on everyone, and packing his iron and tin wares sporadically. He was headed for Connecticut to visit an old friend and had only an hour's drive to make tonight.

But Joe, Maggie, and the Wyndhams were already filling their vans. Joe's books were heavy, so his cartons were small, but he didn't have to wrap books individually, and half an hour after the show's closing he had already packed and stowed half his inventory.

Maggie had filled her portfolios and was stacking them in her van between rows of the plastic boxes she used to display her prints. She moved more quickly and purposefully than usual, keeping her eyes on the vans around her. When Abe was inside the show building getting another load, she stopped Lydia next to her van.

"Lydia, may I talk with you?"

"Maggie dear, you know I'd love to talk with you. But Abe and I aren't quite finished packing. And we have to get on the road. We have a show to do outside Boston on Tuesday. We're headed there tonight, so we can set up tomorrow."

"Lydia, I really need to talk with you." Maggie looked her straight in the eye. "In private."

"Well, if you must, dear, just step into my van. There's nobody there, and Abe won't be out for at least five or ten minutes. He's packing the smalls on the back table, and he's getting older, you know, and everything takes him twice as long as it used to. So, whatever you need to say, we'll be quite private." Lydia's van was parked between Maggie's and Gussie's. "I don't know what could be so important to talk about now when we've had all weekend to chat."

Maggie hesitated. Then she followed Lydia through the open van door.

Despite the late-day sun, it was dark inside the van. Its few windows were covered by stacked boxes attached to the sides of the van with bungee cords. The living space wasn't much larger than she'd remembered, and it smelled more. The Wyndhams must not stop at Laundromats too often, or at least not to wash their bedclothes. The folding bed they obviously slept on, sat on, and, to judge by the crumbs covering it, ate on, might once have been spread with white sheets and a striped red-and-black blanket, but now everything was a shade of dusty gray. With some pink in it, Maggie found herself thinking. Maybe they had washed all the bedclothes together. Several years ago.

Lydia gestured toward the bed, and Maggie reluctantly sat on its edge. Lydia stood by the door, which had slid shut, cutting off most of the available light. Maggie fought off the feeling that she was trapped in a small metal box and forced herself to say what had to be said.

"Lydia, I know what killed Susan."

Lydia nodded, reaching over to adjust one of the cartons she had just placed in the van. "AIDS is a horrible disease, dear. Horrible. You have no idea."

"Yes, it is." Maggie watched her closely. "But people don't just die of AIDS. They die of a disease that is able to take over their body because their immune system doesn't work anymore."

Lydia looked at her. "That's right. But if it weren't for AIDS, then they wouldn't die. And they die horrible deaths. Sometimes pneumonia keeps them gasping for every breath. No matter what doctors write on the death certificates, or what families want to call it, people die of AIDS. Susan was dying of AIDS."

"But she didn't die of AIDS last night. She died because she was poisoned."

"That's what that policeman said, Maggie. But don't you be getting yourself all turned round because of it. He didn't know what could have caused her to die, all sudden like that. She was tired, and in shock. People with AIDS can collapse anytime."

"You know a lot about AIDS."

"Well, I read a lot, you know. In the van, when we're on the road."

"Lydia, didn't you tell me you were a botany teacher back in Iowa?"

"I taught high school botany for twenty-seven years. And for seven years I taught at night, too, at the local college."

"Iowa's big farm country."

"It's beautiful country, Maggie, but this is not the time to talk about Iowa. We both have things to do. You're upset about Susan, of course. We all are. But we have to get on with our lives. Which means packing up our vans and going wherever we're supposed to go next."

Lydia turned toward the door. "If you'll excuse me?" She gestured toward Maggie.

"Lydia, I know how Susan died. So do you." Maggie took a deep breath. Lydia turned toward her, and she saw the short woman's eyes focus directly on hers. "If you don't tell the police, then I'm going to."

Lydia walked over to where Maggie was still sitting on the edge of the bed and sat down too close to her. An odor of sweat and stale air and the thick scent of Lydia's perfume filled the narrow space between the two women. "Maggie, I don't think that's smart. You really don't know anything; you're guessing."

Maggie looked straight back at her. "I mat a lot of prints. Most of the herbs and flower and tree prints come with botanical information. A lot of customers find that interesting, so I copy it or mount it on the back of the mat. While I was looking through my stock for the coffee and tea prints you wanted, I found a beautiful print of azaleas."

Lydia put her head down, cradling it in her hands.

Maggie paused a minute. Maybe this was going to be easier than she thought. Maybe Lydia was going to admit everything and give herself up.

Maggie continued, "Azaleas are poison. Especially to farm animals. In Iowa, azaleas are especially common, and the University of Iowa has published several studies pointing out the dangers to grazing animals. And, in particular circumstances, to people. Of course no one, except maybe a child or a cow, would eat azalea flowers or leaves. But azalea nectar, and honey made from the nectar, is toxic. In ancient Greece, soldiers were sometimes poisoned by eating too many cakes made with honey from azalea blossoms. And the only thing more toxic than the honey is a strong solution of azalea flowers. It looks just like a pale yellow herbal tea, and it takes a couple of hours to work. First it burns the mouth a little—not much if there is a lot of honey put in the solution. Then it numbs the tongue and lips. That makes it harder for the person poisoned—especially someone who is already weakened by another disease—to vomit. In a case like that, a victim can choke to death on their own vomit. Or they can go into a coma and die anytime up to six hours after ingesting the solution."

Lydia hadn't moved.

"The only thing I don't understand, Lydia, is why you did it. Why kill Susan?"

Suddenly, there was a flash of light as the van door opened wide. Maggie felt herself thrown backward, toward a pile of racks and steel cases full of jewelry. The pain in the side of her head merged with the sensations of being off balance and unable to breathe.

As she pulled herself up, she watched a narrow red

stream of blood dripping down onto her shoulder from the side of her forehead where she had hit the corner of the metal stands.

Lydia was standing over her. In her hand was a small gun. Abe was standing by the door he'd opened, staring at them both.

"I don't want to have to hurt you, Maggie. But you're thinking too hard. Sometimes it's not good to think too hard."

"You can't kill me, too."

"Dear, I'm afraid I can. Guns are very simple to use, you know. And I grew up on a farm. I know how to use one."

Maggie looked at her. It was hard to focus on the person standing directly over her without focusing on the small silver gun pointed directly at her head. It looked like a toy. It wasn't.

Abe slowly put the open carton of silver miniatures he was carrying down on the front seat. "Lydia, why get her involved? There's no reason."

"There's reason. She knows about Susan. Maybe she knows more."

"There are people around. They'll hear. We don't use guns unless we have to."

"We don't have to kill her here." Lydia's voice was getting impatient, as Abe glanced with concern at the parking lot in back of him. "She'll stay with us. You finish packing. How many more cartons?"

"Two or three."

"Then you put that carton away and go get the rest, and we'll be off. And somewhere between here and Massachusetts we'll stop at a rest stop and leave her there."

Lydia hadn't taken her eyes off Maggie. "Dear, you won't be able to tell them much with a bullet in your head. And we'll get rid of the gun, too. I don't need this one anyway. We have others."

"Others?" Maggie tried to glance around the crowded van, but didn't want to lose her view of the hand with the gun. Her head was throbbing, and if she lost her focus on the gun, she might lose her focus on Lydia.

"Two old people on the road all the time need protection, don't you think?"

Maggie had no doubt that Lydia could use that gun. And at this close range there was no chance of missing. Her blood was staining the front of her silk blouse. Cold water would take out blood. She needed to get to a sink of cold water. She forced herself to focus on Lydia.

"Why, Lydia? Why did you do it?"

"Well, you might as well know that part; you figured out the rest." Lydia almost relaxed her expression. But the hand holding the gun remained steady. "Susan was sick; she was dying. AIDS is a horrible way to die. It's God's way of punishing those who have sinned against His word. Its revenge is slow and painful. Susan was in pain. What happened was a kindness."

"How can murder ever be a kindness?"

"You're young, Maggie. Have you ever watched anyone die a slow and painful death?"

Maggie shook her head. Just keep her talking. "No. Never."

"It's not pretty. And AIDS takes everyone close to it down with the one who has sinned. That's what happened with us, wasn't it, Abe?"

Abe was still standing in the doorway. His height blocked the light. Maggie wished she could call out, but the gun was too close, and the way the bed was angled she couldn't see through the windshield so she had no idea who might or might not be nearby. Her van was the nearest, she knew, and no one would be there. Gussie and Ben were loading on the other side of the Wyndhams' van. Most people were still packing up inside the exhibit buildings.

Abe nodded his head, looking sadly at Maggie. "It comes like a sickness from hell, destroying all in its path. It took our Danny, and it took our life. It has to be stopped."

Danny. Their son.

"Your son died of AIDS?"

"He left us to live in Chicago, and the forces of evil defeated him. He had always been a good boy, but he was contaminated by Satan. Then he returned to us, broken and ill of the plague. The wrath of God had brought him down."

Lydia glanced back at Abe, who was still standing, almost like a statue, in the doorway. "That's right, it did. And we nursed Danny and took care of him. It took two years for him to die. At the end his skin was covered with lesions, and he was blind, and he could hardly breathe without pain." Lydia's voice was full of anger, not sorrow.

"God sent all of the plagues against him." Abe intoned the words as though he were in a pulpit.

"There was no place to turn. Danny had no health insurance. He was just twenty-four. He had no place to go but home. And the neighbors turned away from us. The people in the church said Danny had to repent. He was stubborn, that boy. He wouldn't pray to the Lord."

"He turned his face away from the face of the Lord." Abe said it like an incantation.

"We had no friends to turn to. I had to leave my job because there was no one else to care for Danny, and then Abe's supervisor told him they really needed a younger person at the bank, so we had no income. And all the time Danny was getting weaker, and weaker, and more in pain. Abe would sit by his bedside for hours, reading to him out of the Holy Book. But Danny wouldn't repent and be saved." The hand holding the gun wavered slightly. "The people we'd grown up with, the people who had been our friends, left us alone. They were afraid of being contaminated, by the AIDS, or maybe by Danny's rejection of the Lord. But they stayed away. One July night, on the kind of dry, hot night when you leave all the windows open, hoping for a breeze or a shower to end the heat, we were in Danny's room. Danny was pretty bad then. We were all together when we heard the cries and shouts."

There were tears in Lydia's eyes, but the eyes were hard and angry. "They'd lit a cross on our yard. Flames were shooting from the cross, like a wall of fire. I couldn't see the faces, but I saw people running. The flames followed them, across the grass, because in the heat and the drought the grass caught fire. We called the fire department, and they came. Fast enough so no one was hurt, but the front of our house was black with the smoke from the fire, and there were no bushes or flowers left in our yard."

"Like a sign from God; the bushes burned."

"That was the night Danny died."

What a nightmare. Maggie wanted to reach out and hug Lydia, but one look at Lydia's eyes said that was not an option.

"We left. We knew it was a word from God. We had to end the suffering; end the plague. God had spoken through the burning bush." Abe said it in a monotone.

"We sold our house, and we started in the antiques business," Lydia continued. "At first I thought we could escape the pain if we just kept moving, but the pain followed us. There are so many suffering men. Wherever we went, we found them. Some we were able to help, and some we weren't. But we tried. God had put his hand on them and condemned them. Burning in hell is enough of a punishment. We did what we could to end their suffering."

"You killed Susan to end her suffering?"

"She would have been in great pain, Maggie. Alone, and in great pain. It was for the best."

"And—Harry?"

"That was Abe's stupidity." Lydia shot a glance at her husband. "We saw Susan's AZT on Friday, and we knew she had the sickness, and so Abe assumed Harry had it, too. We felt especially moved by Susan, since she was the first woman God had asked us to help. It only seemed right for them to go together; they had been so close, and they were both to die anyway."

"But you didn't poison Harry."

"Poison is the easiest and cleanest way, but sometimes you have to use other ways." Lydia spoke simply, as though she were explaining alternative methods of making pie crust. "Abe found one of those bronze lion statues when he went over to her van Friday night. It was just sitting there on the ground. He was going to see if he could get any of her pills, so we could fix them to help her. She wasn't there, and the door was locked, but Abe picked up the lion, thinking Susan had left it there by accident and would want it returned, and then God led him to Harry." Lydia made it sound matter-of-fact.

Abe nodded. "He told me what to do. He told me to smite the enemy with the weapon He had given me. So I did, and it was as the Lord said, and then I returned the lion of God to its resting place and went to pray."

Which explained why Abe wasn't among the dealers who gathered when Harry's body was found. He was praying.

And Abe and Lydia had been at the Westchester Show.

"Did you—help—John Smithson, too?"

"Indeed we did. He was so easy. Not like some of the young men. His booth was near ours, and the Lord asked him to leave his medication right there, in his booth, when he took a break. He is at peace; the end came quickly."

Some of the young men. Maggie wondered how many.

"Didn't anyone ever suspect what you were doing?"

"The Lord knew. We did His bidding." Abe smiled calmly.

Lydia held the gun steadily as she chattered on. "We were on the road most of the time. There was nothing to connect us with any of the men. We didn't help everyone in the same way, either. That would have been too easy. God creates each man separately; he would want each man to have his own special way of leaving."

"But I don't have AIDS. There is no reason for you to 'help' me."

"Maggie, not everyone would understand our mission. You asked too many questions; you know too much about us. You are not a part of the plan, but I need to stop you from telling anyone. You said you would go to the police."

"You are interfering with the plan; Lydia is right."

"Abe, we're talking too much. You still have to get the rest of the cartons in the booth."

"Two, I think." Abe picked up the carton he'd balanced near him and reached over to pile it above where Maggie was sitting. The van door slid closed again.

Let him block the gun, just for one moment. That would give me a chance. Maggie concentrated on Lydia's hand. If she could knock the gun, maybe she could catch Lydia off balance.

She heard the sounds of dealers outside the van. Car and truck doors opening and closing; the sound of dollies loaded with furniture. Voices. How close were they? How long had she been in the van? It felt like hours, but she knew it was probably only a few minutes.

Suddenly a siren blared, the van door opened, and screams filled the air.

This was Maggie's chance. She struck toward where Lydia's gun had been. As she heard the gun go off, she stumbled against Abe, whose carton had fallen and knocked against both of them, pushing her toward the front of the van.

The gun was on the bed; Maggie reached for it just as figures filled the van doorway.

Officer Taggart's gun was drawn as he reached out and pulled Lydia's arm behind her back. She struggled, trying to reach for the gun with her other arm, but her tiny size was no match for the officer's.

Abe had slumped on the bed; blood was beginning to soak through the small hole in the side of his shirt.

Taggart called to another officer outside the van, "Call an ambulance. And bring in an extra set of cuffs." He turned Lydia around, cuffed her, and pushed her toward the door, focusing his attention on Abe and Maggie.

Maggie grinned. "Did you hear everything?"

She reached inside her bra and removed a small microphone, which she handed to him.

"Down to the last syllable. But sure looks like you'll have one hell of a headache in the morning."

"I'll be okay." Maggie followed Taggart and Lydia out of the van.

As one of the other policemen went back in for Abe, Gussie and Ben grinned at her, and Ben gave her a thumbs-up.

"We did it, Gussie."

Will appeared next to her, obviously relieved. He reached over and hugged her. "Maggie, if you'd needed some help packing up, why didn't you ask me?"

Maggie grinned. "Could I ask now? I still haven't finished packing, and I wouldn't want to get blood on any of my prints."

Chapter 27

—◦—

The Constellations *(set of six hand-colored steel engravings: two circular and four square),* from E. H. Burritt's *Geography of the Heavens, 1856, New York. Each view of the heavens covers three months and, in addition to showing the placements of the stars themselves, includes illustrations of the constellations and the mythological figures they represent. Price: $2,000 for the set.*

It was late Sunday night, and Gussie's motel room was full. Maggie's head was bandaged, but, thanks to Will and Ben, her van was packed.

The doctors at the hospital had told her to take it easy for the night, so she would spend one more night in the motel and make the four-hour drive to New Jersey in the morning.

Ben and his parents were there, too, beaming with relief and delight; the weekend's nightmares were over.

Will reached over and put his hand on Maggie's. "My friend in Connecticut can wait a day to see me.

But I still can't figure how you and Gussie did this, and why you didn't ask for any help."

"I wasn't absolutely sure, and I didn't want you to think I was crazy. I thought of the azalea tea when I was looking through my prints this afternoon and found some notes on the uses—or misuses—of azaleas. Of course, the fairgrounds are surrounded by azaleas in bloom, and I'd seen the flowers in the Wyndhams' booth, and in their van Friday night. And thinking about all Lydia's teas, the explanation just made sense. But Gussie's the one who confirmed it all."

Gussie nodded. "I came back here to my room this afternoon and checked the Internet. Sure enough, it listed several studies published by the University of Iowa about the dangers of azaleas."

Maggie broke in, "Lydia was a botany teacher in Iowa, and she taught students who came from farms. She would have known about azaleas. I didn't know why she'd poisoned Susan, but she certainly had the opportunity. And then I remembered she and Abe had been at the Westchester Show last week when John Smithson died. There might have been a connection, since poison was involved both times."

"What about Harry?"

"I wasn't sure about that. But when I looked at the bronze temple lions in Susan's booth, I realized that the front feet of one of them had been cleaned—almost polished. The back feet, and the feet on the other lion, were untouched. It looked as though someone had been trying to eliminate stains or marks of some sort."

"Like blood or dirt?" Ben had been listening.

"Exactly. And since Vince told me he'd left one of the lions outside Susan's van on Friday night, and then

250 • Lea Wait

picked it up later, I figured it could have been moved in the meantime. It could have been Vince . . . but he was with people almost all evening. I got Taggart to put the microphone on me. He thought I was a little off-the-wall, but he agreed to try it. Gussie was waiting outside the Wyndhams' van, and she set off her alarm when Taggart signaled he was ready to break in."

"That was some noise!"

"Jim got the alarm for me last year," said Gussie. "It's attached to the side of my scooter and it's inconspicuous. The idea is to signal for help if you really need it."

"Well, I really did! That was the most welcome sound of the day."

Will shook his head. "This has been an incredible weekend. What's going to happen to Lydia and Abe now?"

"Abe's in the hospital; that shot from Lydia's gun got him in the side, but they think he'll be all right. They're both being charged with the three murders they confessed to—Susan's, Harry's, and John Smithson's—and the police here are going to contact police near all the locations the Wyndhams have done shows in the past year or two, looking for suspicious deaths or unsolved murders, particularly of men who might have had AIDS but who died suddenly of other causes. Remember, she said Susan was the first woman they'd 'helped.'"

"I never guessed when Abe showed me all of those mourning artifacts. It must have been a way of mourning for his own son," said Will. "And maybe mourning the other people he had helped to end their lives."

Gussie grimaced. "Watching their own son die must

have been awful. But what would set them on such a strange crusade?"

Will shrugged. "Who knows what makes anyone do something as perverted as murder? They felt they were on a mission. But at least their mission is over now."

"Speaking of missions, Maggie, what is your antiques schedule for this summer?" Gussie leaned back in her chair.

Maggie smiled. "I'll see you next month, for the Provincetown show, and then I'll head Down East to visit one of my college roommates and her husband. They've just bought an old house, complete with a ghost. I'll do some buying while I'm there, and I've signed up for a couple of shows."

"Maine? Your roommate wouldn't happen to live near Waymouth, would she?" Will had come to attention.

"Right across the river, in Madoc."

"My great-aunt Nettie lives there! I try to visit her several times a year. She saves her household repairs for me to do, and Maine is a great place to pick up old brass and iron items. Maybe I can help you and your friend vanquish her ghost."

"Thanks, but I think after today I can cope with anything that doesn't carry a gun."

"Or wave an azalea branch?"

"That, too. I'll never feel quite the same about springtime blossoms."

Gussie laughed. "Don't worry. This weekend was a once-in-a-lifetime experience. The antiques business is a quiet, safe profession."

Maggie wasn't so sure.

SHADOWS ON THE COAST OF MAINE

LEA WAIT

Turn the page for a preview of
Shadows on the Coast of Maine . . .

"Please, Maggie, you have to come to Maine a day early. I need you. Drew has to fly back to New York overnight and I don't want to be alone. Not in this house."

Maggie Summer kept hearing Amy's words as she gave her excuses to Gussie White. She'd been staying on Cape Cod with her friend Gussie while she displayed her nineteenth-century prints at an antiques show. She'd been looking forward to an extra day of relaxing on the beach, but Amy's call was too strange to ignore.

"Amy is the most realistic, straightforward, organized person I have ever known," she explained to Gussie as she tightened the tops on her shampoo and conditioner bottles before packing them. "In high school, before she got her driver's license she took an auto mechanics course. In college her term papers were always done early, her dorm bed was made, and when she said she wanted to go to homecoming with Joe Smith, that's what happened. She's the last person in the world to be nervous about staying alone. That's why I have to go."

Gussie had given her a hug and nodded. "If you're worried, then I am too, Maggie. You go. Let me know how everything is once you're settled in."

That had been five hours ago. Maggie took another swig of diet cola. She'd forgotten just how far midcoast Maine was from the Cape. Thank goodness she was finally off the Maine Turnpike and heading up Route 1. She glanced at the directions she'd taped on the van dashboard. Madoc shouldn't be far now.

She hadn't seen Amy in a couple of years; not since Amy's wedding to Drew Douglas. It had been an elegant affair at the Short Hills Country Club in New Jersey, with Amy's mother and stepfather looking stylish and proud. And rich, Maggie thought to herself. Maggie had gotten by with scholarships and loans at the state college, but Amy had never explained why, with her family's money and her top grades, she hadn't gone to a private college or university. Maybe even Ivy League. "Montclair State is close to home" was all she'd say, as she crossed off the next item on her day's "to do" list. Amy's daily list started with "healthy breakfast" and went on from there.

Rooming together had sometimes been frustrating for both of them, Maggie remembered. But she had always known whom she could borrow deodorant from, and who would have an extra box of typing paper the night before a report was due. Amy was reliable. And she put up with Maggie's bed not always being made, and Maggie's casual social life. Amy would never go out for pizza without scheduling it ahead of time. Never.

When Amy had called in May, Maggie had been glad to chat, as always. She had sat down in amazement when she learned Amy was not calling from her condo in New York City near the ad agency where she worked and uptown from Drew's office on Wall Street, but from a small town in Maine.

"You have to come and visit. It's a wonderful house, Maggie. Built in 1774, on a hill with a great view of the river. You'll love it. And you can give me advice on historic preservation. You know about these things. And, of course, I'll be needing a lot of antique prints for these old walls, so be sure to bring some from your inventory."

Maggie's time was her own. She wasn't teaching summer courses at the college this year; all she had planned was doing several antiques shows. Since her husband Michael's death last winter, she had been restless. Besides, Maine was a great place to find new inventory to add to her business, Shadows. Shadows of past worlds; shadows to share with the present. Maggie loved her print business's name. She loved her life, even if it was a lonely one just now.

Amy was right; she couldn't say no to a trip to Maine to see an old friend.

So here she was, driving her faded blue van up the coast

through postcard-pretty towns full of two-story, white houses, art galleries, gift shops, and BEST LOBSTER ROLLS HERE signs. Many of the antiques shops looked inviting. But not today. She would stay a week or two; there would be time later.

Amy's house stood on a hill, rising above the road and a line of pines close to the Madoc River. Maggie drove around the curve in the road that made up two borders to the property, then made a sharp left turn into the driveway. She parked near the ell that joined the barn and the house in true New England fashion. She didn't need to see the pickup truck already parked next to Amy's Volvo wagon or the ladders leading up to the roof to know that the old house needed work. A lot of work. The roof was probably only the beginning.

"Maggie!" Amy came running from what must be the kitchen door. "I'm so glad you're here!"

"What's happening? Why the emergency?" Amy looked as always—short blonde hair in place, fitted designer jeans, and a NEW YORK CITY navy T-shirt. The only unusual part of her attire was a wide, white bandage circling her left arm. "Are you hurt?"

"I'm fine, now that you're here. I'll tell you all the gory details and you can tell me I am absolutely crazy after you get settled in and I open a bottle of wine."

"Speaking of wine . . ." Maggie reached behind the faded red Metropolitan Museum canvas bag that served as her travel pocketbook and pulled out two bottles of a good Australian chardonnay. "I can never resist those New Hampshire wine prices." Despite her bandaged arm Amy managed to balance the bottles while Maggie picked up her duffel bag. "It's a beautiful site, Amy. No wonder you love it. I can hardly wait to see the house."

"Tour coming right up." Amy seemed more relaxed than she had sounded on the phone that morning. But Maggie noticed Amy didn't look directly at her and was chattering more than normal. As they started toward the house, several old wooden shingles tumbled from the roof and fell directly in front of them. "Giles! There are people down here!"

Maggie could now see a big man and a teenaged boy balancing on the roof of the ell, holding hammers. "Sorry, Mrs. Douglas. They slipped again."

Amy shuddered. "Well, be more careful." She turned to Maggie as they entered the house. "Giles and his son Brian are doing the roof, and I hope they'll have time to help with some other work. Depends on how many calls Johnny Brent's construction company gets this summer."

Maggie looked around in delight. The kitchen was large, full of light, and lined with high cabinets. Storage space! The appliances were 1930s vintage, and the walls could use paint, but the possibilities were limitless.

"Crystal, this is my college roommate, Maggie." The attractive blonde teenager who was washing dishes smiled at them. "I'm hoping she will be staying with us a couple of weeks."

"Nice to meet you." The girl wore tight jeans and a short, bright pink tank top.

"And since I'll have company, you can go for the day after you finish the dishes. I'll be fine."

Crystal nodded. "If it's okay, I'll stay till Brian is finished. He said he'd give me a ride home."

"No problem." Amy turned back to Maggie. "Just wait until you see the rest of the house! After apartment living for fifteen years, I'm loving the space. There's a small room just off the kitchen; I'm turning it into my study. I'm not sure yet what I'll do there—maybe take up oil painting—or learn to quilt—but it will be all mine!" The small room was indeed cozy. It was almost filled by an executive-office-sized wooden desk covered with piles of papers and a floor-to-ceiling bookcase half-filled with books.

"Looks as though you've already got at least one project going."

"I've been checking the town archives for information

on this house. I'm curious about who lived here before us."

"This must have been the birth and death room," said Maggie. "They were usually small rooms, easily heated, and close to the kitchen for warmth and accessibility."

"I knew you'd be able to figure this place out. Just wait until you see the view from the living room!"

The house was just as Maggie had imagined it: a classic New England home with a central hall, fireplaces in most of the rooms, and four bedrooms on the second floor. A space that might have been for storage at some time had been made into a bathroom, and there was electricity, but otherwise the house looked as it must have a hundred or more years ago. The faded wallpaper still hanging on the cracked clamshell-plaster walls was definitely late nine-teenth century. Possibly earlier.

"Drew is using one of the bedrooms as his study," Amy explained as Maggie touched the crumbling black-and-white-speckled plaster and wondered how complicated it would be to repair. "And this is our guest room, all yours for as long as you can stay." Maggie hoped the cracks in the buckling ceiling didn't indicate problems of immediate concern. Amy had found a bright modern brass bed and covered it with a quilt. The quilt was no doubt made in China, but it was patchwork. The room was bright and cheerful despite the crumbling plaster.

Amy and Drew's bedroom was the most finished of the rooms Maggie had seen, with new yellow paint and small-sprigged wallpaper that made it cozy and welcom-ing. And the four twelve-paneled windows had the same wonderful view of the Madoc River as the living room below.

"And this"—Amy smiled, opening the door to the fourth bedroom—"is for the future." The room was a per-fect Saks Fifth Avenue display nursery. A white crib topped by a lace canopy stood in the center of the room. In one corner an upholstered, navy blue rocking chair waited, next to a bookcase filled with picture books. Floor-to-ceiling shelves held an assortment of stuffed animals and toys near a newly built closet. Of course. A house of this age would not have been built with closets.

"You didn't tell me! Congratulations!" Maggie grabbed Amy and gave her a hug. "Oh, how wonderful! I have to tell you, I'm a little envious!"

"Not yet," Amy said, as she closed the door and walked into the hall. "No congratulations yet. But we have plans. You unpack your clothes and then let's break out some of that wine."

Plans? Amy would not be drinking wine if there was a chance she was pregnant. Maybe they were adopting. But why hadn't she said so?

By the time Maggie had unpacked her clothes and hung them in a pine wardrobe, she found Amy on the front porch overlooking the river. Amy poured the wine into red bohemian glasses and offered a plate of wheat crackers and Brie.

"Mmmm." Maggie settled into the green-and-white-striped cushions on the Adirondack chair and looked around. "I'm set. You may have to move me after a while, this is so comfortable." She sipped her wine and then turned toward Amy. "So what is happening? Why did you call this morning?"

Amy hesitated. "I don't know, Maggie. That's the problem. Or one of them. Nothing seems to be turning out quite the way I planned."

Maggie remembered Amy's lists and plans in their college days.

"Like?"

As Amy poured more wine, Maggie noticed Amy's fingernails were carefully polished in creamy pink, but badly chipped. The Amy she knew would have touched up those nails immediately. Although it would be crazy to try to keep nails polished neatly while working on an old house.

"This place has so much potential. We fell in love with it the first time we saw it, and the price was right. The owner was leaving the country and wanted to sell quickly. But—I know this is all going to sound very strange, Maggie. And not like me at all. But right after we moved in, I felt something was wrong. And the woman next door, Shirley Steele, who is also the hairdresser in Waymouth, told us there have always been stories about this house."

"Stories?" Maggie's wine was slightly dry, just as she liked it, and she couldn't imagine any stories that would make this house less lovely. "You mean you have ghosts? What fun!"

"Sometimes at night I swear I can hear a baby crying. But it stops almost as soon as I notice it. And one night Drew and I both saw shadows that looked like a woman in a long dress, moving across the moonlight on our wall."

"A house that has been home to as many people as this one has, over so many years, must be filled with memories," Maggie answered. "And it's so different from your apartment in the city, or from Short Hills, that you're probably just very conscious of everything. Plus"—she paused for a moment—"it's so quiet here! You can hear the birds. Those are chickadees, aren't they?" She listened again. "And I think mourning doves."

"And we can hear every car that goes by, and every lobsterman who checks his traps on the river at five in the morning. Yes; you're right. At first we thought maybe our imaginations were just filling the silences. But that's not all."

"What else?"

"There are the accidents." Amy looked down at her arm. "This one happened yesterday. I opened one of the windows, to try to wash the outside. Most of the windows are the old blown-glass kind, with bubbles in it. We don't want to replace any that aren't broken. But suddenly the glass shattered, and I jumped a little, and the window came down on my arm. It took an hour in the emergency room to take out all the little pieces of glass and stop the bleeding. My arm is pretty badly bruised."

"A nasty accident," said Maggie. "But it's an old house. Things do happen. It looks as though no one has done anything to maintain it recently. The ceilings in a couple of rooms look pretty precarious. But that isn't ghosts. It's just part of fixing up an old house." Maggie tried to sound knowledgeable. Several friends had restored Victorian homes near hers in New Jersey, but she couldn't begin to imagine the time and money they'd spent. She usually got involved only when the owners had reached the point of decorating and wanted authentic Victorian prints to match their furnishings. One couple had hung Currier & Ives prints in every room of their house. Maggie was happy to have them as customers, but she preferred a more eclectic look for her own home.

"It's not the only accident," Amy continued. "There are the shingles that keep falling off the roof. You saw some today."

"But the roofer, Giles? He said he was sorry. He must have dropped them."

"He always apologizes. But they fall even when he's not here. Even when we know he has checked and assured us they're not loose. And the lights flicker at strange moments. And there are noises in the pipes."

All just part of owning an old home, Maggie thought.

"And then there was the fire."

"Fire?" Maggie sat up straighter.

"Thank goodness we had installed smoke detectors as soon as we moved in, so we knew, even though it started in the middle of the night. It was in one of the empty rooms in the ell. I called the local volunteer fire department, but luckily we had two fire extinguishers in the kitchen. Drew was able to put out most of the fire before anyone got here. A fireman told me we were lucky; a house this age can go up quickly."

"What started the fire?"

Amy shook her head. "That's one of the scary parts. There was no wiring involved, and no one had even been in that room recently. We had cleaned it out and left it empty. We thought we'd eventually use it for storage. We're working on the main house before we get to the ell. There's no heat there, no gas lines, no materials to catch fire. In fact, one of the walls in that room is brick."

"Strange."

"The firemen thought so too. One of them asked Drew if we knew anyone in the area who would want to make trouble. Of course, we just got here. We haven't been here long enough to make many friends, and certainly not long enough to make any enemies." Amy smiled weakly at Maggie. "After that we started getting weird hang-up calls. The phone would ring, we'd answer, and whoever was on the other end would hang up immediately."

"Heavy breathing?"

"Nothing. No background noise; no voices. Some days we'd get a dozen calls. The ones in the middle of the night really freaked me out. Last night I was having trouble sleeping; my arm was throbbing, and it was hard to get comfortable. I had finally gotten to sleep at two-thirty when one of those calls woke us. And then after the call we both heard the baby crying. Drew hadn't heard it before; he thought I'd been dreaming. We looked everywhere; we don't know where the sound comes from. It lasts about thirty seconds. One night I timed it by the minute hand on our clock. It's a horrible sound. Almost an echo. As though the baby was crying a long time ago, and we're just hearing it now." Amy took more than a sip of her wine. "I'm sure you think I'm crazy. But I couldn't sleep after that, and I couldn't face being in the house alone tonight. Drew had to fly to the city to talk to one of his old clients. The guy wanted his old financial adviser, and Drew's company was glad to pay to keep the man happy. Drew will be back tomorrow. That's why I called you."

"It does sound awful," Maggie said. "But I assumed you were just here for the summer. Has Drew left the brokerage house?"

"Didn't I tell you? We both left our jobs. We decided a less stressful lifestyle would be best for us, and for our children. Someday," Amy added quickly. "Drew is thinking about teaching, and maybe I'll write the great American novel."

"Whew. You've taken on some major lifestyle changes." Amy had always loved the city; the pace, the excitement, the theaters, the clubs.

"And the changes will work. I'm sure they will. I've planned it all out. But something, or someone, is making the transition harder than we imagined." Amy took another gulp of wine. "I was the one who suggested this move; Drew was always reluctant. Expenses are higher than we thought they'd be, and with the strange noises, and the fire, and the telephone calls . . . Drew's been drinking a bit more than he should and is beginning to talk about going back. That's one reason he stayed over in New York tonight. I'm sure he could have flown down, had his meeting, and come back today. But he's meeting some friends for dinner."

"He'll probably have a wonderful time, miss you terribly, and be home tomorrow. And tonight I'll be here to help cope with telephone calls and crying in the night. Have you called the telephone company about the mysterious calls?"

"The lines out here are old; we can't get caller ID. And the caller never hangs on long enough for them to trace anything."

Maggie poured herself another glass of wine. She was glad Drew would return tomorrow. There must be more to this story than Amy was sharing. Maybe Drew would have more answers.

The phone rang.

Maggie and Amy looked at each other. One of them would have to answer it.